praise

"*She Receives the Night* masterfully exposes the yielding cracks and deep crevices of humanity in all their grit and darkness—and, with equal precision and splurges of hope, bathes them in light."
ELIZABETH DAY, AUTHOR OF *LIVING WITH GUSTO*

"The depth and glow in Robert Earle's writing comes from living in the world, and fearlessly seeing beyond its surfaces. The elegant prose, complex characters, and plots that carry you off like falling in love, make his work a rewarding pleasure to read."
GINGER MAYERSON, AUTHOR OF *DR HACKENBUSH GETS A JOB*

"Stories full of the pain of life shot with hope."
MARTIN CHIPPEFIELD, PUBLISHER, *34THPARALLEL*

"Earle has an eerie way of drawing the reader deeply into the inner worlds of the women he writes about, transmuting lived experiences into poignant tales that remind us that though the night is long, dawn eventually breaks, and we are all the stronger for it. Overall a stirring and insightful collection."
MEHREEN FATIMA ASHFAQ, FICTION EDITOR, *THE MISSING SLATE*

"Robert Earle's brilliant new book, *She Receives the Night*, is a dazzling collection of short stories that you'll find difficult to put down. Earle's precise, confident voice guides us from the nightmares of the dispossessed along the rocky paths and vast range of human experience to fully realized acceptance of the human condition. These rewarding and compelling stories present vivid characters in sometimes exotic settings that will stay with you because they are true and profoundly human. In the closing story, the narrator reminds us of the journey we've taken, thanks to Earle's mastery of the written word and keen eye for *'Unimportant but intimate things, tender things, frightening things, all shared in a kind of rattle of words between dips in the suspect waters of the Atlantic full of seaweed and who knew what else.'* I strongly encourage you to read and enjoy these memorable stories."
GEORGE KOVACH, EDITOR, *CONSEQUENCE* MAGAZINE

"I couldn't help but think, as I read Robert Earle's sterling and cosmopolitan collection *She Receives the Night*, of that experimental writer Henry James. Earle is a master de-laminator of that stratified Jamesian character depth, excavating earned and earnest transparent, but amplified epiphanic stares (boketto on steroids) into the slipping and stuttering machinery of night. 'Experimental' in that he wrangles, like Henry, the new dynamic birthed from the Hieros Gamos of unconscious inner impulse and viral traumatic software, playing out the many permutations that are still percolating of secrets kept and revealed. Robert Earle—empathetic Brahmin of voices, gestures, and telling looks—out-looks James, out-Jameses James, in this lavish laboratory of sublime emotion and rare earth reality."

MICHAEL MARTONE, AUTHOR OF *MICHAEL MARTONE AND WINESBURG, INDIANA*

about the author

With more than 100 stories in print and online literary journals, Robert Earle is one of the more widely published contemporary writers of short fiction. He also is the author of the novels, *Suffer the Children*, *In the Blood of Herod and Rome*, and *The Way Home*, and books of nonfiction, *Nights in the Pink Motel* and *Identities in North America*. He was a diplomat for two decades (Latin America, Europe, Middle East) and has degrees in literature and writing from Princeton and Johns Hopkins, respectively. He lives in Chapel Hill, North Carolina.

Visit Robert online: *robertearle.me*

She Receives the Night
Copyright © 2017 Robert Earle
All rights reserved.

Print Edition
ISBN: 978-1-925417-36-4
Published by Vine Leaves Press 2017
Melbourne, Victoria, Australia

This is a work of fiction. Any similarity between the characters and situations within its pages and places or persons, living or dead, is unintentional and coincidental.

Cover design by Jessica Bell
Interior design by Amie McCracken

National Library of Australia Cataloguing-in-Publication entry (pbk)
Creator: Earle, Robert, author.
Title: She receives the night / Robert Earle.
ISBN: 9781925417364 (paperback)
Subjects: Short stories.
Women--Fiction.

she receives the night

short stories

robert earle

Vine Leaves Press
Melbourne, Vic, Australia

table of contents

To Mary

trouble sleeping

When Elizabeth answered the phone just after midnight, she immediately pictured Marta Carrasco's youthful but bleak face. The one with the five children. Painfully reserved, seated on the two-person sofa in her tiny, undecorated living room, no photographs, no tchotchkes, answering Elizabeth's questions in uncertain English when she could, Spanish when she couldn't, her oldest girl, Corazon, retreating after she had placed two tea cups and a sugar bowl between them.

Elizabeth pushed her hair off her forehead with her free hand. She whispered so as to not disturb David further. The phone was the old black one you couldn't carry around. "What is it, Marta?"

Marta said in Spanish that she didn't know.

Although Elizabeth had told Marta she could call her anytime, she'd assumed that her uncertainty in making the offer would undermine its sincerity, a gesture by another human being, not an official from the Office of Policy Assessment in the Department of Immigration and Citizenship. But the woman was so young; she had so many children; she seemed so numb. Knowingly violating protocol, Elizabeth went ahead and reached out. It wasn't like her at all, adding to the unease Marta surely sensed in her and making it unlikely that they ever would speak again. Yet now they were speaking again, or trying to.

"Something is troubling you?"

"Sí. Yes."

Elizabeth imagined the two-year-old, Luz, asleep in Marta's room. She pictured the two boys, Fausto and Tino, in the middle bedroom. She envisioned the girls, Corazon and Magdalena, in the last one. A post-war brick slab of a building, two units facing each other on every level, first the parlour where she'd spoken with Marta about her family's experiences in Australia as refugees from El Salvador and then, down the line, the kitchen, the bedrooms, and finally the loo. Marta in a pink Lacoste polo shirt and mannish gabardines. The children arrayed in gaudy synthetic sportswear, except for Corazon, who'd worn a tightly fitted white blouse that flared over her hip hugging jeans, a girl of fifteen in full sexuality. As a group, the family looked like a piano manufactured by several different companies—the keys different lengths and widths and surface tones except for the inky black hair (they all had that).

"It's difficult to put into words?"

"Yes. Afraid if …"

"Marta, there is nothing to fear." Elizabeth didn't know how she could say this with such certainty. She couldn't, rationally. What she meant was that now, at this immediate moment, there was nothing to fear. David was asleep again. Melbourne was asleep. Australia was tethered in its harbor beneath the world.

But think about everything that could make her afraid, all the categories about which Elizabeth had interviewed her— housing, health care, education, food, clothing, employment assistance, even the basic issue upon which their conversation now depended, a working phone.

Her supervisor objected to Elizabeth going out to do inter- views about these things. "It's not the best use of your time," Lew said, implicitly referring to her PhD. But she had studied Spanish during a year abroad in Spain, and she had analyzed interview data for twelve years. When this project came up, she felt an unsettled need to disrupt her routines of professional competence. David, an historian, only reinforced her intuition when he, too, attempted to dissuade her by telling her about the brutality of the civil war in El Salvador—a radicalization of the peasantry along neo-Marxist lines that generated a counterattack by the privileged "fourteen" families of El Salvador, supported by the United States. "We're right to take their refugees, but that's not the big issue. You can document how well our bureaucrats administer this refugee program all you want—it's not going to make the world a whole lot better until the United States buggers off. You won't like what you hear about that."

Marta Carrasco's interview, despite her monotone responses, in many ways had been evidence of success. She already had a job housecleaning just off Yarra Parade where she was welcome to bring the baby, Luz. Tino, sixteen, was enrolled in a large machinery vocational school where his deficient language skills were not a problem. Corazon, fifteen, was studying English in the morning and taking a nurse's aide course in the afternoon. Fausto, thirteen, was in a middle school. Magdalena, bright as wet glass, was enrolled in a multilingual grammar school. They'd all had their teeth repaired and inoculations given. Three of the children received glasses.

So far, so good, but then Elizabeth had realized, during the sequence of questions that dealt with emotional wellbeing, that Marta was being untruthful. The key false answer was that she was sleeping well. Immediately Elizabeth recognized something in Marta that was wrong. She could see the uncertainties of the night in Marta's tired eyes, and she could feel the same thing quicken within herself. Hearing that lie was when, surely, she had been motivated to offer to take Marta's call whenever she needed to speak, but at the moment, she'd simply recorded the falsehood that Marta had no trouble sleeping. It wasn't until the interview was finished and Elizabeth was getting up and closing her briefcase that she'd nervously pushed her card out at Marta with her home number written on the back. "Absolutely any time," she murmured.

Now Marta said that what disturbed her sleep was fear. She said she had not mentioned it to Elizabeth during the interview because it was completely absent during the day; she claimed that it left her alone until, in the night, it made her terribly uneasy.

"Do you fall asleep and then wake up?"

"Yes."

"When you wake up, what do you think might happen?"

"I don't know."

"Your neighbourhood is safe, Marta."

"Yes, nothing can happen. The door is locked. There is no one in the street. I look out. I don't see anyone." Marta said this in English and Spanish and English again before she began hyperventilating and squeezed her sobs into a muffled silence that sounded as if she were speaking with a pillow covering her face.

Elizabeth felt herself instinctively turn locks in herself that paralleled the safety checks Marta had made, but these were not connected to doors and windows. They were efforts to stifle anodyne suggestions, the apology that she was not a trained social worker, the explanation that in her family David was the sympathetic one to whom the children turned. Elizabeth simply clutched at the one thing she was sure mattered—being alive on the other end of the phone.

Eventually, Marta's gasping subsided. With its departure, her nameless terrible fear relented. She begged forgiveness and promised she'd never call again, but Elizabeth insisted that she should ring her at any time if the fear returned, and she told herself that she must change out the old phone in the morning. She knew Marta's fear would certainly return, and she had to be able to take the receiver into her dressing room and shut the door so as to not disturb David and therefore unintentionally betray her solemn pledge to Marta: no one would know that she had called.

But having agreed to that, the ethics were not clear. This woman's tears and sobbing were not therapy. They would not make her better. Fear of what? David was fully awake and waiting for her to speak. He was angry lying there, not at her, at the world, but she didn't want to hear it. She listened to the night, the insects in the garden, and imagined driving through Melbourne to Marta's apartment building—the clarity of nocturnal urban solitude, night's way of averaging the upscale and downtrodden into a mean of sprawling mystery, Elizabeth not knowing where anything ultimately led, no captions, no charts, no directions, her dreams before dawn wandering up and down the avenues, peering into darkened windows.

***

In her second and third calls, Marta began telling the story that she would modify later on. She'd lived in a village southwest of San Salvador that operated as a collective under the terms of a land reform, but the coffee the collective produced was still bought exclusively by the finca from which it ostensibly had been detached. Neither the guerrilla nor the rightists associated with the big landowners and the government were happy about this, so each preyed upon the collective in different ways. The rightist paramilitary stole part of the crop; the finca owners blocked the roads that would lead to other markets; and the guerrilla taxed foodstuffs and kidnapped children to replenish their cadres of fighters.

Elizabeth sat listening to this in her dressing room with the door closed and knew that these were accurate but not crucially important details. They were a lead-up to a certain night in which certain things happened, or began to happen, about which Elizabeth became vague, falsifying at first, then edging toward the truth without committing herself to its burden of fear.

By the fourth call, both women knew—as did the children in Marta's apartment, no doubt, and David, for certain—that sleep and night terror were not precursors to their speaking. The first call yes. Afterward, there had been no sleep; there had only been waiting for a time, that certain time, when the raw stuff of consciousness overflowed its cup.

***

Initially, Marta said her house was the first one attacked because her husband was one of the cooperative's leaders. He was dragged outside and shot. Then, when the house was set on fire, Marta ran toward the forest with her two children and the children were shot and a guerrilla tore her from them and lunged at her and she struggled and managed to get away.

The shooting spread quickly, as did the fires. The guerrilla formed a semicircle and splashed gas on house after house and on some of the people trying to escape, transforming human beings into human torches. Marta scrambled out of her hiding place and pulled a child into the bush with her where she hid—Corazon. She saw two more children racing through the flames and chaos and again ran out and grabbed them and pushed them into the corncrib to hide—Fausto and Magdalena, who was clutching a newborn, Luz. Then she saw Tino firing a rifle and begged him to come protect her and the girls in the bush. And when the corncrib was set on fire, Marta ran out and pulled off the planks in the rear and helped Fausto and Magdalena escape.

By now Elizabeth understood at least part of the confession Marta wanted to make.

Share my lie: these are not my children.

Marta fled with them for three days toward San Salvador. There she said that all of their documents were destroyed, the whole village was destroyed, and her husband was dead. The Australian relief representatives heard about this desperate family and asked if they would consent to being expatriated to Australia as refugees where they would be provided everything they needed to start a new life.

Somehow Marta negotiated all this while wracked with guilt. Her own children had died but not she. Her husband had died but not she. These children had lost their parents, and Marta feared she could not protect them from the terrible force reposing in the wicked night that eventually would tear them away from her and consume them like all the rest.

If Marta Carrasco were Elizabeth's sister, a schoolmate, a colleague or a neighbour, Elizabeth would have tried to explain survivor's guilt, about which she had read at some point in her studies, or knew intuitively and felt stirring in her own breast, but it couldn't be now, not yet, not for either of them. This wasn't the end. Hearing Marta talk about the completion of the paperwork, the stay in the hotel in San Salvador, the plane flight across the Pacific—that all happened, but it was not the end. Elizabeth didn't know when that would come. There were so many details Marta had to share first.

She described each of the children's parents, whom she had known all her life. She described her husband, Santos, and her own children, a boy named Ricardo and a boy named Abelardo. Elizabeth had children, and she listened almost chemically, the physiology of her body at the mercy of Marta's words. She sat by herself afterward with the phone in her lap, visualizing the hillside village among the coffee plants, the nineteen dwellings, each a room or two, the slopes and gullies and tree-fringed precipice where raw rock and erosion hurtled toward a deep-set mountain stream, the sunrise and sunset, the mists and little afternoon storms, the piles of burlap that young girls and old women stitched into sacks, women crying out, men shouting, guns firing, the flames roaring … somewhere that was nowhere and everywhere cracking open suddenly like the spontaneous violence of lightning revealing its invisibly accumulated force.

She waited until she was certain David had fallen asleep before she returned to bed.

***

At the office she made no mention of these calls. She continued her interviews, appalled by her own fear, forcing herself to risk meeting another Marta, *knowing* that these people, the women, the men, the children, the elderly, were all Marta but telling herself that they still needed social and health and education programs that worked, the whole program—the collective—had to work, and that was her job, seeing whether it did.

There was a birthday party for her daughter Claire, twenty-three now. She and Claire joked that they were both working girls, and she gave Claire a black leather handbag into which Claire, so beautiful and intense, immediately transferred all her things. David sang a few of his favourite old ballads. Claire's brothers, Curtis and Rand, bought her a week's vacation in Hong Kong. The family sat around the large glass-topped table in the garden behind their steeply roofed Victorian, a striking silhouette in the descending gloom. Rand's wife Penny made Elizabeth sit still while she served the coffee and liqueur after the ceremony of the cake.

Elizabeth could hardly see their faces in the wavering torch-light, but the swimming pool by the south wall did cast an opalescent glow back up into the tranquil Melbourne evening, intensifying the shadowy features of each family member, their essence ineradicable despite the absence of details, the loss of an eye to swiftly-striking night, the erasure of the back of a head, the way hair merged into the skeins of unfolding blackness. Time and again Elizabeth's gaze wandered toward the quiet, silvery pool. Her three children and daughter-in-law cleant up. David chuckled and joked with them as they did, clumping behind them up the back steps, across the porch and into the kitchen, whose lights now clashed with Elizabeth's geometry of sadness, crushing the pool's glow, the torches' flicker, the shadows in the shrubs.

***

Marta began to tell her the final truth by saying she had told Elizabeth everything. She was calling to thank Elizabeth and end her confession with a lie. Elizabeth didn't know, as she sat in her dressing room, if that was better for Marta, but for her she was certain that it was worse. She found herself trying to end the conversation with reciprocal platitudes— how important it was that they talked, how grateful she was to have gained Marta's trust. For a while it seemed Elizabeth herself couldn't stop lying until finally she moaned, "Oh, Marta, Marta, Marta …" and couldn't go on.

Marta was quiet for some time. At last she began to speak again. "There is more," she said. Elizabeth leant forward and pressed the phone hard against her ear. "Yes, Marta, I am listening."

Marta said her husband was shot in their doorway, and she didn't take the boys and run. She ran to her dying husband, and a man charged at her and grabbed her and then she got away and then the boys followed and then they were killed and then she got Corazon and Tino into the bush and Fausto and Magdalena into the corncrib but Magdalena wasn't clutching a baby and then the corncrib was set on fire and Marta ran out and freed Fausto and Magdalena and the man who had shot her husband grabbed her and pulled her away and threw her down on the ground and violated her and after that another man came and violated her and then there was a third man who could not achieve an erection but pretended to violate her and groaned as if he were finished and rolled off and the other two saw his flaccid penis and laughed at him and called him a queer and he lifted his rifle and shot one and the other shot him and then aimed at Marta to shoot her and Tino rose up with his rifle and shot him three times, his body jerking and quivering on the ground beside her each time Tino fired another bullet into him.

Marta spoke as if nothing could stop her, as if what she described had never stopped and Elizabeth listened with the vivid map in her head, all the features of the hamlet overlaid with flames, flames for houses, flames for people, flames for animals and paths and stones.

What could possibly be said? They didn't say anything until Elizabeth said, "Is that all?" and Marta said, "No," and Elizabeth said, "Oh, Marta, I know, I know, I know."

***

Marta did not call again for a week, then two. During this period, Elizabeth was not well. David, the children, and Lew could see that. David suggested some time off, perhaps see the doctor, perhaps go with Claire to Hong Kong. Lew was concerned that Elizabeth had discovered that the refugee program really was not working well. Elizabeth told him it was working fine. "What is it, then?" he asked. Elizabeth didn't answer, or answered vaguely, "Trouble sleeping."

Each night she turned off the light with an immense sense of failure. She lay flat on her back and waited until Marta would call and then pass the time when she would call to when she knew Marta wouldn't call. Elizabeth felt guilty that she had never been asked to survive or required to survive. She felt guilty that she felt guilty, ashamed and appalled, but there it was, irreducible and inescapable. What happened somewhere happened everywhere. What happened to someone happened to everyone. One night she reached over to pick up the phone and cradled it to her breast like a child, both hands clasped around it. Hadn't the poor woman lived through enough? But Elizabeth got up. She went to her dressing room and closed the door. She looked out at the darkened garden and then dialled Marta's number with no idea what to say.

you must tell us

Constance didn't like taking the van with the other Park Hill residents, all females. Eve Gagne. Lisbeth Fields. Sunny Coulter. Lucy Kemp. Dot Plank. Audrey Widman. Side by side, hip against hip. Freddie the patronizing driver telling them, "You're going to enjoy this, ladies." Who was Freddie Marchetti to tell them what they would or would not enjoy? Ah, men. Men flaked away like dandruff, bits of skin. Husbands, boyfriends, short-timers, and what were they called? One-nighters. Constance hated women giggling about one-nighters.

She irritated people herself. She was born in Southern Rhodesia long before it became Zimbabwe. Was that so complicated? Yet no one knew either country existed. Grew up in London, a London awash in brown fog, brown cigarette tobacco and brown beer, everything brown, but delicious, racy. Decided never to visit the Tower of London, confounding everyone then and now. Hadn't seen the crown jewels? No, I had better things to do, didn't you? Afterward, Africa again, Massachusetts, the divorce, Florida, the second divorce, then fellows who couldn't zip their pants or find their glasses and what about the left slipper? Where was the goddamn left slipper? She remembered Pete limping past it twice, driven by his obsession with not walking barefoot, even inside, certainly not onto the balcony for his coffee.

All the hens had these stories. Constance didn't want to hear them. Eve Gagne lectured her after only two days at Park Hill: "You don't listen, Constance. You say something, a person responds, and there is this 'no reply necessary' look on your face, as if we're all stupid. We're not all stupid. Remember that."

"I shall," Constance replied, the "shall" a perfect example of what galled the others. She'd gone to boarding school in England, learnt proper English, and been on the stage by the time she was fifteen. So she said "shall." No one said "shall" in New Jersey but Constance.

They climbed a cedar-lined drive. Freddie parked under the portico. Constance had entered the van first and exited last, her movements synchronized with neither rushing nor dawdling but with the requirements of endless self-castigation. She'd done this to herself, no one else to blame. Sold out in Miami and followed poor Jerry to Park Hill so he could be near his daughters, who despised Constance.

What a terrible death, the purple blemishing of his limbs gradually deprived of oxygen gave his bones a friable quality, one dissolving after another as if he were a large biscotti being dipped into coffee, a foot falling to the bottom of the cup, a hand, a whole arm. She wanted out, but the terms of entry had required almost everything she had. She couldn't afford withdrawal. Meanwhile Jerry's girls blamed her that an eighty-seven-year old man was crumbling. Hah. Hadn't touched him in years. The idea of loyal friendship seemed beyond them, but that's what put Constance in his will, infuriating them still further. If he wouldn't change it, they wouldn't visit him, or thought they wouldn't, but they did. He would lie in bed fantasizing he was talking to one of them, and Constance would reply, playing a daughter's role just as she would as an actress. Old men on their deathbeds have such sweet, watery, defenceless looks. If he bleated, "Lorna?" Constance answered, "Yes, Daddy," and it brought a smidgeon of peace to his troubled brow, the furrows inflamed, red as jellyfish stings. If he said, "I'd like to go to the beach, Karen, okay?" she told him okay. That soothed him, too. There was no going to the beach, but what did it matter? He was out of his mind. No lawyer would allow him to change his will even if he wanted to, which he didn't, so at least now Constance had a little money. He'd loved her, was among her best beaux, and she missed him.

The women sat on seven of the forty folding chairs in the multipurpose room. Four pubescent boys came out, led by a man with a dashing, if thinning, widow's peak and the rest of his hairline deeply receded. We are so glad you're here, ladies. All that. A brief performance for you. All that. But he had a sincerely enthusiastic look about him, and when he pivoted and raised his arms, his whole body trembled with excitement like a leashed dog that has just seen a squirrel. Three of the boys were white, one black. Naturally Constance looked at the black one. Black people had been her ground since infancy, her nannies and playmates, effectively the human horizon arrayed around the garden, the city, the countryside. They'd lived in Africa after all, and there weren't any indigenous white Africans. Even as a child Constance knew that. The sun washed them out. What remained was the deep authenticity and substance of glorious black skin.

This black boy began to sing, couldn't be other than the soloist, seizing his moment the way a twisting river follows the path of a deep gorge and finally plunges into the free fall of the cataract. His three accompanying cherubim formed a kind of aural cape, spreading out behind him. They sang little things, perhaps reflecting the music master's judgment about what old ladies could take, not too much about death but yes a little about love, the kind of love he perhaps imagined they had experienced decades ago and still cherished: "Down by the Salley Gardens," "Robin Hood and Allen-a-Dale," "John Henry," "Die Zufriedenheit." A few others. The harmonies were delicious, likewise the tenderness of the boys' voices, their unblemished belief in the eternal companionship of music and life, never one without the other, always together, forever and ever.

How loudly can seven old women clap? Not loudly, but they can croon and sigh, and one, Constance, could leap to her feet and shout, "Bravo!" as if she were at the Met, irritating all the others who did not want to get up until it was time to go, which eventually it was.

"Oh, no," Constance said, "let's stay a bit and talk to the boys."

"I really have to get back," Sunny Coulter said.

Eve Gagne said, "The boys do, too, I imagine. We've taken up quite a bit of their time."

"No, no," the music master Charles Feveral said, "it's been their delight, hasn't it boys?"

The boys said nothing. Their smiles were very small and abashed.

"Here now," Charles Feveral said, "let's pull up chairs and chat a bit. Let's do exactly that."

The boys arranged some folding chairs so that everyone sat in a kind of circle. The white boys were named Tom Malinowski, Richard Locke, and Allen Weymouth. The black boy was named Algernon Custade.

"That's an Italian name, isn't it?" Lucy Kemp asked Agnes Gagne in an indiscrete whisper.

"I have no earthly idea," Agnes replied.

"It could be, you know … a kitchen thing, the dessert," Lisbeth Fields said.

"Why on earth would it be a 'kitchen thing'?" Constance snapped.

She couldn't take her eyes off him and couldn't care less about his name. Visually she touched his nose and ran her fingers—thumb and forefinger, actually—down its bridge to its nostrils; she traced his ears, again with her eyes' fingertips; she recalled that surprising, somewhat disturbing voice. Well, it had descended heavily, hadn't it? He'd been making an effort. In fact, this could be the very last afternoon he sang before its change grew irrevocable. Every boy's voice changed.

She knew that. As a young actress, she'd lived with it, the unpredictable crack and screech generating unwelcome, unintentional laughter as those ghostly English lads blushed, almost died, of embarrassment. They wanted to hold onto the success of their boyhood, but they were plummeting into manhood, every one of them.

The music master had a plan, and the women, all experienced in what was coming, grew reserved, even severe, as he sketched it out. From the Warner Boys' Choir School every boy would be going somewhere else. Tom, Richard, and Allen already knew where—schools up the East Coast. The issue was where would Algernon go, and how could it be financed? Year after year the school faced the same problem. Mr Feveral cooperated with a number of choirs in South Carolina to get just the right boy and bring him to New Jersey for sixth, seventh and eighth grade, but then?

Agnes asked, "Why couldn't he simply go back to South Carolina when his replacement arrives?"

"Where in South Carolina?" Dot Plank asked.

"Saluda," Mr Feveral said, "which isn't much of a place, to tell you the truth."

"Who were you singing with in Saluda?" Sunny asked Algernon directly.

"The church choir, ma'am," Algernon answered.

The three white boys looked at Algernon with a mixture of envy and pity. They were embarrassed for him, but Feveral kept going.

"When I first heard him it was just in the nick of time. He had a voice beyond belief. Already they were making him sing too much and too often. The congregation loved him and passed him to other churches. He'd sometimes perform four times in a weekend!"

"Who paid for him to come here?" Lisbeth asked.

"A judge in Saluda, but he's done all he can. In fact …"

"He's passed away?" Lucy asked.

Feveral looked at Lucy with wry consternation. How did

she know?

Algernon sat before them utterly expressionless. His hair was short, he had full lips, and wore a white shirt that was a bit brown at the collar.

Constance asked him, "What do *you* want to do, Algernon?"

Algernon didn't answer. He was almost, Constance sensed, the epitome of thousands of youngsters she'd seen in Southern Rhodesia for whom such a question would be meaningless. What did *they* want to do? What did *their* wishes matter? Who had wishes? She felt torn, fearing she might add permanently to his embarrassment, but the idea she had in mind required an answer or there would be no point. He had to be able to speak, he had to be able to demonstrate that he could defend himself with more than his pure voice while also enduring its change. He couldn't be inarticulate and hopeless. She'd never been either. It was how she survived and explained how she could sit there thinking what she was thinking despite the fact that the other women were looking at her with impatience and what might be called dislike.

"You must tell us, Algernon, or there is no way you can be helped," she said.

"Oh, Constance," Dot murmured, "don't push him."

Feveral seemed to agree, sensing his gambit would bear no fruit. "We'll work something out. It will just take a little more time."

"He'd probably rather not have his future discussed in public like this," Agnes said. "Perfectly understandable."

"I agree," Sunny said.

Then surprisingly Algernon spoke. "I'd like to go to Europe, I think."

This statement roiled the woman, all except Constance. An unstated suspicion arose that perhaps he was saying he wanted to reverse his ancestors' voyage to America. That thought came first. Next came the financial implications: Europe cost a fortune.

"Do you speak a foreign language?" Audrey Widman asked.

"He can sing in German, Italian and French," Mr Feveral

said, "but none of them *speaks* a foreign language."

Constance began talking. She said she'd been sent from Southern Rhodesia to a school right by the Halls of Parliament in London and she was utterly miserable for the better part of a year, but it was a wonderful school then and a wonderful school now with one of the finest music and theatre programs anywhere.

"If you like, Algernon, I'll contact the school and if we can work out admission, I'll pay for you to attend. It's a pre-Oxford sort of school. Not just music. Everything."

Lisbeth Fields didn't explicitly say what she wanted to say, but she conveyed the idea anyway by using the word homogeneity, meaning, Would there be any blacks there?

Constance remembered arriving and finding that no, there weren't any blacks there, not even the porters and maids and so forth. Lots of brown ingrained in everything, but no black. Consequently she'd felt bereft. She'd cried every day for months. She written home, begging and then demanding to be allowed to return. Her father said the political situation was such that either she stayed where she was or moved on to America. Africa was out. Or so he thought.

Eventually it became America. Eventually it became all over America and now this afternoon in New Jersey accompanied by some rough calculations as to whether her share of Jerry's estate would do the trick, and whether the boy whom, if she'd been thirteen, she'd want to marry, would now find enough black post-colonial companionship to survive being thrown all the way across the Atlantic. What was London like now? It had to be better. The empire had collapsed and so many talented blacks had nowhere to go but there.

"Please, Algernon, will you consider this? I don't promise they'll take you, but if they do, I'll pay your way through."

Music master Feveral was jiggling in his seat, overjoyed; now he was the joyous squirrel who'd scampered away from the barking dog. The other women pulled their rumps back and straightened up.

Eve whispered, "Constance, do you realize what you saying?"

Constance answered, "I should think so, otherwise I wouldn't have said it, would I?"

Algernon looked at his schoolmates. Their smiles couldn't be as beautiful as his simply because they didn't have such a wonderful contrast between their teeth and their skin.

"Now you all go back in the van with Freddie," Constance told the other ladies. "I'll call a cab once Mr Feveral, Algernon and I have sorted a few things out."

Thus they departed without her, and the other three boys left the room, too, and Constance begged Mr Feveral's and Algernon's forgiveness because she simply had to take a few moments to cry.

the woman in yemen

My wife and I dispute over Annie. Are we going to her house for Thanksgiving to protect Annie's family from itself, or Annie from her family? Not clear which. See, our families are largely dead, so we adopted Annie's, or Annie's adopted us … not clear on that point either. I have my view, she has hers. Who needs mercy more? I say them, she says us.

With nothing settled, she hops out of the car and I drive off in search of a place to park. Having found a distant spot in the leaves along the curb, I realize I would rather just walk around the neighbourhood, enjoy the misty November dusk, the perfect comfort each scaled house bespeaks   solid, weather-worthy, full of warmth and good smells. But I have to go into Annie's little brick cottage where everyone's arrayed in a suspicious circle, holding out against this annual ritual of unrequited love.

A boy with curly brown hair plays a game on a handheld device. His mom's not there, that's one absence. Seems she and Annie's brother, Mike, plan to divorce. Another absence is Tom, sister Toni's second husband. Tom died last summer. Too fat; heart attack; forty-seven. Their son Peter is a half foot taller this year and getting fat, too. Perhaps to compensate, Toni's daughter, Kelly, by her first husband has showed up. Never joined us before. Pretty Kelly doesn't say anything. Like Toni, she's bipolar, sometimes in up quark mode, sometimes in down quark mode. Definitely down tonight.

Sam, Annie's husband, doesn't care. He's drinking diet Snapple secretly laced with vodka that mixes well with his Vicodin. Not saying anything, either. His father-in-law, Grandpa Ray, who's eighty and used to smack Annie across the face when she was a little girl, is sitting beside Grandma Gwen, his wife, on the couch. They don't look at one another. Smile in different directions. Up from Florida. Aren't going to go into anything except storm damage and memories of the Korean War, when times were so bad they were good.

Then there's Annie's other brother, Bill, who owns the largest collection of old Volvos and spare parts in the country and his harried wife with that fugitive look beneath her helmet-like hairdo. Last year she said she couldn't go on teaching kinder-gartners. Couldn't shut up about it. This year she can't shut up about the new principal who tried to put her in middle school to ease her pain. But she resisted and now has seventeen preschoolers, two to four, which is impossible. Here's how preschoolers work: When gathered in the same classroom, the four-year-olds regress to three, the three to two, the two to one. Piss and poop everywhere.

I count on my past experience—no one will ask me anything about myself—and sit next to Annie's son Caleb (by her first marriage) who has been in a large law firm since June. This firm begins firing new hires after three years. Historically, only 2% make partner. Caleb tells me he expects to keep lawyering after he's let go while later telling my wife he wishes he could put on a backpack and just walk. Anywhere. Both futures can't be true, but he's smart. Had a full scholarship all the way through law school so he could get this good job from which he'll be canned. Lawyers, as they say, can do anything.

Grandpa Ray says he has a lawyer friend who was in the north tower on 9/11 and the loudspeaker said no one should move. After ten minutes, the lawyer friend told everyone to move anyway. They all lived. That's a hero, Korean War stuff like back in Grandpa Ray's day. Other heroes are the guys who fought on flight 93 in Pennsylvania. Brother Bill, Grandpa

Ray and I agree we'd have fought, too. More Korean War stuff. But what about landing the plane if we prevailed? We debate whether auto-pilot can do it. Bill says no, and we must defer because he owns all those Volvos and saw a *60 Minutes* piece where five non-flyers were put in simulators, and only one was talked through landing safely. The others crashed big time before they could make the auto-pilot work.

I say I love giant machines. Soon-to-be divorced Mike says he was a logger years ago and used to drive oak trunks down mountainsides six at a time. His rig had a snow plough to aid in both braking and steering. He'd keep it low and if the rig wandered, he'd drop it and redirect or slow his progress by cutting into the roadbed.

"Why did you stop logging?" I ask.

Mike says loggers only stop logging for one reason, they go broke. Best job he ever had, steering with his snow plough.

We begin talking about the mahogany tree on Grandpa Ray's condo grounds in Florida, all beat up by the last storm. It's got to come down. Dropping nuts on people. One old lady tripped, broke her ankle, and sued the community association. I say sell the wood. Ray says there's no market for it. Mahogany? I ask. There's different kinds of mahogany, he says. This one's all knotty and burly.

"Well, that could make it especially valuable for table makers and even sculptors," I say. "They could make a movie about you old guys finally making the killing of your lives."

Brother Bill laughs, delighted by the thought of his father finally winning the Korean War. Grandpa Ray smiles, skipping over this filial funny-stuff. His problem is the county says they can take the tree down but must replace it with two, and there's no room for two. He wanted to put in a royal palm and was told it didn't generate enough oxygen. So back to the drawing board. Maybe a silver buttonwood.

Have we seen Annie? No, we haven't seen Annie, but now here she is, small, wiry, wearing her apron like chainmail for protection. She announces dinner: squash, mashed potatoes with cheddar cheese, turkey, of course, stuffing that includes oysters, green beans in vinaigrette, salad, chocolate cake with a cheesecake centre, coffee and Grand Marnier for those who can pass her breathalyser test. We toast her before cramming into the little dining room, Sam with his Absolut Snapple, me with my fourth glass of wine.

Toni says her grief over losing her husband sometimes hits her like one of those wandering waves in the oceans; otherwise she's okay. Her son isn't, though. He breaks down in class and is sent to the psychologist's office two or three times a week. And she can't travel, just when she wanted to most because she's a sociologist tracking the effect of Twitter on the Arab spring. People all over the Middle East tweet once, sometimes thousands of them in a second, then go silent, so no one can trace them, but there's a woman in Yemen, a node, who bravely retweets what she's pulled in from the suffering folk of Egypt, Libya, Tunisia and Bahrain. Toni would like to meet her. Her apartment in Sana'a must be set up with more computer equipment than Google in California.

The disturbed boy still has his gizmo in his hand, ignoring his mother's lament. The rest of us nod and cut and chew. Annie stays safe in the kitchen. Won't let Grandma Gwen come help her out. No room in there, all taken care of, desserts are on their way.

The old regime, the one that brought us here, the genetic defects, deaths, moments of questionable passion, close calls, ancient abuses, and lingering mysterious ties, can't last forever. That's now clear. Grandpa Ray's mahogany tree is already gone; my sixth glass of wine is almost done; Kelly is telling Toni she's heading off; the boy who lost his father now says he is not feeling well, too much cheesecake not the cause.

An inaudible whistle blows through us all. Game is over. Time to go.

My wife and I step onto the front porch, together for the first time since we arrived. Our car is nowhere in sight. She begins to ask me why, as always, I have parked so far away. I begin to frame my defence. But she stops herself. I do, too. We know the woman in Yemen is listening. Our grumbling is nothing she needs to hear.

through the ice

I

Out of the blue Suzanne received an email from Allen Federman telling her that he was moving to the Land of Zim and saying goodbye. She asked herself what could have drawn Allen to Zimbabwe and what he meant by "goodbye." Had he met someone in the gold mining business when he was posing for a jewellery ad? She wrote back, "I don't know what to say except good luck. From what I read, it's now the worst country in the world. You must have your reasons." Allen replied, "I do." That's all. Just, "I do." She found this ominous. Was he saying he was dying without wanting to be clear, which would be exactly like him—punishing her for ignorance he himself created?

She'd had the longest and most difficult relationship of her life with Allen and brooded about him a great deal the next few days. As she engraved a block of boxwood with her burin, one part of her mind was silent but another part spoke.

She remembered that when they were together, she'd sometimes say, "I'll end up in the Land of Zim." By that she meant she wouldn't be able to survive as an artist in America and be deported. Zimbabwe, like the letter Z, was her symbol for the end of the line. (She didn't think about it as Southern Rhodesia anymore, the name of the country she left when she was nine.) But she'd laugh, curious about what it would be like to return to the beautiful place where she had been a child, though now as a member of the dispossessed. Her father was furious at her for not taking US citizenship; she didn't because she thought it was unwise to surrender the things that made you who you were. You only ended up like him, impoverished in ways that were truly painful, not simply impoverished in the literal sense. That never scared her. She'd always find some way to make do.

She and Allen were together for five years during his final cruises as a nuclear sub captain and before he became an international male model. Their relationship was like the beating of a heart, full of blood, then empty, full of blood, then empty. The alternating eroticism of presence followed by absence. All the anticipation, the entrancing mystery and enigma of who he was and who he thought she was and her reckless acceptance of everything he gave her without ever asking for it. He set the terms. Twenty years older. In command except for the extreme moments of lovemaking (the whimpering, the pleas) and whatever he thought as he pondered her work.

They met in New York during that dismal post-college period when she was selling things on the street. He bought three prints one Saturday morning in Washington Square and came back Sunday to buy two more, a man in his forties with compelling eyebrows and inquisitive blue eyes and leanness everywhere and the pure, unsunned skin of the submariner. He asked her to lunch that Sunday. She hesitated but agreed. Afterward she was too embarrassed (and wary) to let him tote her portfolios back to her dismal flat on the Lower East Side.

She told herself that he couldn't really be interested in her; it had to be her work. She was too young and unkempt (his pet name for her became Raggedy Suzanne, shortened to Raggedy, also the name of the doll he gave her quite gravely one day, the way another lover might present a ring), and still pudgy with baby fat, and just not sophisticated. That made New York hard for her. You had to be assertive, but you had to preserve your solitude, too.

This is what Allen taught her, how to steer herself anywhere without getting lost. "I knew I was meant for submarines the first week at Annapolis," he said. He needed the confinement and danger and discipline of guiding a nuclear-powered vessel through canyons miles below the waves. But he confessed that long undersea journeys wore on him and everyone on board. After they took the first dive of a cruise, the real depths they entered were the depths of time.

"The pressure builds but you can't admit it, certainly not the captain. The captain must remain relaxed. No sunlight. Everything made out of metal. Temperature always the same."

"What do you see?"

"We don't have picture windows. Even if we did, the water is blacker than the darkest night. Could you engrave that?"

"How would I?" she giggled.

"I don't know. Variations on ink?"

"Are there any variations?"

"You think you feel variations—water temperature, currents—but that's just an extrapolation from your instruments. You couldn't see them with your eyes."

He had bought prints of Suzanne and a little friend of hers (white girl and black girl), a man driving a donkey cart with a boy on the donkey's back, worshippers exiting the Zim cathedral, sinewy men hauling tobacco into the auction house, and a portrait of her mother in a room she almost never frequented, the kitchen. Her style in those days was a mixture of influences: Van Gogh, Kollwitz, to a lesser degree Max Beckmann. Her shapes were blocky, stable, and elemental. The heads were disproportionately larger than the bodies. There was a certain amount of crowding. She did not restrain herself early in her career; she was too caught up in trying to turn a wood block into a movie screen. Had to squeeze in a patch of crumbling wall, a knife-slice of face cropped along the print's edge—Ernst Kirchner.

"Will you take my prints with you on your next cruise?" she asked, not seriously. But he said yes. Apparently this was a serious matter to him. He always took a portfolio of images with him at sea in a tubular leather chart case whose brass end pieces doubled as weights to keep the charts from curling up when they were removed. She asked what other works he'd take along.

"Just yours."

She said she didn't believe that.

The romance began the next time Allen was in New York. He bought another piece of her work. (Suzanne and her friend, Amadika, having tea in the grass, her father reading a book on the porch, her mother staring down into the garden reprovingly from a second floor window, and her sister Alma, if you looked carefully through a ground floor window, in a bassinet: not actually Alma, just the reed bassinet in which she nestled, and not Alma's nurse, just her black hand on the bassinet's rim.) Afterward he invited Suzanne to a restaurant she couldn't go into because of her clothes. He remedied this by cajoling her into letting him buy her a blouse and skirt in a store across the street. Then he marched her back to the restaurant, almost as if she were his little girl, her temperament flaring. Was she angry with him? Flattered? Turned on? She didn't stop struggling until they were settled at the table. Then she asked him questions about his life at sea because she was too timid to ask him about his life right there on land, where he struck her as a gorgeous marine creature that had been evicted from its shell, leaving him in a state of vulnerability that was almost prenatal, his armour and even skin peeled away to the delicate, iridescent cells beneath. Every private tissue and membrane and electric connection between their nerves and thoughts and pleasure centres spun together as they sat there having sex across the table without even touching.

This quirky first date set a template that they followed, more extravagantly, even after she'd moved up to Connecticut, where he introduced her to the people at the Art Barn, and she established her studio and managed to buy the tiny farm house with its half acre of apple trees. He would return from a voyage, and they would drive to Manhattan in his Alfa Romeo, and he would buy her some new "outfits," as he called them, because he was a sailor who always wanted a new woman when he came into port.

She couldn't imagine submitting to this benevolent dictatorship now, but then she had no money for clothes, and women's fashion fascinated him. He would walk in a store, look around, say, "Not for you," and lead them right out. Or he'd stop before a display window and sketch out a full strategy before they went through the door—those boots, that bag, this sweater, and perhaps a scarf or a shawl to go along with these blouses. He could be difficult with the sales people. His eyebrows grew oratorical, expressing dismay and disappointment. His eye for the precise length of cuffs, the cut of collars and shoulders, and the flow of fabrics was impeccable. No one else she knew in the arts who didn't have a rich husband could dress this way. There was never a proposal, however, just the clothes, which served her well in the studio when people came in from Greenwich and Darien and Old Lyme and were taken by her elegant formality in striking contrast to the increasing daring of her work, her subjects less naively portrayed and enjambed.

They would make love two or three times a day in their hotel suite—before they went out, when they came back, before they slept. She was a young woman who set no conditions on her free days, didn't care if she got a thing done, and wouldn't always stop when he stopped, continuing on, much the same way she did at the table on that first date, their companionship uninterruptedly sexualized by her drive and eagerness for more. But he'd take his time, stirring things up with long interludes of faux crescendos and insertions of normal life as foreplay. This was the Eros of him as the captain and her as the ship, until that desperation she saw in him but never mentioned when he was the ship and she was the sea.

After shopping they visited galleries, starting with Tommy

DeMarco, to whom Allen had introduced her and who now carried her work, the first big break of her career. When Allen recounted her life story, he made sure people knew she was African, enjoying their ambivalence about her whiteness. He told how he found her selling her work on the street. He seemed to adore her if not love her. She didn't know if he was capable of love. Maybe she wasn't, either, preferring these wind-whipped trysts, boat and water lost in the foam. What did she know about love with a family—mother, father, sister—that always split emotions in two, or ten, or a thousand, like crystals refracting light? Warm became cold. Laughter incited tears.

At night he hired a car. "Where to, Harry?" he'd ask.

"Sir, I'm drowning in good ideas," Harry would say. "I'm thinking you need to see Feathers. You need to see Club La Frontera. You're going to die when you hear the singer at Mr Morgan's. Years of second string opera, then bam—the city's best chanteuse, Ingrid Bierstadt."

"What a name!"

"What a voice, sir."

Allen asked Suzanne if she could sing. Suzanne said no.

"But have you ever tried?" he pressed, apparently thinking she must be wrong about herself.

Suzanne laughed and looked out the window, not answering.

"I'll bet you could," he insisted.

"No, I couldn't. Now stop it."

In a way she grew up with him. He was like a marker against which she measured her progress through her twenties (more self-confidence, more assertiveness) although he remained the grown-up in their relationship.

And yet sometimes he would talk to her in a funny child's voice as they lay in bed, treating her as if she were the doll he'd given her. He'd say that he wished they could nestle together forever. He'd say that he wished he could hide her in his cabin on the submarine, his dear Raggedy.

Suzanne teased him once by suggesting that he take the doll

along on a voyage since he couldn't take her. "Just hide it in your things, no one has to know." She thought the idea of a submarine captain with a doll in his footlocker was hysterical. Allen grew furious—really furious—when she kept laughing about it. He got dressed and left and wouldn't accept her apology.

They squabbled. If he was too awful in a store. If he tried to give her hairdresser instructions. If he lectured her instead of asking her about German expressionism. He could be unbearable when he tried to sound better informed and more worldly than he was, or when he was making up for sixty dry nights at sea by drinking too much.

"How do you go so long without a drink?" she asked.

He said that he went without almost everything when he was at sea.

"That doesn't bore you?"

He said that land bored him more.

"I'm here on land."

He ignored her protest, insisting that he was more aware of things when he was at the bottom of the ocean. "The isolation keeps me engaged."

He made her feel that he wanted to hurt her when he said something like this, deriding the erasable quality of terrestrial life, its lack of what he called danger, or, on occasion, necessity. (His highest praise for a piece she or another artist produced was that he found it necessary, it couldn't be otherwise, it had to be exactly as it was. He detested things he found arbitrary.)

It was better when she had moved to Connecticut, and they limited their New York sprees to two or three days, and she could get back in her house and return to her studio while he did follow-up reports and planning and training exercises, often staying at the sub base and not coming to visit her too often. This was good. She had to work to make her living, and she liked working. Any day was too long if she didn't work. She took one day off per week, but only one, Tuesday.

Allen had never married. She assumed that he never would.

This didn't prey on her mind because in some ways he was like a child. Who would marry a child, or have a child with a child? He bored her sometimes with Cold War bluster and tales of undersea roughhousing with the Soviets—tedious accounts of war games, moves and countermoves. She preferred hearing him describe surfacing through the polar ice cap, and what it was like to mount the conning tower in a field of nothing but white. He said the sky couldn't escape the white and the air couldn't escape it either. He felt something like panic. You can't be here, he thought; this wind will consume you; why have you surfaced in this nowhere?

"If I could draw or paint or engrave anything," he said, "that's what I'd try to do. It was the exposure. I felt so exposed."

"It would be a sheet of white paper, or a blank canvas, I suppose."

"No, that wouldn't have the right gnawing quality." He was very troubled by this memory. "I'd wanted to come up through the ice for years; you have to do it; but I never had. Then you go up and have a look and nothing can prepare you for how desperate it makes you feel. For weeks you've been encased in your vessel, and there is always a restricted line of sight. Then you're caught up in the whole epic of ice. It will grind you down to your bones in a matter of minutes. It's unbearable."

She would have given anything to see the polar ice cap and welcome its terror. Equally, she would have given anything to know how to place her hands on the ice inside him.

She asked him once what he did for sex on his cruises. He turned the question back on her. "What about you?"

"When you're away? Why should a girl tell her secrets?"

"Do we have secrets from one another?"

She joked that everyone had secrets. His whole job was a secret, and wasn't he a secret inside his job? "With all you've told me, I still don't understand who you are."

"Are you saying you really want to?" He was referring to what he did for sex on the submarine as if she were being literal, which she wasn't. She was trying, actually, to be close. "Don't I make love to you enough when I come back?" he pressed.

"Okay, let's drop it."

"No, I'd like an answer. You seem eager enough when I show up."

"Exactly, you have nothing to worry about."

"But you think you do?" His head was cocked at an angle that was unfamiliar to her, making him seem not just irate but aggressive. His tone was alarming.

Suzanne thought she should work her way out of this exchange. "I was only asking, the way lame-brained people do, how the whole question of sexuality gets sublimated. I know you can't be having affairs on a submarine. That's obvious."

"Is it so obvious? Don't you think there's ever a time we have to deal with that?"

"If you mean blowjobs in the bathroom, I don't want to hear about it."

"What do you know about blowjobs in bathrooms?"

"I don't know anything."

"I've never even heard you use a word like blowjob."

"I shouldn't have this time either."

He said she could be an awful hypocrite. He told her that her suggestiveness was spoiling her art now. She'd lost her early vision, which sometimes happened to artists, unfortunately.

She laughed at him. A thought that had been on her mind for some time came out in that laugh. His superiority for being more sophisticated and a submarine captain and spoiling her had worn out. Her laugh dismissed his judgments and obsessions about her and her art.

He hit her. The blow landed on her right ear so hard that she found herself on the floor without knowing what happened. When she tried to get up, she pulled over a lamp. Its glass globe broke and sliced into her temple, which began bleeding profusely.

Allen shouted, "Look at what you've done!"

She tried to scuttle away from him, but he grabbed her and picked her up and hurried down the stairs to get to his car, now moaning in his familiar, little boy voice, "We've got to get you to a doctor, we've got to get you to a doctor," as if whatever possessed him to strike her didn't exist anymore. But Suzanne was furious at him. She scratched at his eyes. She tried to bite him. They fell and struggled in the dirt behind the house. Finally, he hit her with the butt of his palm below the sternum, rendering her breathless. She was almost grateful to him for stunning her this way, but it was a ghastly experience, followed by their embarrassment at the emergency room as they lied about what obviously had happened and were told she might lose her hearing in her right ear.

Afterward, he tried to look after her, bringing her meals and paying the bills for her ruptured eardrum. "This won't ever, ever happen again. Please believe me."

"How can I believe you, Allen? Why did you do it? You haven't told me."

"I don't know why."

She didn't like being alone with him. She asked him to stay away and give her time, at least until she got rid of her cane and wouldn't be tempted to hit him with it.

"You could hit me all you want."

"Oh, please," she said. "Look, if we can be friends, let's be friends."

"I can't be just your friend. You mean too much to me."

"Allen, I am not going to be your … whatever."

"The word is lover."

"Is it?"

He said he wanted to return to who they'd been.

She said no, regretting that it was too late tell him she wouldn't mind if he led a double life. The only thing that made no sense to her was people lying about themselves.

A cruise intervened, making things easier for her but apparently not for him. When he returned, he wanted to hold her if not make love, just hold her, forcing her to tell him to stop calling her Raggedy and accept how things had turned out.

He choked out that he was going to retire from the Navy.

Was he saying he feared she would reveal what he had done? She wouldn't but didn't want to say so. Any intimation that she was judging him might turn him against her again. That's what she must guard against, just as she must guard against him drawing her into responsibility for his decisions and their consequences. They had grown together, their strange, sensitive skins intermingling, for Suzanne was a creature without much of a shell, too. Now those interconnections had to be torn loose.

In the face of her resistance, Allen seemed to give up. He began discussing retirement the way a person normally would, not a person who was panicked about where he would hide if the oceans were going to be sealed against him. He drew a cloak of practicality around himself, dissecting offers he'd had in industry and international trade—counting the money and comparing the benefits, showing her pictures of the kind of ketch he planned to buy and talking about moving to Washington, which he had always disliked, or perhaps Annapolis, which he had loved since his days as a midshipman at the Naval Academy.

Suzanne regretted his newfound conventionality, but they needed to secure a truce; and this is what did it. And they never, in subsequent years, reflected on how differently he managed his retirement from how he foreshadowed it, or how much becoming a model revealed about him, although he always brought his latest magazine ads when he dropped by her studio and talked about them so much that there was never time to discuss her new work, which he would glance at surreptitiously and anxiously but never again buy.

II

Shortly after receiving Allen's email, she received a letter from a man who wanted to commission a personal study. (Did that mean nude?) He wanted to give it to someone who was leaving the country as a farewell gift. Would she meet with him to discuss this?

She called the man and told him to come to her studio, remembering to point out that she was in the Periscope Plant now, not the Art Barn, which had burnt. Of course, he wouldn't have written to her at the Art Barn if he hadn't come across her through something or someone from the past—Allen, for instance?

William, the letter writer's name, was just beginning to surrender his second adolescence as people do when they're approaching thirty. She contemplated him as a print as soon as he walked through the door—the scalloping between the corners of his eyes and the bridge of his nose, the dominance of the high forehead, the scrollwork of his ears, his springy black hair, his chin padded by a buttery knob of flesh. He called himself a fashionista and was wearing a black jumpsuit he'd copied from the Italian carabinieri. He said he made it himself. All the lettering and unit symbolism and marks of rank were meaningless variations on the originals, as decorative and impenetrable as Koranic quotations on the walls of mosques.

"Do I look like someone you could do?" he asked, blushing at his unintended double entendre.

She wasn't hiding the fact that she was scrutinizing him. His smile generated parentheses at the corners of his mouth, but he wouldn't be smiling in the print. She wondered what that would do to the parentheses, and how he held his head when he wasn't animated.

"You said a 'personal study.' What did you mean by that?"

"I meant all my person."

"Nude?"

"Yes."

She couldn't see much of him in his jump suit, but he would be sinewy. She thought of her sister Alma, also sinewy, a former dancer. Had William been one, too? His bony knees, elbows and shoulders would anchor his long spine. He would have a flat, fish-like belly, chevroned with black hair. There was never any predictability about a model's genitals. The penis and scrotum were as specific as the male face and more difficult to render because of their constant mollusc-like squirming.

Did he plan to talk about the friend who was moving abroad for whom this study was to be a gift? Wasn't he an emissary from Allen? Weren't the email and the letter too linked in time and topic to be coincidental? Allen did not look well when she last saw him; he looked older and hoarier, but still good enough to attract someone as compelling as William, and, being Allen, Machiavellian enough to send William to her to confess through him what he could never say in person. "I'm gay, Suzanne, but now William is over and the only thing left for me is Zim." Was Allen dying? Did he have AIDS?

William, however, said nothing about the friend who would receive the print. He chose to talk about himself, self-centred but cheery, energetic and friendly. "I want to give you the opportunity to know me as you work on me. I mean, after all, look." He pointed at her work surrounding them on the walls of her studio. "I know you."

She did not believe that the artist and the work were one and the same. Only in the moment of creation. "Okay, why not start now? Tell me about yourself."

William said he was barely making it in the fashion business. "Very small runs for very small vendors, and a lot of disappointment in production. I have to wear the manufactured pieces and keep my handmade studies in the closet so these machine jobs don't suffer by comparison." He held up his arms.

"Are you telling me that isn't one of your handmade pieces?"

William giggled. "Well, of course it is. Today's different. I'm modelling for you, not selling!"

He had his things produced by his former neighbours and high school classmates in Millville, Tennessee, where he grew up. He said he didn't want to be sexist, but he had to teach them all how to sew, which he had learnt how to do right at the Fashion Institute of Technology. He got his ideas from second hand stores, military surplus stores, and industrial clothing manufacturers. "Everything I do is a variation on something else. I'm about roles as much as about style and elegance, but I do try to get past the clichés."

"Does everyone have to be built like a dancer to wear your things?"

"Oh, even with your curves, we could fit you," he laughed. "Maybe as a grease monkey? Sunoco had wonderful coveralls."

"I'd try anything," Suzanne confessed, liking him.

He had slipped onto a shipping container. His eyes flickered at the blocks she had arranged like books on three long shelves above her worktable. "You said the Art Barn burnt. I guess I got confused looking at your website so that's where I wrote you. You didn't lose anything?"

"A few of us were spared. I was one of the lucky ones."

"I used the periscope downstairs to watch you working up here. It's amazing. You could have been on the moon."

"That periscope probably gets more people in here than the art."

The centre of the building was an open well, permitting periscope assembling and calibration during World War II and for decades thereafter. Three catwalks encircled the well, providing access to studios that occupied the upper floor space once used for machine work and mirror grinding.

"Where do you live, outside town?"

Again, William seemed to know something, but it was out of date, the way Allen would be out of date—he hadn't come to visit her in more than two years; he didn't know about the changes in her life.

"I moved into town when we came here. I bought a little row house a few blocks away."

"I mean, I don't think I could pose here, could I?"

She had already considered locking the door, putting up a closed sign and hanging a curtain. It wouldn't work. They wouldn't have the things they might need to give him context, a bed, a sofa, a doorway, a table, unless she simply studied him sitting there on the box, naked as if he were a one-man show in a theatre. Had anyone ever done that, walked on stage nude, taken a seat, and told stories? What effect would that have, the man (or woman) oblivious to the impact of nudity, wrenching the audience away from the body self to the talking self, the observing, reflecting, feeling self?

After Allen hit her, male-female moments were uncertain for her. She doubted she wanted William nude in her house, but that was the logical, perhaps only, place for this.

"You said this is a going away present for someone moving overseas?"

"Yes."

Maybe he didn't know what he wanted to say about Allen; maybe he'd been bullied into this; maybe he had rethought why he was there; maybe he assumed she had figured it all out.

"If it's a nude, would it be a lover? Do you mind my asking?"

William's face darkened slightly, but he wasn't blushing. "Well, that's over, and everything else."

She waited for him to say more. He wasn't going to. He was stubborn because he was upset. That upset her, too. Allen might be dead, and this might be, who knew, a work that William would burn and sprinkle into Allen's ashes in his chart case before dropping it into the sea.

III

The following Thursday William drove up from New York in the white van he used for trips to Tennessee. He had agreed to model for a full morning and pay her $2500 for the print that emerged without precluding her from selling more from the same block. Perhaps that really was enough, Suzanne thought; perhaps it was better that he didn't reveal why he had come to her. There was a reason why she had never done a print of

Allen or any other lover. What she did with a subject didn't correspond to what she might see and feel walking down the street holding someone's hand. She saw and felt other things and did not want anything to alter that.

Her narrow row house had a small living room, dining room and kitchen downstairs, and two bedrooms and a bath upstairs. William tramped around a bit, eyeing everything, commenting on the fact that there was no food in the kitchen and letting his hand graze her worktable in the dining room. She didn't have her own pieces on the walls, just things she'd received over the years in trades with other artists. He said he was sorry about that. She didn't reply, already studying him.

"How do we do this?" he asked.

"You take off your clothes, and when you're ready, I'll take pictures with this little camera. Then I'll make some sketches."

"It's funny. I watch models undress all the time, but now we're talking about me."

She could feel the tug of his abashed arousal, the aggressive-apologetic way a man stood square to a woman he knew didn't want him. "It was your idea," she reminded him.

"Well, is there somewhere I should go?"

"I think you should go wherever you want to. The light's good in the kitchen, but kitchens aren't that personal."

He was wearing a Mao suit made of heatherish wool with yellow piping sewn into the cuffs and around the buttonholes. It gave him a penal, runaway look.

"Do we pretend you're not here? As though your place was my place?"

"Take that thought as far as you want."

"Me as you?"

"Maybe not that far. We want you to be you."

"But I hide in these clothes. Why do you think I make them?"

"I was fourteen the first time I drew a nude male," she said to reassure him.

"I'll have to go upstairs. That's where you undress, isn't it?"

"We're talking about you, William."

William climbed the steep staircase. Suzanne waited a few minutes, listening to the floorboards squeak overhead, the sound of a man urinating, the rush of the water closet. Then she heard him open the door to the front bedroom where she had a daybed and many racks of clothes because she didn't ever throw clothes away. She heard metal hangers sliding this way and that. He was riffling through her blouses and dresses, going back to things Allen had bought her, the very beginning of what could be called her wardrobe. Was he nude yet? Had he left his Mao suit in the windowless bathroom?

She climbed the stairs and looked at him running his finger-tips over the sleeve of a white mohair sweater she wouldn't wear again in a million years. He was barefoot; his legs were lean but not especially muscular. His penis resembled a young deer's budding antler, thick and furry, just poking out of the tuft of his black pubic hair. Then his finger-like ribs, his broad collarbone, and the arc of his nose and depth of his eyes settled beneath his cloudbank forehead.

She took several pictures of him inspecting her clothing, each article doll size in his large hands but with no doll inhabiting them. Did he already know these pieces? Had Allen told him about them? Suzanne had an uneasy feeling about Allen, who didn't know this house, whose gifts no longer fit her. Her baby fat was gone; and Suzanne didn't sew well enough to alter the things he'd given her, which was the question William seemed to be asking as he held up a pair of trousers like a valet inquiring of his mistress whether it really made sense to keep them.

He walked to the double casement window and stared down into the street, letting her photograph him from behind. His buttocks were plumper than she expected, reminding her of the pad of flesh on the point of his chin. His back was long, the vertebrae prominent.

He turned and sat down on the floor, leaning back against the wall below the window, letting her study him with the grocery store across the street visible in the background, his knees raised, his genitals hanging free of his groin, his expression something that did not have a name as she worked. (There was no time for a name, nor did she have any interest in a name.)

He got up and walked past her into her bedroom. Finding the bed unmade, he crawled into it and lay on his side looking out the window toward the sagging row houses across the alley.

Was he going to tell her that he had been getting nowhere? That he one day decided to put on a French sailor's suit and hold poses in Washington Square? That a man came, that the man invited him to lunch?

No, he said it this way: He said he was still in love, of course he was still in love, but there was no remedy and the image had to be, obviously, as dark as the feeling, which he could express now, working his way down into the sheets.

"As dark as the sea?" she asked.

"As dark as the sea," he agreed. "I mean, you're particularly good at that."

"People seem to think so."

"Well, I'm not. He won't even tell me where he's going."

Who, Allen? She waited for him to say so. But he didn't, afraid she would explain to him what the Land of Zim meant, or could mean: that Allen had found a way not to hit someone to say goodbye; that Allen finally found a way to love someone; that William should be happy, even if Allen was—what else could he be doing?—going away to where you died.

"But I found your stuff rolled up in an old leather case, and I'm putting this print in there, too, and when he opens it wherever he's going, I'll be there, too."

William turned onto his back and looked across the foot-board at Suzanne, a gloomy look of triumph on his face, her sheets swaddling him, his forehead as bold as an infant's. This was his pose, she knew, and he knew it, too.

after apple-picking

They started taking things from her. First, the marriage, then the job. She should have been chosen as deputy county attorney. She knew it was because she was a domestic abuse victim who divorced her husband and made sure he went to jail. Watching the rising sun bless the day above the Sandia Mountains, she decided to appeal not being picked. She had more years on the job, more convictions, and more awards than Ted Billings. How could he be chosen over her?

The county attorney, Rafael Moon, said, "There's no appeals process on this, Angela."

"I don't mean a process. I want you to reverse your decision, or whoever made the decision."

"What do you mean by that?"

"Maybe someone spoke against me."

Rafael's office was spare, a New Mexico state flag in the corner, the statutes in the bookcases, on his desk pictures of his grandchildren, their hair raven black in contrast to grandpa's high-combed silver mane.

"I make my own decisions, and I chose Ted."

"Why?"

"Because I did."

"That's no answer."

"Then let me put it this way: You're great in court. That's where you belong, not helping me evaluate cases, write reports and keep the other assistant attorneys happy, which you wouldn't. You second guess everyone, never ends."

"You didn't even interview."

Rafael possessed unshakeable *dignidad*. For him 2007 might have been 1777, when his family received its land grant from the king of Spain. *Yo, el Rey.* "I think we're finished."

Angela didn't recall raising her voice, but Rafael's secretary, Mary Ortiz, stepped in and stared at her. No one could speak to Mr Moon that way. Or threaten him with a sex-discrimination suit.

He suspended her without pay for a month to cool off. Her cases were distributed by Ted Billings to other attorneys. Three times she was told to leave the county building when she returned to plead for reinstatement.

One morning she awoke in a kind of paralysis. She had a frame and stucco two-story, not an adobe, that had creaked in the wind all night like a ship crossing the high desert, and the journey left her exhausted. What if they extended the suspension? What if they made it a firing?

The light in the bedroom was blazing white, but she was a dark bundle on the bed, clutching her quilt as if she had fallen there. She had nothing to do and almost no money. Tearing her ex-husband to pieces had cost her a fortune, even acting as her own attorney. Now she had the mortgage, utilities, and upkeep. She put on overalls and walked down the staircase into the barren kitchen with its terra cotta tiles. No coffee? Through the patio doors, she looked at the apple trees, sagging with fruit. She went out and picked an apple and polished it on her overalls and ate it. Then she walked around the house to the garage and got a stack of baskets and began harvesting the apples.

Anyone who hasn't harvested apples doesn't know what heaven is like. Even those who have can get it wrong. She read the Robert Frost poem in 11th grade and understood he was looking for death wherever he could find it, even where its opposite, eternity, held sway. Apple-picking is ambrosia.

Apple-picking is no way that God would ever expel you. It's more like God in your hands. Reaching deep among the fragrant branches you really know that life is good. She wrote this and received an A+. Her teacher, Mr Moore, read the essay out loud. "Listen to how Angela captures the intoxicating scent, the beautiful striated shades of the skin, the effortless way you twist a ripe apple's stem to free it."

She picked for an hour and thought, What will I do with all these apples? She carried two baskets into her kitchen. She'd pare and bake them, she'd slice and dry them, she'd make and freeze pies, breads, tarts ... but first, maybe she could sell some. So she drove to the Grange market and sat in the cool shade of the front porch with her apples, ten cents apiece, fifteen for a dollar. Out on the glittering gravel parking lot, they were beginning to roast peppers that day, some on charcoal grills; others in barrels that had holes poked in them and could be filled with peppers you rotated over a mesquite-wood fire by slowly turning a handle, the tumbling peppers giving off the acrid scent of capsaicin that bit your nostrils. Up here beyond Albuquerque you didn't get the hottest of the hot. Down south in the Jornada del Muerto the peppers were more fiery. But people still were drawn to the Grange market by the smell that drifted from the whispering cottonwoods along the shallow river across the green grey sage flats toward the mesa lands, and they would buy fresh roasted peppers and come over and pay Angela more than she asked for her apples. She made seven dollars. With that she bought a gallon of orange juice, a loaf of bread, and a half pound of coffee and went home to pick more apples and return to make more money, $9 in the afternoon.

In a few days she had sold so many apples that other apple sellers showed up, so it wasn't worth it anymore. Another thing taken. Now she had to decide, no heating oil or no electricity. She paid the electric bill, letting one more thing go: warmth. She asked herself what else she could sell. She decided half her wardrobe and her computer and printer because she still had an electric typewriter. She packed the car tight because she didn't want to waste gas on two trips to Albuquerque. It was a Square-backed VW, taxi green, a project car. She'd bought it used twelve years ago, but it still ran, and she'd learnt how to work on it herself. Her ex-husband had wanted her to get rid of it as part of buying the house, take out a little extra mortgage and get something new. He said her junker humiliated him. She told him it didn't humiliate her. When he was being nice, he said it chugged the way she chugged. When he wasn't, he said they would have a nice, white stucco house set against a pasture with twenty apple trees on the property yet people would think he had a woman spending time with him who drove the county, making rounds. Doing what, cleaning? she asked. No, not cleaning, he said. She told him he was disgusting.

She consigned the clothes and found a trade/buy computer store off Central Avenue. A dismal place.

The owner was a pimply neat geek in a vest who said, "That piece of shit is worth $400, printer included. I get $200, you get $200."

She asked, "Who do you sell to?"

He said, "University kids mostly."

"$300 for me, $100 for you."

"Okay, sell it yourself."

This was an Apple machine that had cost $1500 four years ago. Angela took it outside on the footpath. When people approached the shop, she said she was selling it.

The owner came out. "No way, lady. You're raiding my customers. It's illegal. Where's your permit?"

She said if he wanted to go to court, she wouldn't need a lawyer, he would, because she *was* a lawyer. He called the cops. They came into two cars and walked at her from either side because the owner had said she was "a kicker." At the moment she was involved in a sale. A guy said if they went to his place, and it worked, he'd buy it. She said she would go with him if he gave her $200 up front. The cops asked if she was soliciting for prostitution.

"I'm selling a computer!"

The shop owner lurked in his doorway. "That's her cover. She's got these horny undergrads all over her."

The cops didn't believe him or her. She was in her overalls and wearing an engineer's cap. If she was a woman in there, you couldn't see it.

It came to the buyer to speak up. "I came to buy a computer, not a whore."

She lost it. "Who are you calling a whore? I'll sue you for slander."

Things got nasty. There was some kicking. After the cops separated everyone, they checked her I.D. and called Rafael Moon to confirm her identity and let him know there'd been a question about the sale of used computer equipment or possibly prostitution. Ended up citing her for conducting business without a license and impounding her computer and printer. She'd receive her notice for a court appearance within ten days. She also spoke to Rafael who said he was extending her suspension another month.

She sat a long time in her VW Squareback looking through her windscreen at the lifeless streets of Albuquerque. Something else had been taken from her, more of her good name, more of her time, more of her hopes of paying the mortgage on a house that no longer had heat.

That night, wrapped in her bathrobe as well as her quilt, she felt the long intake of breath that quieted the house before the thunder and lightning storm hit, shaking and crackling the skies and making the house not only creak but sway. She lived near the end of what the hot air balloonists call the Albuquerque Box. The winds could cut either way, out to her from the south or down upon her from the north. These were north winds that had crashed across vast stretches of barren high desert before channelling into the Rio Grande valley. As the night wore on, it got colder. She went downstairs and used her torch to check the apple trees. Frost already? If they didn't take her back, could she practice on her own or become a public defender? If she did, she knew she would have to rent the house at least for a while or she'd never catch up.

The next morning she walked to Gail's place bordering the acequia. Gail's wolf dog Howlie spooked away, presenting no problem—he knew Angela—but Gail's door was so thick it took time to wake her. A woman in her fifties with thick braids and huge breasts, Gail saw that Angela wasn't eating or thinking right. She fixed her eggs, juice, coffee and sopapillas. Her cinderblock place was a dump, the ragged carpets worn thin as dollar bills, the wood-framed windows warped, half broken and half shut, but the furnace was on, and that felt good. All the warm things felt good, including in Angela's stomach.

She asked if Gail would rent the outbuilding where Howlie slept and Gail kept her picks and shovels and such.

"For what?" Gail asked.

"I might have to rent my own house. I'd need somewhere else."

"There's no bathroom, no kitchen. It's not insulated."

"You've got a wood stove in there."

"Are things that bad, Angie?"

People in the village stood their ground, Gail too. She collected the overdue acequia fees and did odd job trash removal with her surplus deuce and a half dump truck. She was saying no, but Angela wasn't accepting it.

"I just need some breathing room. The divorce and things."

"Move into my spare bedroom."

"I couldn't."

"Why not?"

"I need to be alone; it's just my way."

Gail wondered how she could make things easy, though as assistant county attorney Angela hadn't made it easy for a lot of people she knew.

"I feel like they're taking things away from me," Angela said. "I need to be where that won't happen anymore."

"What would you do with your stuff?"

"Sell it," Angela said.

"Why not sell the whole house?"

A bolt of anger descended Angela's spinal cord. "No, whatever happens, I'll get it back. I need to save money, live cheap."

"You'd want to use my kitchen and bathroom."

These were foul places. The slime of food and human waste lay upon them. Angela did not want to become like Gail. All she wanted was for Gail to be a mountain range that stopped her from blowing away.

"I'll clean them for rent and anything else you want done."

"What about Howlie? He sleeps in there. Never comes in here."

Howlie really was part wolf. See him slithering through the trees, trotting away from you, and you would know it—not just his long legs and mangy coat. Gail's sign on the fence said: *Do Not Ever Look Wolf Dog Straight in the Eyes.*

"He can still sleep there."

"He won't come if you're there."

Angela thought perhaps he would. She thought something about her now would appeal to him. He was a lanky, shifty beast Gail never petted. If she sprawled in the hammock, he might lie down ten feet away, but if she shifted or farted, Howlie disappeared. He had his trails and byways among Gail's never-tended apple trees, weeds, brambles and vines.

"It just won't work, Angie," Gail said.

Angela said, "If you'll stop calling me Angie, which I don't like, I'll make it work."

Gail laughed and gave in.

Angela posted a sale notice on Craigslist. People from the South Valley came in pickups and bought everything but her books, which Albuquerque and Rio Rancho people bought. Things moved quickly and pointlessly and uselessly. Who couldn't live without a curling iron, a spade, a tool set, a Walkman? A first year law student bought her text books for $30. She sold her backpack for $7, her spinning rod for $5. All she held back were her remaining clothes, the typewriter, the receipt for her impounded computer, her bike, and her Squareback. Altogether she cleared less than $1,000. Then a man offered her $500 for the Squareback. She had to hold onto herself, not attack him. He was talking about taking something from her, but he meant to pay for it. This was different, but it felt the same.

"I don't think I want to sell it living out here," she said.

"I thought you were renting the house."

"Yes, but I'm going to live up the road, still in the country."

"$600," the man said, silver-bearded, bald, and intent. "I like to fix those old things up. We were all young once. Had one myself."

Some equation struggled to take shape in her mind. "Seven," she said.

"Deal," he said.

He drove it off, following his wife in a brand new Escalade. What she had left fit easily in the outbuilding where Gail had put a cot as far away as possible from Howlie's sleeping mat.

For three days Howlie stayed clear. During those days Angela scrubbed Gail's kitchen and bathroom. During the nights she rolled herself twice in her quilt and wore a wool beanie pulled over her ears and stared at the dying embers in the stove. She sometimes imagined Howlie slipping in and lunging at her. If he did, she'd pull herself deeper into the quilt, turtle-like and pray for the dog in him to quiet the wolf.

The fourth night Howlie crept in and lay there apparently sleeping, but Angela didn't think he was sleeping anymore than she was. They were looking at one another in the blood-flamed darkness, wide awake.

Gail had an arrangement with the village council. She tramped the dusty paths along the acequia and hammered on deadbeats' doors, demanding their overdue irrigation tax, keeping half for herself. She said if Angela kept her company, she'd share her half. So the two women spent many glorious blue sky New Mexico days on the dusty trails lacing through the village. The fear of Angela, ostensibly an assistant county attorney, worked wonders. Gail said things like, "Pay or we'll cement your water gate and your property will dry up and blow away in a year." Or, "It's way overdue, sweetheart, so watch out you don't end up in jail, right, Angela?" Angela would say yes, right. Then trash and rubble jobs came up. Angela rode with Gail all over the village and up in Rio Rancho. Gail had piles of questionable scavenge items in the passenger's side foot well of the deuce and a half, but no problem, Angela was short. She just rested her feet on things.

Working in the kitchen, she typed a letter to Rafael Moon, requesting reinstatement. The next day a sheriff's deputy hand delivered a letter saying not until the court date was set for her citation in Albuquerque. Angela rode her bike to the village library and read the classifieds, looking for work. To do that she had to pass her house. A couple and two boys lived there now. She studied everything for damage and once stopped to clear away a cobweb between the gutter and the garage door. The husband asked what she was doing. She explained. He said he wished she would leave that to him.

"You wrote the contract tight enough I know the house has to be perfect when we leave."

"You might want to wash the dust off the exterior window sills then," Angela said.

He turned on the hose and did that, and she knew she should back off. No more citations. In court she was given six months probation, a $200 fine and a restraining order—the street on which the computer store was located was off limits to her. Rafael Moon then wrote her that once her probation was complete, she could return to work. So six more months of this? She didn't think she could make it.

Howlie came in every night and lay there watching her.

One Saturday morning at breakfast, they looked out the kitchen windows, which Angela had repaired and cleant, and saw a spectacular armada of hot air balloons drifting up the Albuquerque Box. Howlie began howling. The sound was fearsome, yet laced with fear. Every year those resplendent monsters floated up the Rio Grande and their yellows and reds and blues and periodic whooshes of flame sent him all over the property, trying to make sure they didn't get in.

The pasture lands that backed Angela's house also backed Gail's.

"My God, one's heading right for us," Gail said.

"That's never happened before," Angela said.

"Howlie's going crazy."

They walked over to the fence that was only there to keep Howlie in. He was near, but invisible. The balloon was purple and white with black fleurs-de-lis decorating its rippling silk envelope. The basket came down and the balloonists expertly ensured that the envelope settled gracefully on the grasses beside it, light as a smell.

Angela stared at the balloon a long time, enchanted, feeling like a little girl. Gail was happy, too, but Howlie was in a frenzy. For him the invasion was complete. The skies of New Mexico had been conquered. Now the land was at risk. He didn't know what to do about it, but clearly he felt that something had been stolen away from him, this fence wasn't enough, he had to get out, and he did, leaping it and taking off.

Gail and Angela didn't wait to watch the trailing pickup come get the balloon and its basket. Gail grabbed the deuce and a half and Angela got on her bike. They went all over the low-lying, twisting, sprawling village. No sign of Howlie. Was he hiding somewhere, under something, in something, quivering and unable to think of his next move?

They didn't find him. Gail said he would come back. He didn't come back. Angela thought maybe he would do so at night, but he didn't, and she took it as a sign. No sleep came her way, either. The final apple had fallen, frightening her, too, with its soft silent descent to earth. Somehow she had to lift herself up and float away. The next day she took her typewriter up to the kitchen and wrote Rafael Moon a letter, asking if he would give her a good recommendation if she did not return to the county attorney's office. The reply came hand-delivered fast. Yes, she could count on good references forever. Obviously he never wanted to see her again, and when her ex-husband had served his own six months, things would get worse. He'd find her. She'd defend herself. Trouble was no one-way street.

She made arrangements to sell her house and cleared $21,000. With that she went to the man who had bought her Squareback and found that he had reupholstered and repainted it. He didn't want to sell, but his wife saw a chance to influence things in the garage where the old man kept her banned. She did this from the doorway to the kitchen, helping Angela turn him around.

As a last protest, he asked, "I mean, if you're not a collector-restorer like me, what do you want it for?"

Angela gave him what would pass for a yellowish look if she were a wolf dog and said it was time for her to move on and start over somewhere else. Maybe Colorado. $3900 was the price.

That afternoon she packed the car and then spent her last night with Gail in the kitchen. They drank too much wine.

Gail said she would probably go back to living like a bum. "And you'll get a job and live in a nice place and have the sterile, boring life you've always wanted. No one fucking it up. Throwing six guys in jail every week."

This was said with both humour and anger, which Angela noted.

"No, I think I'll drift," she said. "I'll be just like a balloon but never come down."

Gail snickered. "Wonder if Howlie will come back when you're gone. You plus the balloon were just too much for him."

Angela stumbled to the outbuilding and wrapped herself up. She could smell the wine on her breath because she was tucked so deep in her quilt, and then she began smelling another foul, stinking breath on the other side of the shack.

He was there. She knew he was there, over in the darkest

corner. Take me, she thought he was telling her. I know you're going, and that's what I need, too.

As the sun crested the Sandias, its light penetrating the shack's cracked and shrunken boards, the woman and the wolf dog stared at one another, seeing each other clearly now. She moved very carefully, not approaching him, putting her few things in the Squareback but leaving room for him if he wanted to jump in. Then she peed in the weeds and he came out and peed in the weeds. The two of them remained stock still a long time after that until, at last, he ambled over and sniffed the Squareback's bumper and leapt in and lay down and she closed the rear hatch. That's where he stayed as she drove past what once had been her house, her apple trees, her life.

the frying pan

Pee brush teeth let Frank shower snip beard nose eyebrows choose right suit right shirt right shoes pull on robe wake Alissa Teddy Sealie downstairs everyone milk orange juice waffles

one kid after another smoothing their wild hair with her wet palm reaching to sink for more and

hey I said hey how do I look

you look great where did you get the tie

at Nordstrom's where do I get everything

and into her blue blouse blue slacks

no makeup white ankle socks white shoes

back into the kids' rooms

go go go out everyone into the van

while he is sitting down with his coffee and almond milk and soy patties convinced there are ways to make an impression with your fitness and clothes and good health and the look in your eye

his look in his eye

and she's driving along Westmoreland smoking a cigarette past houses she doesn't see across intersections she doesn't see thinking the thought of him flossing then slapping his face with astringent and combing his hair

and coming his hair

and down into his Lexus

and she's hanging up her coat with patients end to end
to scrape away their tartar
poke their gums
wondering about her breath she's tried to gargle smoke-free
in the ladies before Doc comes in with his perfect smile
because you can have this too yes you can really you can
but oh my god unbelievable back teeth mucky in the cracks
gums tender and bloody red spider webs everywhere vacu-
uming away sucking right out gone gone gone that too over
there and there
work like you're swimming Doc's advice
next and next and next
stroke and stroke and stroke
no effort
no worries
in happy tooth city
but it's not no it's not
as she glances at the computer looped picture frames of
their families in which she didn't put Frank and the other
hygienists didn't put their husbands just Alissa Teddy Sealie
really Cecelia Frank's mother's name dead and she HJ because
her real name's too embarrassing had it changed when she was
eighteen in front of the clerk and said yes
HJ just HJ
six hours straight eating nothing only water people with the
Brooklyn Bridge in their mouths the Luray Caverns incisors
that would tear flesh off a live cow
she swims that long
she's got the figure
needle through the fabric arrow through the air
patients she likes
ones who tense
  don't care almost sleep take pleasure in her body leaning
across their chests pulls politely away keeps on working
has Doc come look reschedules fills plastic bags next
appointment cards complimentary floss and

over wow over
sits in the van
smokes
feels nothing 100% nothing
heads for the biker bar and orders a glass of beer and fries
and looks at the photos of Annie Oakley and Wild Bill
Hickok and his beard Frank would never tolerate or the
bison's head same problem awful beard never trimmed poor
bison and movie posters John Wayne Gary Cooper and Free
Beer Tomorrow sign and bikers in two groups
Goats she calls one skinny malnourished gang with wispy
chin sprouts
and Hippos the other fatsos with beards like their bellies
and she can't finish all the fries
but have another beer one Goat says sliding glass her way
thank you but I couldn't
it's there got to be drunk
no way
takes a sip to be polite
just people after all he comes down and says go on another
now like a good girl won't kill you you're too skinny
oh this uniform makes me look awful I'm a dental hygienist
me I kinda do computer stuff
two Hippos staring at a beautiful tobacco-brown girl behind
the bar in tight black T-shirt yellow lettering Cowboy Café
why café who drinks coffee here
she takes another all right another
him staring I've seen you here
she smiles be nice last sip no more
goes into the cowgirls' room sits on the toilet and he follows
her in and she looks at him leaning back against the door and
he says I own my company and am bored out of my mind so
I do this come here
but not in the ladies' room please
I just want to talk to you
but not here please

okay no but we could take a ride
I can't take a ride
I've got an extra helmet
no please
come on
no no
yes up you go now atsa girl kiss me hey kiss me
his lips tender and soft and hands gentle on her back and
fingers up in her hair but with her pants around her ankles
come on please please
okay okay I shouldn't have
I just I just
pushing him away
bending
pulling herself up him looking at her crotch twisting zipping
can I go out please
course you can
no hard feelings
no hard feelings
thank you you're very kind
not as kind as you are lovely
me
yes you but I won't do this again unless I ask you he laughs
and she slides around him out into the dark midday bar
the Hippos watching her in the mirror and gets into the van
goes home straightens up looks through the mail pays bills
gets them dinner makes them eat it puts the plate she fixes for
Frank in the refrigerator chases all three into homework and
he comes home at eight after his workout at the gym and is
angry the plate is in the fridge and not the stove
cold instead of warm
doesn't want to nuke it in the microwave
told you that and told you that why can't you wait for me
because these kids have to eat they have homework listen
how quiet it is isn't that what we want
what I want what I want why don't you get just as preoc-

cupied with me and all the work I do

    she doesn't want to say

    he knows she doesn't want to say

    because I'll tell you this isn't edible when it's nuked you can't nuke fish don't you know that

    was it this bad when you gave it to them

    he throws the whole plate into the trash

    she gets the plate back and puts it in the sink

    he grabs it and puts it in the trash again

    she gets it out again he grabs her arm and she pulls away and he pulls her back and snatches the plate and breaks it on the kitchen floor where she kneels with the dustpan and Sealie is in the door

    what's wrong

    nothing dear I messed up Daddy's dinner

    do you want me to cook you something else Daddy

    he grabs her and lifts her and says no he'll do it himself

    then just go do your homework Sealie

    but I'm finished

    then watch TV if you want or phone time I don't care put her down Frank let her go it's okay Sealie go

    she dumps the plate and contents into the trash and kneels again to the floor with the sponge and he says we wash dishes with that sponge you idiot not the floor aren't you a hygienist don't you know that

    she gets up and pushes the sponge in his face and rubs it all over his beard he is furious looks at his reflection in the window over the sink

    his beard his beard

    he smacks her face and she loses her breath

    Frank Frank listen to me hear me I want you to hear me

    I am leaving you

    no you are not

    yes I am

    taking the kids and we are going

    he grabs her and pulls her back to him

she fights loose grabs her keys off the hook by the back door runs to the van drives to her mother's house where her sister lives

Frank follows

her sister tries to block him at the door

he pushes through

her mother sits on the sofa her mouth open HJ's father used to smack her kicked her once the sight of Frank like this now the dead back from the grave

HJ sweetheart HJ we'll put this right

no we won't no we won't

her sister says we've got room for everyone here except you Frank get lost this isn't your house HJ doesn't need you neither do the kids

oh really try to get the kids try

believe me they'll come on their own

not before I figure out what she's up to

what do you mean by that

I mean where does she have her sex if she doesn't have it with me

women don't need sex like men do Frank

eight months is more than not needing sex

Frank Frank

you were so nice what happened

I grew up I took responsibility I've made my way

oh did you her sister says

then tell me what you do for it when you don't get what you want at home why so pretty why so neat why so groomed

who're you slipping it to on the side

what's her name

HJ hasn't even thought of that really hasn't hasn't gotten anywhere near sex in mind or body until that Goat pressed his lips against hers and she was excited because he was excited and Frank is never excited this is the first time she's seen him excited in who knows when she can almost feel something going on between him and her sister as he lifts his arms above his silver head with her sister up there he is that strong what will he do

is he going to throw her somewhere

she kicks and struggles

her mother runs to the kitchen comes back with the big cast iron frying pan

what are you going to do with that I'm going to hit you in the face and she hits him smack in the face just like she says and he drops her sister and doubles over and stumbles and hits the wall and his nose is bleeding onto his shirt and tie and jacket

and she realizes of course she'd never have gone into the Cowboy Café if it was just for the beer and fries

you could get beer and fries in the Safeway

you couldn't get sex in the Safeway

that's not where they sell it

Frank Frank she cries going to him he bats her away oh Frank Frank she keeps calling weeping and him yelling all right take the kids if you want move here live here do whatever you want

I don't want anything

that's the problem with you all of you you make me sick

he gets up the three women don't know what he'll do

he goes to the door and slams it behind him her mother still has the frying pan in her hand and is crying the two sisters are crying I've got to go get my kids she says no I'll do it her sister says she pushes HJ back onto the sofa slams the door behind her just like Frank HJ sits there staring at her mother with the frying pan in her hand and her mother says it was what he deserved and she will burn in hell because she never did it to her father and let HJ think there is any other way.

not that, this

Julia went into the vet's for glucosamine chondroitin for Polly, her beagle. A young woman on the bench by the window was sobbing into her hands. Andrea the receptionist was crying, too.

Julia paused a second out of discretion. The young woman noticed her and began talking.

"This guy ... he picked up my kitten and threw her against the wall. Now she's bleeding from the mouth. Why didn't he just hit me? She's just a little kitten."

The word kitten caused her to convulse. Julia lightly put a hand on her back. Andrea told Julia the kitten was in with Dr Moore.

The young woman began talking again. She was in her mid-twenties with black hair, ivory skin and scattered birth marks. Her pale pink lips moved as quickly as hummingbird wings. "I can't pay for this. What do I do?"

Julia said, "The kitten's with Dr Moore. She's a very good doctor. You've done the right thing."

"No, I haven't. I'm the stupidest idiot on earth." The moment was a wave that kept swelling, impossibly swelling, higher and higher, tossing Julia and Andrea both up into the frightening air. "Like a baseball! He threw her like a baseball!"

Julia tried to calm things by introducing herself and asking the young woman's name, which was Trish. What about the kitten? It didn't have a name yet. Trish thought they would name it together, she and this guy.

Julia scanned what she could see of Trish's flesh for bruises and cuts. She saw none. But what about her covered torso? Julia and Andrea looked at one another. Andrea shook her head, indicating there was little hope for the kitten and perhaps not much more for Trish.

Dr Moore came out and sat on the other side of Trish. Julia removed her hand from Trish's back.

"I can't help a great deal with internal injuries, but I've called Hind Paws. They're set up for things like this. You've got to get her there right away."

"Where is it?"

"Little River Turnpike, near Route 50."

"I don't have a car, and I don't have any money. I just ran out of the apartment with the kitty."

Julia said, "I'll drive you. We'll work out the money."

"But—"

"Don't worry, Trish. This is settled."

Dr Moore signalled to Andrea to get the kitten, a tabby, about six months old, not bleeding any more but still streaked with blood around its tiny mouth and nostrils. Barely breathing.

The things Julia had planned to do that morning vanished; she couldn't think what they were; she concentrated on how to get the turns to Hind Paws as fast as possible. Trish sat with the kitten in her lap. She began telling her story, her painfully rising and falling voice intermixed with even more painful quivering, self-accusatory pauses.

"He's this army guy from my home town in West Virginia and we hooked up back there in high school, and now he's here and said come on out to DC. Like a dummy, I packed a bag and got a bus and my mother was yelling at me all the way, and I get there and he's in an apartment with nothing but a mattress and some garden furniture and his clothes on the floor and he goes icy when we're having sex and can't finish and I tell him it's all right, he's been in hard places, you know, these wars? And I said, look, it's okay, no war anymore, let's be friends then, or partners, or whatever, and I got this idea yesterday and went to the animal shelter and they gave me this pretty little kitten, this pretty little kitten, and …" Trish had grown deathly pale staring at the kitten's miraculous tabbi-ness, the subtlety of hairs that were many colours bordering other colours and ending in the soft brown hairs on its nose so short they were immeasurable, hairs Julia herself had stroked and put her lips to when she'd had a tabby as a girl; the first creature she ever kissed except her parents was that kitty. She always kissed the same way thereafter: delicately, no matter whom she kissed, it was her kiss, a kiss no man, even her husband Harry, could make her change, a brushing of lips, no more, her best kiss no matter what anyone thought because she knew where it came from.

Trish pulled herself together. She began talking again. "And he comes home after his night shift and what's the cat doing there, who's idea was that, who was feeding a cat when he could barely feed me? I said I wouldn't eat. He said all right, eat me then. He said that. It was so crude. He begins storming around. He comes at me. I think he's going to do something. I don't know what. I've got this kitten in my arms, and he grabs it and he turns and he throws it at the wall, and that's it, just that. I ran to it, and it was bleeding like this." She looked down at the kitten. "Down in the lobby they told me about Dr Moore and the guy there, he gave me cab money. Do you think they'll say kill it? I don't want that!"

Julia had no training in any of this but she was sixty-three and could see that the kitten and Trish were one and the same being now and the bloodlessness in Trish's terrified face mirrored whatever blood had burst from the kitten's organs and flowed out of its life, that minuscule wash of vanishing urgency, thin and red and precious.

Somehow they reached Hind Paws. A young man in whites came out to meet them as Julia parked.

"This is kitty?" he said, opening Trish's door. "Here. Let me get her into the doctor. We're waiting."

"What will you do?" Trish asked.

"Doctor Cynzeski will do everything she can, I promise."

He cradled the kitten in its little cotton blanket. There was another aide at the door, a girl, holding it open for him. He disappeared across the lobby into the examining and treatment rooms.

Trish turned to Julia to thank her. Julia said she'd stay with her. Trish said no, she'd already done so much, but Julia took Trish by the elbow, and they walked into Hind Paws, and sat in a corner where another assistant brought them paper cups of water.

Julia still couldn't remember what she was supposed to be doing this morning. Go here, go there. She'd never gotten Polly her pills. That was all she recalled. Beyond that? Her minister had told her that women are widows for a reason. She'd said, "That's a cheery thought. God said, 'Let Harry die,' so Julia can find out about being a widow'?" Harry was the person she never discussed anymore because she couldn't bear to. Instead, she did things. What things? What did they matter? The dressmaker. The dog pills. Have lunch with Gracie, read Proust, call her children when it didn't seem too soon since the last call and avoid talking about the only thing that mattered. She was a widow. Harry was gone. She was lost.

She looked around Hind Paws's lobby, done in crayon blues and oranges, an infantilizing kind of place, some tacit acknowledgement that pets were childish artefacts, dreams of what humans couldn't be again after they grew up, couldn't wander in the grass and woods anymore, couldn't drink out of ponds, couldn't climb a tree, couldn't sleep all day and prowl all night, couldn't protect anyone the way Polly protected Julia, barking at anyone who came within five feet of her, an old beagle, grey the way Julia was grey, sad-eyed the way Julia was sad-eyed. "We have seen too much, haven't we, dear?" Julia would say to Polly, and Polly would look at her with the infinity of a beagle's eyes, the totality of all experience and evolution, and probably wonder what the woman was yammering about. What is too much? Too much suggests there is a reasonable limit in life. But there isn't any reasonable limit in life. Life goes on, life doesn't care.

Julia said firmly, she didn't know why: "They'll save kitty."

Trish said soberly, exhausted, "Like I told you, even if they did, I couldn't pay. I shouldn't have come here. Do they charge you for putting animals down? God, I'm an idiot."

"You have to stop saying things like that. They'll save kitty, and after that, I'm taking you home."

"There? With him?"

"No, I mean where you came from. In the meantime, you'll stay with me. If he gets near my house, I'll call the police."

"But ma'am—"

"—Julia, call me Julia."

"Julia, you don't even know me."

"I don't have to."

"—Believe me I'm not worth it."

"Everyone's worth it."

"What about my stuff?"

"We'll get it. I'll get it for you."

"You can't do that. He'll kill you!"

Sometimes in her loneliness Julia wouldn't mind. Sometimes travelling to see her children and grandchildren, she wished the plane would crash. She knew there would be no photos of Harry in their houses, not until she left, because Grandma couldn't bear looking at him.

"A man who did what he did is a coward."

"He's a trained killer, that's what he did over there."

Julia stared into Trish's eyes. The words flew out of her. "You don't have to be trained to kill, you have to be trained to live. The problem is they don't give that training. It's do-it-yourself."

Trish grew docile. After a while, she asked for the bathroom. Julia said she needed to go, too. They tinkled in adjoining stalls and then went to adjoining sinks and looked at themselves in the mirror, both of them were a mess. At one and the same time, they leant over and splashed their faces until all traces of their smudgy, runny make-up were gone. Neither had eyebrows anymore. They laughed.

"We look like Little Orphan Annie," Julia said.

"Who?" Trish asked.

Julia didn't answer. Her own thoughts were breaking down, too, she realized. Get Trish's stuff? House her? What was she saying?

Dr Cynzeski came out into the lobby. She kneeled before them, actually got down on her knees. Another young woman, her brown hair loose, her brown eyes wary. Trish and Julia drew back in their seats.

"I think kitty's going to make it," she said. "We've given her some coagulants and we're helping her breathe and keeping her sedated so she has a chance to heal."

Trish asked, "Is she in pain?"

Dr Cynzeski said, "If humans had animals' pain tolerance, we wouldn't know what pain meant, but I'm going to want to keep her for a few days."

"I can't pay for this."

Julia said, "I can."

Dr Cynzeski said, "Don't worry about that now. Just be grateful you got here in time. Again, I think she's going to make it. Do you want to see her?"

She led Trish and Julia into the infirmary. Kitty lay still in an oxygen-enriched incubator. She had a new cotton blanket.

"Now we get your bag and things," Julia said when they were in her car.

"I can't let you do this. It's too dangerous."

"Where is the apartment?"

Trish held out. Julia pressed. Finally Trish said, "Seminary Road."

In the apartment tower's parking lot, Trish wanted to go in. Julia forbade it.

"But you won't know what's mine," Trish protested.

"Yes, I will."

"He won't let you in."

"Yes, he will."

"If you're not back in ten minutes, I'm calling 911."

Julia said, "That's a good idea."

Julia didn't know what she was feeling as she entered the lobby and spoke to the attendant and then took the elevator to the twelfth floor, but when she stepped out into the dismal, endless hallway, door after door identical, she realized it must be adrenalin. She felt as though she was in command of the wave that swept her along now, riding it, gliding upon it. Fear what? Dread what? Walking down that long lifeless hallway was ominous, reckless, and perilous, yet thrilling. She wanted to be there. She liked being there. She came to #1256 and knocked.

A shirtless man in khakis opened the door. He was a drunken, bleary-eyed brute. "I help you?"

"I came to get Trish's things."

"You came to get Trish's things?" The man laughed at this for no particular reason except perhaps some inexplicable contempt for Trish. "Trish can get her own things."

"No, I will get them, or in five minutes the police will be here, and they will get them."

"Lady, I don't know you, and what the fuck have the police got to do with this?"

Julia was small, and this big angry man was looking at her as if she were a bug he planned to step on. She didn't know what to do except look at him as if he were a bigger bug.

"They'll explain when they get here if that's what you want. Just let me collect Trish's things, and it won't come to that."

He let her pass. As Trish had said, there was almost nothing in the apartment. It was bleakly anonymous. Parquet floor. Unadorned walls. A shallow balcony looking out on a panorama of similar apartment buildings where tens of thousands of soldiers and federal workers and contractors lived.

In the bedroom, a heavy woman lay sleeping. She wore a sleeveless T-shirt. Her large breasts puddled on her chest. Her mouth was open and her two front teeth were neatly chipped, creating a perfect little triangle in the middle. Her pocketbook and clothing lay on the floor beside the bed. The room smelled of alcohol, cigarettes, and sex. Obviously this man wasted no time.

He stood right behind Julia, almost bumping her. When she moved, he moved. She spotted Trish's bag and a pile of her clothing and stuffed it inside. She went into the bathroom and got Trish's toiletries. She went into the kitchen and saw a crescent of bloody drops on the wall beside the refrigerator.

"Is that where you threw the cat?" she asked.

"Lady, get the fuck out of here. You got what you came for."

Julia retraced her steps down the long gloomy corridor. She was hurrying. She didn't want the police to come. She wanted Trish still in the car. She wanted the kitty to live. She didn't want to be a widow anymore.

who has a real castle where i can hide?

Na Cheon would put her father's enormous high-crowned general's hat on the floor of the room they used for being together. The hat was olive brown with green piping. The red five-pointed star on its badge stood out brightly against a white enamel background. She wasn't allowed to wear the hat, but she could pretend it was a castle that kept her safe. No one could scale its height—too steep! There was room inside for pantries, schoolrooms, armouries, little baby rooms, big people rooms, her brothers' rooms, her mother and father's room, cellars below and attics above. Her mother called her a squib, and she could hide anywhere inside it. Sometimes she pictured the Beloved Leader magically appearing on the patent leather brim her mother wiped for her father before he went to work each morning, ensuring no dust or fingerprints. Those were special moments; she could barely breathe as she imagined the Beloved Leader telling the world how courageous and efficient her father was supervising the fieldworkers who were insects, not human, in his section of the camp.

"When I became lieutenant general, my colonel general gave me this hat. It was his when he was lieutenant general," he told her.

Her mother, her father's second wife always said then, "We are so sad your first wife could not live to see you wear it that day."

"I didn't see it, either," Na Cheon said.

"Because you are only five. You weren't even born!" Chin Ho, one of her half-brothers said.

The great music and praise came through the speaker in the wall, but she scarcely heard it. She wanted to hear what her other half-brother, Jae-Hwa, would say.

"Our father, servant of Great Beloved Leader!" he said.

Na Cheon helped her mother clean their house in Camp 22. They sang patriotically as they worked. Afterward she joined the other officers' children to dance and turn somersaults and bend over backwards to stand on their hands, the slowest one rising receiving the most applause.

Then the colonel general came to visit one day and saw Na Cheon on the floor playing with her father's hat.

"What is this?" he asked Na Cheon's father. "Lieutenant General, your hat is on the floor!"

"My daughter pretends it is a castle."

"A castle! It is a lieutenant general's hat, not a castle! What is wrong with the girl?"

Her father bowed his head in shame. Tears welled in his eyes. "I put it on highest shelves, but she climbs and gets it."

"A symbol of your honour in such disgrace? How can you put a hat on your head that has been on the floor? I gave you that hat! How many times has it been on the floor?"

Her father begged forgiveness. His whole body trembled. "Na Cheon is a child of misfortune. My first wife bore me brave strong boys but now this second wife, look at what she has done, giving me such a wretched child."

The great music and praise poured from the speaker in the wall but no other sound. Na Cheon grew so afraid she tinkled.

"Look!" her half-brother, Chin Ho, cried. "She fouls our home!"

"Na Cheon, you disgust me!" Her father pulled her into the air by an arm. "Insect! Insect!"

Her mother pleaded. "Please, honoured sir, let her go!"

"Let her go? No, take her where no one is human!" He

swung Na Cheon at her mother. "Take her and stay there yourself!"

Na Cheon and her mother were pushed out into the cold as the colonel general watched and Chin Ho slammed the door shut behind them.

Her mother banged on the door to be let in. Her father stepped out and kicked her. He had his hat on. "Go! Go!" he cried.

Guards came running. He ordered them to take his second wife and Na Cheon to where the not-human women lived with their not-human children.

Over her father's shoulder, Na Cheon saw satisfaction on the colonel general's face and despair in Jae-Hwa's face. The soldiers pushed her and her mother down the hill to where the not-human women lived with not-human children under six because after six not-human children became orphans and lived only among themselves.

***

Na Cheon had never dug in the earth with a sharpened stick, never pushed a barrow on its wooden wheels, never eaten weeds, never seen women push up their behinds for rabbit sex when men got near them, never slept with her face between her mother's breasts and her mother's hand over her bum so no one could finger it at night, never heard about the pigeon torture, the water torture, the kneeling torture, or the box-room torture, which she thought would be worst. What if she could crouch in the box but not pull in her hands and feet? What if they cut off her fingers? What if they cut off her toes? She asked her mother when her father would rescue them. Her mother said never.

"But he is a lieutenant general!"

"No! Because of you the colonel general took back his hat. Father is brigadier general again."

Na Cheon still thought a brigadier general could save them,

but when she was six, she was relocated to the not-human orphans' barracks where the other children knew her story and abused her, and the guards never stopped them. They did not even remove the bodies of children who died working in the fields. The bodies lay there; they puffed and turned green and the real insects gnawed them and the other children came over and pinched the insects away and ate them in turn, worms and maggots and shiny green flies that looked as though they had been dipped in oil. Na Cheon ate them, too, better than weeds. She also had a secret rock where she dried worms in the sun to make them taste better.

***

One night a general's jeep chattered to a halt in front of the orphans' hut. The general threw open the door and flashed his light so that he could see the children lying on the floor. Children who were taken away on such occasions came back sworn not to tell what had happened, but they did. Was it better or worse to be taken? Better. Sometimes they got food although sometimes they only got what came out of the man, the white stuff.

The general's torch reached Na Cheon who like all the girls pretended to be asleep. So she did not realize that it was her half-brother, Jae-Hwa, in her father's uniform wearing her father's brigadier's hat. He snatched her up and drove to the not-human women's hut and dragged out her mother. Then he drove down a long road and said he had killed his father and Chin Ho with a kindling axe and used the kindling axe again on the guard at the camp's fence. Then Jae-Hwa pushed his stepmother and half-sister out of the jeep and ran it into the fence and there was a tremendous flash and blue fire all over the jeep, but he had leapt out, returned, grabbed them, and said if one fell, the others must keep running, and if one was swept away by the river, the others must keep struggling, but he would carry Na Cheon on his shoulders and hold his stepmother's hand and they would escape to China and find a South Korean who would get them to Seoul where the Americans would keep them safe.

***

China was not worse than Camp 22 but similar. There was desperate hiding, there were days when Jae-Hwa went out to look for the South Korean helpers he had heard about and came back not having seen one, or having been told it was all a myth, there were no South Korean helpers, but if he wanted to work and eat, he could work and eat. So he would take apart bulldozers and lower their transmissions and axles and engines into acid and wipe the acid off and put the bulldozers together again and be given food and return to the place in the rocks where Na Cheon and her mother hid, not even a real cave, and share it if he had not succumbed and eaten it on the way and then wept with shame and grovelled at his stepmother and half-sister's feet.

One day a man told him to go into the alley behind the garage. A blind man sat there smoking a cigarette and said that he could take Jae-Hwa and one more, but that was it. Not three, two.

Na Cheon's mother said she would stay in the rocks. Na Cheon said she would stay with her. Na Cheon's mother said no.

"But why?" Na Cheon cried.

"Because he can carry you if he has to, and he cannot carry me. I am too used up to survive. Look at me! I am dead!"

Na Cheon and Jae-Hwa saw her face wasted away from her teeth, her eyes fallen deep inside her head, her patches of baldness, her inability to stand up.

They left her.

For the next three months they travelled under the floor of truck beds, in crates, on night-long icy walks, on horses, and once in a container house that was being moved south in a convoy of container houses to create a new camp near a mine. A Chinese woman snuck into their container house and taught them Chinese phrases she said would save them if they were ever found out: *We come from Jilin Province where there is no food. We are father and daughter. We want to live. Please help us. We will do whatever you want if only we can go to Beijing.*

Why Beijing? Because there they would live in a tiny apartment across the street from the South Korean embassy and one day there would be a car crash at the changing of the Chinese guards, giving them a chance to run through the gate and be safe for the rest of their lives.

Na Cheon made it through, too small for the Chinese guards to grab. Jae-Hwa was caught. She never saw him again, but when she thought about him, she pictured him in her father's uniform, wearing her father's hat. That hat kept Jae-Hwa safe if only in her mind. There in her mind he had a house and children, including a little girl like Na Cheon, and a jeep and men who served him and insect non-humans to punish. But then she thought of her mother singing tearful songs as they walked away from the place in the rocks, and she didn't want to think anymore. *Think nothing!* she told herself. *Stop!*

***

They said in Seoul she must be eight. Okay, eight. Her name could still be Na Cheon. Okay, too. She was near the American base because Americans paid for the house in which she stayed. Very slowly—for her own good, they said—she was starved a little less and a little less and grew strong enough to go outside.

There a large man in a uniform took her hand and touched each of her fingers and said, "One ... two ... three ... four ... five." The next time she saw him he did it again and said, "Four are fingers. Other's your thumb."

She took his hand in hers and said, "One ... two ... three ... four ... five!"

"That's right!" he laughed.

"Fingers … thumb."

"Right again! You're a smart little booger."

Also there was a ball on a grassy field with no weeds. The girls and boys kicked it and screamed. At first she couldn't run, but eventually she could a little bit. She even kicked the ball a few times, but like so many things, this made her cry. She didn't like kicking the ball.

The American woman in the house where she lived gave every girl going into the showers a little dab of green jelly. Na Cheon ate it. All the other girls laughed at the bubbly vomit spewing out of her mouth. The American woman took off her clothes right there and got into the shower with Na Cheon and washed her hair for her. She was a heavy woman with enormous blue-veined breasts, a fat belly creased like a stairway, fat behind, great big thighs and enough hair to cover a whole head between her legs. Na Cheon pressed her face up between the American woman's breasts. The American woman said she mustn't do that. Na Cheon thought this was a game and pressed her face there again. The American woman slapped her.

"Wash your hair yourself and don't ever do that again. I was only trying to help. Don't you say I wasn't, you hear?"

When the soldiers came out of the base, they didn't hit anyone or kick them. The first soldier … the second soldier … the third soldier … different kinds of friends. Candy, a comb, words:

"Hey, what's up? Where you been, sweet pea? Haven't seen you, feeling all right? How about a little kiss? You smile okay. What else you do? Pretty hair, pretty girl, I your guy? Call me Charlie. What's your handle? Na Cheon? Where'd you get that name?"

A general's car drove past. She pointed at it. Knew what it was.

"General gave you that name? Really?"

She nodded.

85

"Well, fuck me square, a little general's girl. Tomorrow I come back, okay? Show you a little something. See this? Money. Know what you can get with it? All the candy you want. Make-up. Clothes. Ain't just generals got it in America. We all do. They tell you that? Someone did? Who? I got to teach you to say what's on your mind. All this nodding and smiling. Something about you, I know that much. You look odd. No one ever feed you when you was little? Didn't hurt your teeth none. Guess you didn't use them much, huh? You a runaway from North Korea? Yes? Whoa, baby, you could be worth more than you know. Them Northie gooks come sweep you right off the street and ship you back to what? Nothing, they got nothing. All the something is here. We got it in the PX. South Koreans got it, too, and who gave it to them? Yep, me, you got that right. Whatever you want, any kind of music or car or you name it—cartoon shows!—came from America, my home sweet home."

In the classroom they taught her the words the soldiers used. The woman in the house talked that way. The other girls liked it, talking American. Who could do it best? They all tried. Bathroom. Wee-wee. Over the top. Give me some. Who came from North Korea? Three did: Na Cheon, Park Pok-sun, and Hei Ryung. Each learnt new special phrases: *We're from the countryside, we lost our parents, we don't know how. No mother, no father, no brother.* These phrases would make it easier to get a soldier to be your brother daddy and give you whatever you wanted and take you to America. Yes, they worked, and when she saw how easy it was, she offered rabbit sex in the alley. She liked the money Charlie gave her and how he laughed that he was fucking a general's little girl.

"Tell you what. He can have his long as I get mine. Men say they can fuck all night but they can't. Women's the ones. Why be selfish? Spread the wealth, what I say."

She had money so she bought clothes. She had money so she bought presents. The North Korean girls taught the South Korean girls about rabbit sex. Two or three Americans and two or three girls in the alley or a basement across the street. Quick fuck, quick money.

Some Seoul women caught them and chased them and yelled at the soldiers to give them business, not these girls. Na Cheon and her friends hid and watched. Not so rabbit. Beautiful breasts, eyes and hair. Different sex different ways the men liked.

"Oh, sweet pain, mama! Sweet, sweet pain! Spread your legs wide 'cause here comes the train."

A Korean man grabbed her and Park Pok-sun and pulled them into an elevator. Then he pushed them off the elevator into an apartment where he said, "You love these Americans?"

They said yes, they did, very much.

"Well, I have news for you: men in Pakistan pay ten times what these guys pay. You work once, twice a week, the rest of the time you eat and do your hair, whatever you want. I can make that happen. Interested?"

Park Pok-sun asked what kind of work.

The Korean man laughed. "What you do right now but in a great big bedroom with a real soft bed. No basements, no alleys, all cushy as can be. You like it, it likes you! The Punjab, sweeties, boat ride to paradise. What about it?"

***

How could they know? There were women old as mothers on the ship, a big room where everyone waited, and little rooms where they went with the sailors. How old was Na Cheon? Twelve now? Not every sailor wanted her. No titties yet. Where was her period?

"What is period?"

"The blood between your legs," an older woman explained.

"I have no blood between my legs."

"Don't tell me you're pregnant, Na Cheon. Where did you come from, you and Park Pok-sun?"

"The countryside."

"Oh, come on. The truth. You came from the North, didn't you?"

"I don't know."

"Yes, you do."

"I don't know. Seoul, like you, like everybody."

"All right, say that if you want, but here's what we've learnt and you will too: all men do the same thing to all women wherever they're from. This is what happens, exactly this. You can be rich and work in hotel, you can have a little house, you can be here. All the same. They do what they do so they can do this, so we are special, we are the reward. Men worship us. We're queens, you're princesses. Bow down, bow down, praise your holy queens and princesses and seek entrance to their sacred temples. Tell their fat dicks that."

***

At the end of the ship's journey, Na Cheon and Park Pok-sun were taken out of the city to a house by a stream where each had a bedroom and a closet full of clothes and a dresser full of underwear and bathrooms with make-up and perfume. They didn't like sleeping in their own rooms, so they slept together. Park Pok-sun was older and had breasts. Na Cheon pressed her face between Park Pok-sun's breasts and felt the soft warmth. In the morning, a woman came with food. She said things to them they didn't understand. One day a boy their age came. He spoke English and talked to each of them. Was he deciding? He said he didn't dare. They were for his father when he came back from business in London.

Park Pok-sun said she wouldn't tell his father. She pulled off her blouse and showed him her breasts.

He was a handsome boy with dark skin, black hair, and shining eyes. The sight of Park Pok-sun's breasts made him leave. "Cover yourself! I don't want you! You are sin!"

The big house was up a steep hill. There were pens for animals halfway and workers in the gardens and then a fountain and beautiful trees and then the enormous white house.

Na Cheon still couldn't bring herself to say where she really came from. Park Pok-sun could, however. She escaped from Pyongyang hidden in a fishing boat that sailed down the Taedong River. She was five then.

"My life has been long."

"How long?"

"I am fifteen."

"Did anyone come with you?"

"The old woman who cooked for the fishing boat was my grandmother."

"No one saw you?"

"No one. There was a man who told my grandmother he had to leave and would take me into the sea and down the coast if she hid us both. She said she would. When we got on the little lifeboat, they shot. He was hit in the shoulder. I rowed one oar. He could only row the other. Many times we heard calling, but they did not find us. He took me into Seoul to the house with the woman where I met you and I never saw him again."

The father came back. They could see things happening up in the house. Comings and goings. Big cars. Music. Processions. Welcome, welcome! Time passed until one afternoon he came down to their little house and sat with them smoking a cigar and sipping tea.

"You are so excellent and beautiful," he said. "Both of you. I am Irfan. My son Gulshan confessed to me he had met you but not touched you. Did he touch you?"

"No, he didn't," Park Pok-sun said.

"Good. Don't let that happen. What are your names?"

They told him their names.

"Where did you come from?"

Park Pok-sun told her story.

"Now you, Na Cheon."

Na Cheon remembered every detail of what had happened to her but couldn't speak.

"You are far, far away now. You can tell me." He was

a balding man with a jowly face and large brown eyes. He seemed tired. "My heart isn't good," he said. "That's why I was in London. Now give me some talk medicine for my heart, Na Cheon. Lift up my heart so that we both know you are safe and better here. What is your story?"

Na Cheon couldn't stop herself once she began. All of it!

Irfan said, "Well, well, well. It will be a wonder if they don't have someone come after you. Our blasted government is in cahoots with your government. Nuclear matters. And now here I am harbouring a North Korean general's daughter, a general who has been killed. I don't know if this is good for my heart or bad, but I can tell you one thing: Punjab is the best place in the world, no matter how long the world lasts. The food is best, the poetry is best, the people are best, and our only weakness is what the world calls little girls, young girls, tender girls, girls like you, exotic and splendid. So I will cherish you both, but you must promise me never to try to run away until your time here is over. Do you promise me this?"

"We promise," Park Pok-sun said.

"We promise," Na Cheon said.

He liked them both naked with him but not very often, only a few times a month. His heart couldn't take more. How there could be a defective Punjabi heart, he didn't know. He suspected his sister in London had one, but of a different kind: a mean heart, not a weak heart. He would get treated there more often if he could stand her.

"But sadly, no, I cannot. The woman's unbearable. She has an English husband, and I can dress as well as he and speak the Queen's English as well as he, but it embarrasses her when I am with them, which he insists on, never lets us alone so we can talk things through. I know she thinks I am homosexual, you see, because I only have Gulshan, my son, and my wife tells everyone I do not make a good lover to her. But I think, to the contrary, my sister's husband is the one who is homosexual and hangs around hoping to put my sister's false notion about my preferences to the test. You know the truth about me, of course. But does my sister know the truth about her beloved Randall? Marriage isn't sex-based. That's all a lie. I am married in a marriage without sex, not one little bit of it, but I like sex very much, as you know. Randall does, too, I am sure, but not with my prissy little sister. Ah, who knows, who knows. Here, come to me, both of you. Do your little things. This way ... yes, yes, more, yes ..."

Gulshan returned late one afternoon followed by a peacock, the most beautiful bird Na Cheon had ever seen. The peacock circled the house and pecked for things to eat in the bank along the stream. Gulshan wanted to talk to them about Islam. He was nervous but serious.

"I have thought about doing this a long time. My father doesn't want to hear it. 'We will leave that for the mosque,' he says. Okay, but what isn't the mosque?" Gulshan gestured around at the sky. "Allah isn't here?" He pointed at the peacock and the stream. "Allah isn't there?" He pointed at his forehead, where there was a slight rough spot. "Five times a day, Allah is here."

"What is Allah?" Na Cheon asked.

"He is the all-powerful being we must obey."

Na Cheon thought of the Beloved Leader and wondered if Gulshan knew about him. She dared ask.

Gulshan said of course he knew about the Beloved Leader. "We work with him, don't you know? But Mohammed revealed Allah to us, perfect Allah, and He is our beloved. He is who will punish all the unbelievers, burn them to ashes and then burn their ashes, too."

They thought Gulshan was interesting and could see him struggle as he looked at them. He did not quite know what to say about Allah except that there must be jihad at all costs to defend Him. Nor did he know quite what to say about two Korean whores, which is what he called them, living in the bosom of his ancestral estate, because they could see he wanted to possess them. Any girl could see the heat in his eyes, the puffiness in his lips, the restlessness of his hands and knees.

"You're the daughter of a general. We should send you back," he told Na Cheon. "North Korea is infidel but our friend. What is my father thinking? I will do this. You must be punished."

Park Pok-sun saw the tears in Na Cheon's eyes—Irfan had betrayed her secrets!—and stood up. She undressed completely and approached Gulshan who fixed his eyes on her navel, did not look below or above. She kneeled.

"Don't say that about Na Cheon," she said. "We will be your friends. Let us show you."

Gulshan knocked her down and pulled off his belt. Na Cheon leapt forward to stop him. They fell on top of Park Pok-sun. Na Cheon pushed his face between Park Pok-sun's breasts and reached into his loosened pants where he was excited.

Gulshan came back many times and every time he told them they were devils, they lived in hell, burning hell and sometimes he cried and asked them to leave him alone, stop this, send him away, beat him, why couldn't they beat him, take his belt and beat him? Finally, Park Pok-sun did this.

"And slap me! Make me soft!"

Na Cheon slapped him, but he grew harder, bigger. She straddled him and when his white stuff shot out, she had never seen so much. Park Pok-sun smeared it on his face and lips. Yet he was still hard.

***

"I asked you not to touch him, didn't I?" Irfan said. "Now do you know what he did? I had important people to our home to take a meal with us. This was to be an ecumenical affair. There are Christians and Jews in Pakistan, did you know that? Yes! Well, I am on all sides, but Gulshan is not. He told someone that I keep the daughter of a North Korean general as my whore. He led this someone to the edge of the garden and pointed at this house and said I fuck you here even though North Korea is our friend in nuclear matters. Did you teach him the word fuck? I have never taken him to England so he wouldn't learn such things. Off you go now. I can't have you here. The fanatics will create a scandal. It's back to Karachi for you both. Quick, quick, pack. By nightfall, I want you gone."

***

They were taken to Karachi and left in a place where a man approached them right away. His name was Iqbal.

"You work for me, I take care of you. Food, doctors, everything, but only if you work for me, do you understand?"

He was a big strong guy who tested them both in turn.

"Okay, good. Real good. Now I have other women there and you get along with them or we shave your head. Want your head shaved? No? Then don't fight. Do what you're told. Let the doctor have some if he wants it. Let the madam if she wants it. Everyone else pays."

There was in fact a Cambodian woman who had her head shaved and a Nepalese woman and a Vietnamese woman. Why? Because when women fight, they pull each other's hair, the madam said. Answer: cut it off. She stroked Na Cheon's long beautiful hair and said it was a gift Na Cheon should never surrender even though all the other women could see that the Cambodian, Nepalese and Vietnamese women got lots of men anyway. Many men would look at their shaven skulls and want them.

Sometimes Na Cheon was taken to a hotel. One man wanted her to hold his Bible as he had sex with her. He said Christ meant this. She asked who was Christ, like Allah?

"No, not like Allah! You don't know about Christ? Lie down and hold your arms up over your head and don't let go of that Bible and all His glory will pour down on you while we make love."

Some of the others had done this with him. The Vietnamese woman was Catholic. She explained Christ was God on earth, descended to save those who believed.

"Do you believe, Na Cheon?"

"How can I believe?" she asked.

"Because we're all in the Bible, all of us, prostitutes, men who kill, the Romans. Everyone!"

Cho Sun was from Korea. She told about the Reverend Sung Wei and said that God told him to finish Jesus's work, marry the world in love, save everyone in peace.

"Who do we marry?" Na Cheon asked.

"Japanese. Then we have real jobs, one husband, children. No more of this."

"Not whores anymore?" Park Pok-sun asked.

"Who said whores? Don't say that. Sex workers!"

Na Cheon asked, "If we could get back to Korea, how would we find Sung Wei?"

Cho Sun said Sung Wei would find them. He came from North Korea and survived. He went to jail in the United States and survived. He built his prayer and study centres and churches and survived.

Na Cheon wanted to survive and began wondering about how she could leave Karachi and Pakistan.

"Well, how did you get here?" a man asked her one night.

"By boat."

"Then go back by boat. I'll take you to the docks and find you one."

But their master, Iqbal, could never know. Their house madam, Afia, could never know. The man who would help said this himself: "Iqbal would kill me."

"Why do you do it then?" Na Cheon asked.

"I'll get paid, don't worry. Give me time."

Time passed, the night came, five of the women, not just Na Cheon, left the house in different ways and met Na Cheon's customer on a distant street. He took them to a freighter called *The Chemise*.

"Go now! Musa the Malay is ready for you. All you have to

do to get to Korea is work along the way. Nothing more. Go!"

***

When the ship left the wharf, that was one moment.

When the tug let go, that was another moment.

When they could not see the lights of Karachi anymore, that was the real moment. All her life came back to her from when she was a little girl on the floor of their house in Camp 22 to Beijing to Seoul to the Punjab to Karachi and her bond with Park Pak-sun with whom she still slept if she could.

And now there was this to know: The sea birds, the sea itself, Captain Musa inviting them into his cabin, the other crew, and an American who was a passenger called Walker with an ugly soft round brown wool hat on a hook on the wall. She donned the hat. It made her tremble.

"What's wrong?"

"Nothing."

"You look good. It's an Afghan hat called a *pakol*. Do you want it?"

"No." She put it back on the hook. "What happened to it? Where is the brim?"

"There isn't any. That's not how they're made."

She put it back on again, pulled it down to her ears, thinking about her father's hat.

"Could an Afghan general wear a hat like this?"

"Yes, he could."

"What kind of a general?"

"The fighting kind."

"Why all so much fighting all the time?"

"I don't know, Na Cheon. Did you know a general once?"

"My father."

"He was a general?"

"Yes, in camp."

"What kind of camp?"

"A camp for insect not-humans in North Korea."

"Insect not-humans?"

Na Cheon sat beside him, her slender body needing only a few inches of the bunk on which to perch.

"I take the hat off now, okay?"

"Okay, take it off."

"You want sex?"

"Yes, but I'd like to talk more. I'd like to get to know you."

"Why?"

"I just would." His eyes were soft brown and warmed her. "I've never met anyone quite like you. How old are you?"

"Nineteen."

"It's been a long time since I was nineteen." He had a beard that was grey-brown and hair that was grey-brown and a low voice that was easy to understand. He spoke slowly and said that if she told him what she could about herself, he would tell her what he could about himself.

Na Cheon stretched on top of him and told him where she learnt English and explained why she was in Pakistan and said maybe when she got to South Korea, she would find a preacher, Sung Wei, who said there was no North and South Korea just like there had never been a North and South Vietnam, with which Walker agreed.

"No, there never was. But what if you don't find this Sung Wei?"

"Then I don't know. Marry somebody maybe. It's what they say. What about you?"

Walker smiled a tired smile. "I have no plan. All I know is I left Afghanistan where I lived for over twenty years and I'm not going back."

"North Korea I can't go back, either. What plan is that? No plan. Sung Wei, maybe he knows? But now I am here."

"I am, too. Just you and me."

They laughed. When sex was finished, he kept his arm around her and stroked her hair and sometimes he lifted his head and looked down at her with that tired smile on his face.

Two more times she returned. She wanted him to talk, tell

her his story as she had told him hers from little girl to woman now. It seemed easy for him to say he didn't believe in God or Allah or Jesus or any of that. Not easy for him to say what he did all that time in Afghanistan. Didn't go to America much because one time he returned and visited the wife he'd run away from and it hadn't worked. Not at all. Then during the Taliban years he lived in Peshawar, Pakistan. Taught English. Rented rooms to travellers. Was an interpreter.

"But let's not talk about all that anymore, okay? And if you don't want to talk about North Korea, that's okay, too. We can just lie here."

"I make you hard?"

He kissed her and held her and told her face was beautiful because it was asymmetrical. She didn't know that word. He held his hands up and framed her face the way a photographer would and tilted them, just slightly.

"Sort of like that. Provocative because it's canted a bit."

She went back to the room where the women all sat and looked in the mirror.

"What is it?" Park Pok-sun asked.

"The American says something about my face. Am I beautiful?"

"Yes, you're beautiful."

"Why?"

"I don't know why. Hair for sure."

"More beautiful than you?"

"Yes, to me, yes. Your eyes, you see more. Your lips, they say more. You think, that's what everyone says who looks at you. She must think! How could she not think?"

"But I have been afraid to think!"

"Still?"

"Yes, you know that. All the time my mind dances when I talk to this American with the ugly hat. Americans don't wear those hats. Why don't I say that? He can't have that hat."

"What?"

"His ugly hat. It's an Afghan hat."

"I haven't gone to him. I don't know what you mean."

"Go to him, then. Knock on his door."

"It's never my turn for him when he gets his."

"You want my turn next so you can see the hat and talk to him?"

Park Pok-sun did not hesitate. She was curious about this hat, and why it meant so much to Na Cheon. "Yes, give me your turn with him. I tell him I do it for you, you're too sore, need rest but come back next time ready for more."

They laughed and lay down and Na Cheon put her head between Park Pok-sun's breasts.

"His hat is not like your father's hat you tell me about?" Park Pok-sun asked softly.

"No, no, not like my father's hat, but he says generals wear these hats. Fighting generals. Oh, I am so afraid. What if North Koreans find me in Seoul? What if they drag me back to insect not-human camp?"

"Where else can we go? We are Koreans."

"I don't know. But I ask myself so much: Where can I hide? Who has a real castle where I can hide?"

The freighter throbbed along. They were just over the engine room and could hear the motors grinding steadily. The sound never ceased. Night after night, day after day. On the sea everything seemed forever but nowhere else.

monkey girl

The hazard of selling her own work. Even on a weekday morning, someone like this man might come in and ask her to do a logo for his biotech start-up linked to Yale Labs. He was small, had a hearth-devil aura enhanced by a wispy reddish beard, and wore frameless glasses. A natty, attractive, awful looking man.

"I'm sorry, I don't do logos."

"Why not?"

The Elizabethans would have called him choleric—nowadays "testy." Despite her pretty smile, she could be testy, too.

"I just don't. This is what I do."

She gestured at the wood engravings hanging in her small studio in The Gallery, a large hay barn converted to house graphic artists—a dancer's thigh alive with whip marks of light; two girls, black and white, licking opposite sides of a large lollipop; an insouciant woman in a strapless evening gown looking up into the ballroom lights. Each provocative print was unexpected, but permanent once seen. Suzanne was a little bit like that herself, small enough to be held in the eye whole and always well-dressed. She never wore aprons or smocks while she worked. Only her chafed, ink-smudged fingers suggested how she made a living.

"I like what you do. You're so good, why aren't you in New York?"

"I do sell in New York."

"I've never seen your stuff there. Suzanne Mosel, right?"

"Yes, like the wine and the river. Do you live in New York?"

"Used to." He explained that he'd studied physics at NYU as an undergraduate, then gone into finance, and was now a venture capitalist whose business here in Connecticut was called Eidolon.

Suzanne had never heard that word before. "What does Eidolon mean?"

"It's ancient Greek for 'form.' The root meaning is to see. The word 'wise' comes from eidolon. You're wise after you've seen, and I feel you have seen. That's why I want you to do our logo. We aim to see, too."

People wanted their portraits done, their houses, their dogs, even their lovemaking. Everything but what she saw when she went into her mind and looked. "What does your company research?"

"Medications for people who suffer from vertigo. If you're interested, I could tell you about this over dinner. Are you free tonight?"

She shook her head. "Afraid not."

"Then lunch? Come on, I'll treat you at The Inn Down the Road. It's almost noon, don't you eat?"

"As little as possible," she joked, though it was true. She survived more on nibbling than meals.

His name was Renner Alford. He explained that Eidolon was examining the relationship between sight and balance at a neurochemical level.

"I thought balance involved the inner ear," Suzanne said.

"But what's the inner ear?" Renner ticked the curlicued lobe of his own tidy ear. "In molecular biology, it's not structures—it's systems, it's signals. What's sight, even? You're an artist, what do you see with? Your eye or your mind?"

She found conversations with someone like Renner went better when she didn't try to answer his questions. Men of the world assumed artists knew nothing and liked to prove it. "So how do you approach this?"

He said they used subjects at this stage. Not human subjects—monkeys, although it had all begun with cats. They had come across some research done in the 1950s wherein a cat's eyes were removed and reinserted upside down to see if it would still land on its feet when you dropped it.

"Did it?"

"Yes."

"So?"

"Exactly—so?" Renner chuckled. "No one knew how to take it to the next step. First of all … cats? Come on, felines aren't human. Second, why stop at what the eye can do upside down or right side up? Now we can trace every filament of neurochemistry from the eye to the ear whether the monkey has been 'visually re-oriented,' spun, or simply tested while it's hanging by its tail."

Suzanne had been born in Zimbabwe. They'd had monkeys in the garden her mother detested. She said they weren't native monkeys, just monkeys the previous owner, an Australian, had put there because this was Africa and you had monkeys or what would you tell your mates when you went back home? But Suzanne loved the monkeys. Watching them groom each other with their gentle fingers and swing effortlessly on the limbs of the trees taught her how to see. Her scholarly father loved them, too. As a break from studying propaganda films— blacks about whites and whites about blacks—he often came squinting outside to feed them diced potatoes and crumbled bacon.

"I'd like to see these monkeys," she said definitively.

"Really?" Renner put down his fork. He realized he'd gotten through to her. "You've seen monkeys before, haven't you?"

Zimbabwe was called Rhodesia then. Sun-shot Rhodesia. Cannonades of glorious light shimmering on the garden grass. The tittering creatures fled for the woods when Mama squirted them with the hose. Suzanne couldn't bear losing them to her mother's nastiness like that. So now there often were monkeys tucked into her prints, self-absorbed but watchful, counter-balancing the evolution of human desire and pain. Renner Alford hadn't noticed this.

"Not *these* monkeys."

Renner worried that it was the monkeys, not him, who made the colour in her vivid brown eyes grow deep and liquid. "Would you do our logo if I made that happen?"

Suzanne didn't hesitate. "Yes. Get me in to see the monkeys and I'll do the logo."

So it *wasn't* him. He grew short. "I wish could then, but they wouldn't let you."

"Who wouldn't? You said it was your business."

"The money's my business. The research is run by our scientific director at Yale Labs."

"Have *you* seen the monkeys?

"Of course."

Suzanne fell silent. Since she was a child, this was her stubborn response to blind injustice.

Renner got the point. "Look, I can understand an artist wants to lay eyes on what there is to be seen, but what about the *truth* behind the form, the *secrets* that constitute the form? That's what I want for Eidolon's logo. You've got it in the way you do your work."

Suzanne ignored his flattery. She had to force herself to say anything at all. "Isn't 'logo' the root for 'word'?" she asked.

"More than the root. 'Logo' means word—*the* word. 'In the beginning was the Word …'"

"Then I wonder why you don't just use your word in a nice dramatic script." She picked up the pen next to the leather folder containing the bill for lunch and wrote *Eidolon* on the tablecloth with casual brilliance. "Any graphic designer could do that for you."

Renner blinked at what she'd done to the restaurant's tablecloth. (He wanted to get his hands on it and take it with him.) "Look, here's the problem. Our researchers are obsessed about animal rights people invading them. That's turned specimen labs into virtual armed camps."

"I sympathize with animal rights, but I'm an artist, not an activist."

"So what do I tell them—that you want to depict the monkeys in their cages?"

"Are they in cages?"

The octagonal lenses of Renner's glasses glinted as he looked up at the exposed beam ceiling in an appeal for mercy. "No, no, no. They live in a great big expensive room. They've got an elaborate jungle gym and some bushes and artificial sunlight and special ventilation and a gourmet diet of organic vegetables. All of which I finance."

Suzanne dropped the pen. "I'm sorry, I can't do anything with that."

"With what?"

"With what you're telling me. It's just words. If monkeys are Eidolon's subjects, I'd have to see them to find *my* subject." She wanted to see the hair on their arms, their eyebrows, their wrinkles, their bare palms, long fingers, and big round eyes. And now that the subject had been raised, she naturally wanted to know what she would see if her own eyes were removed and reinserted upside down.

Who wouldn't?

***

Eidolon's scientific director, Dr Nora Almazy, clearly disliked her. Suzanne didn't know whether it was because she could be an animal rights activist in disguise or because she had been presented as an artist, which she'd corroborated by bringing along a catalogue of her wood engravings. Dr Almazy accepted it but wouldn't open it. She said there were safety and ethical concerns no one could surmount. On top of all that, you had to have instruction prior to any contact with the subjects.

"Ethical concerns?" Suzanne asked.

"Yes, ethical concerns," Dr Almazy said. Full stop. Apparently she planned to wear Suzanne out by forcing her to pry up every rock to see what was underneath.

"What would they be?"

"The research community is obliged to preserve the integrity of its work and not allow science to be treated as a showcase, Ms Mosel."

"Mr Alford said you were researching why people lost their balance."

"That's right."

"He said things like vertigo and head injuries and infections and strokes."

"Correct."

Frustrated but determined, Suzanne tried this: "I can see that you have an ethical obligation to get that right. And the connection between balance and sight—Mr Alford emphasized that."

"Yes," Dr Almazy said.

When she was being stymied—when she couldn't hear what was being said at a noisy party, for instance, because she had a damaged eardrum—Suzanne had an alternative. She could look. She did this with as much pleasure as another person might eat pudding. The shape of a forehead or a nose somehow tasted good to her. Her mother thought it lewd. "You're *doing* that again. Stop it! It's nasty!" But Suzanne never stopped it.

Now she sat there taking in Dr Almazy's thick brown hair swept left to right above her strong brow and wide mouth, and in between, best and most fascinating of all, her somewhat orbicular eyes, which must have disturbed her when she was growing up. A girl wouldn't like realizing that she had rounder than normal eyes, eyes comprising thousands of tiny brown and ochre diamonds that encircled her deep black piercing pupils.

"And you said instruction is also required before contact with the monkeys?" Suzanne finally asked, having soothed herself with this good long interesting look into Dr Almazy's eyes.

Dr Almazy, almost hypnotized, said, "Even our lab interns have to start by viewing two hour-long videos. The first deals with intrusions into scientific research by misguided animal rights activists. The second is about interacting safely with specimens."

Suzanne used to sit with her father for hours as he studied the ways in which Rhodesian blacks and whites depicted each other in film. The blacks focused on predatory white capitalist colonialists, seizing control of Africa with lawsuits, crooked politics and lies in the media. The whites depicted their philanthropic efforts undermined by a tiny belligerent faction of uncooperative, unreliable, hateful blacks. German and Swedish foundations paid for the black films; the whites paid for their own. Neither blacks nor whites liked her father looking at both sides of the conflict, and he lost his professorship at the university. To her mother's disgust, they ended up at Michigan State in Lansing. Then they divorced.

"All I want is to look at the monkeys, not touch them," she said. "I'm just an artist."

"Perhaps that's the point. This isn't art, Ms Mosel. This is science." Dr Almazy pushed Suzanne's catalogue back across the table to her.

Suzanne wondered where they kept the monkeys in this anonymous two-story brick building that wasn't even near Yale. She couldn't hear them. They were probably way in the back. Renner Alford said their room was full of artificial sunlight.

"But art, like science, requires something specific," Suzanne persisted. "I think that's what Mr Alford wants his company logo to reflect."

"Well, it isn't specimens. Mr Alford knows perfectly well this company isn't about the life and times of monkeys. We do our work at the molecular level, Ms Mosel. It's about the creation of knowledge; our subjects are simply hosts to an array of neurochemical relationships. If you really want to come up with an appropriate logo for Eidolon, I suggest you study organic chemistry and then some bio-physics."

Dr Almazy's eyes were on fire, but summoning up her courage, Suzanne retorted, "I feel that what I do also creates knowledge."

"How so?"

"Art is human knowledge of some kind, isn't it? Art takes you into the unknown. It makes you aware of possibilities that you wouldn't ordinarily consider."

Dr Almazy smiled a large smile that no doubt had compensated for her eyes all her life, a smile that was somehow both motherly and erotic, but in any case distracted from her permanently startled gaze. "Possibilities aren't knowledge. Knowledge is information that can be verified and reproduced." She tapped the back cover of Suzanne's catalogue with the picture of her in her long leather coat under a leafless wintry tree. "I'd venture to say that not one of your pieces is interpretively stable with any other in substance or approach."

"I don't know what interpretively stable means."

"Probably because it's a concept that doesn't apply to art, it applies to science. I'm afraid we shall have to leave it at that."

"But couldn't I at least see the videos?"

"I've told you that we cannot let you enter our labs. What would be the point?"

"Aren't there monkeys in them?"

"In the second video, yes, but not the first one about animal rights activists."

"I'd still like to see them. Won't you let me do that much?"

"If I do, will you claim you're qualified to take the next step and insist on entering the labs?"

"Excuse me?"

Dr Almazy realized that she'd become needlessly offensive. Her tone of voice had sharpened while Suzanne's had remained soft. "No, no, of course not," she said. She took two videocassettes out of her desk. "Here, follow me."

She led Suzanne to a conference room and put in the first

tape, leaving her alone with it—almost as if fleeing. It was a clinical but turbulent video, dissecting the ways in which animal rights activists tricked their way into scientific labs, applying for jobs and then making secret videos, or initiating frivolous lawsuits and spreading lies in the media. The second video, on managing animal specimens, offered detailed instruction in not getting bitten, clawed and infected. The majority of the subjects were quite compliant, of course, but there were always rogues in any lot who could strike without warning.

After she had finished, Suzanne took the cassettes back across the hall to Dr Almazy's office. The doctor wasn't in so she left them in the middle of her desk on top of her catalogue.

***

When Renner Alford finally dared to come see her, he found a logo print hanging on the clothesline above her press. That was the first surprise. The second surprise was what the logo looked like.

Suzanne had done something—he supposed at first you would call it abstract—which was the most absorbing pattern of interlocked, concentrically organized diamond shapes he had ever seen and somehow given it a sad, humanoid quality with just the slightest convexity near the centre, where Eidolon seemed to float in infinite retreat. If you didn't know it was a word, though, you'd never make it out. You'd think you were looking at molecules, maybe, or an ingenious spill of microscopic glyphs.

And it was a round print—fourteen inches in diameter— single and myriad all at once.

"My god!" he gasped. "It's virtually alive! You could never reproduce that on anything but your own press."

"No, there's no way," Suzanne said.

"So, dammit, we can't use it," he muttered in a low, true voice. But he couldn't stop looking at the wavering tonalities clasped within an enormous gravitational field of counter-poised cuts and stabs—vertigo and balance all at once. "Jesus, I'm stuck. I can't take my eyes off it. How long did it take?"

"Forever."

"What do you call it?"

"Monkey Girl."

"But you didn't get to *see* the monkeys, did you?"

Suzanne shrugged. He kept talking, but it was as if she couldn't hear him. The movie was playing but no sound. Looking at the print, working on the print, she smelled diced potatoes and crumbled bacon, and cut by cut, swung from tree to tree.

with her ear
pressed to the earth

Nikandros told the clerk that he would take Kristina's last
name instead of vice versa. He held the counter with both
hands in a way that suggested he meant to impose this proposition, just as he insisted the marriage take place in San Francisco. To Kristina, San Francisco was full of buildings that
could crumble at any moment as they had in 1906, crushing
her parents. She assumed she survived only because she was so
small, a baby. She had many pictures in her mind of squalling
in the rubble. But they couldn't be real memories. Her real
memories of earthquakes came from the verses her Uncle
Alexei came across in the Bible when he read it out loud at
night. The Bible was full of earthquakes. Every one of them
presaged the end of the world and the Judgment.

"You'd be Nikandros Theodore instead of her being Kristina Popandropoulos?" the clerk asked. She was a middle-aged
woman with dewlaps and a doughy face who seemed wary of
Nikandros. Everyone in the birth-marriage-death-citizenship
office knew him. He came in all the time, often straight from
his father's boat, bossy and temperamental, to take pictures of
ceremonies and events with his prized Speed Graphic camera.
But she didn't know Kristina, standing behind Nikandros
as if she were next in line, waiting for a separate marriage
license. Kristina wore a white cotton Mexican dress with red
and purple anemones brocaded across the bosom. She held a

bouquet of daisies, tiger lilies, and black-eyed Susans, Nikandros had picked on the way to the farm to get her. A friend of his loaned him a truck for the ride to the Tiburon landing, and then another friend took him, Kristina, Alexei and her Aunt Grushenka across the bay from Strawberry Point in his motor skiff. Meanwhile Nikandros's mother and father had the curtains drawn in Sausalito, mourning the fact that he wasn't marrying a Greek girl.

Kristina had a long, straight nose barely fluted at the nostrils, a small mouth and a small chin. She was twenty-nine, but everything about her looked younger: her blonde hair, her creamy skin, her delicate bones. When Nikandros told her about the name, she liked the idea of remaining Kristina Theodore but didn't feel comfortable with him becoming a Theodore, even if the name was Greek—gift of God—which is why her Uncle Alexei had picked it and abandoned the Russian name no one could pronounce. Started with K. Karzov, Karmzov … something like that.

"Now Nikandros," the clerk said, "you and the bride have to apply for the license using your current legal names and then the form says that the bride will take your last name. See the blank where we fill that in?" She showed Nikandros the form. He told her it was a form, not the law. She asked if he wanted her to consult Magistrate Wycoff. He said yes.

The clerk walked past some file cabinets down a yellow corridor toward the magistrate's office. Kristina looked over her shoulder at Alexei and Grushenka seated in chairs arranged so that they faced an open space where the ceremonies occurred. Alexei's lean head had the nobility of baldness complemented by a long face and deeply creased cheeks. He wore a clean white shirt and grey overalls and had his Bible in his lap; he wanted it used in the wedding. Grushenka wore a white scarf and blue dress. Over time her figure had shrunk so that the proportions remained the same but the features and dimensions drew together into a kind of elderly doll, a matryoshka doll. As a girl Kristina had many such dolls and understood early on that they represented the stages of life. First you went from little to big, then you went from big to little. Grushenka had Nikandros's bulky Speed Graphic with the big silver flash attachment in her lap. She also wore a carnation corsage Nikandros had pinned on her.

"If only I had met a man like you," she had said to him while he was doing this in the low-ceilinged common room of their farmhouse.

"What did she say?" Nikandros asked Kristina because Grushenka said it in Russian.

"She said don't stick her with the pin," Kristina fibbed.

Grushenka understood enough English to laugh with Kristina at the nervous men staring at them, the black-haired, heavy-shouldered, thickly bearded groom and the lean almost wispy column of smoke uncle. She had told Kristina many times that she wasn't a man's woman like Grushenka. "What do you mean?" Kristina asked. Grushenka never answered directly. "If I told you, you wouldn't want to hear it. We can't change the way we are. We are born a certain way and die that way. All his life Alexei has thought he could pray his way out of being who he is." And without having to finish her thought, Grushenka conveyed to Kristina her conclusion about Alexei: he'd ended up almost nothing, not the one thing, not the other, a man of potential greatness divided and trapped within himself. What Grushenka did say was a little poem she'd made up. "Men with sails, women with pails. The men sink unless the women think."

The story was that Kristina's father, Ivan, had been a man of words like his brother, Alexei, but of his own words, not the Bible's, and he had married an American woman, Christina with a "C," and that after the earthquake killed them, Kristina came to live with her aunt and uncle across the bay on Strawberry Point with her three cousins—Aaron, Andre, and Deborah. But after Aaron went to sea on her Uncle Dmitri's boat and was the only one who came back when it sank, and then left almost immediately for New York with Deborah and

then Andre following him, Kristina felt duty-bound but naturally inclined to remain with the aging Alexei and Grushenka.

She was an average person, no wanderer, and that was
good—an American girl who got through tenth grade and
spoke English with no accent even if she also was fluent in
Russian and who was a good worker tending the cows in
the pastures with Alexei and vegetables in the garden with
Grushenka. Undoubtedly her special energy and beautiful
skin derived from Alexei's strict Molokan milk regimen on
220 fast days of the year. In California most of the Molo-
kans lived in Los Angeles. That's where Kristina had assumed,
when she thought about it, Alexei would go to find her a
husband, telling the one he chose that the girl waiting for
him on Strawberry Point was beautiful. "Our beautiful girl"
was often how Alexei referred to her even in her presence and
when addressing her. Or, "the one the Lord spared." Kristina
didn't like the latter formulation because it made her think of
her mother and father, who were retrieved from San Francisco
and buried in the east pasture, but without markers. "The
cows grazing over them are their markers," Alexei would say.
"What better marker could there be?" Grushenka, detecting
Kristina's dissatisfaction and unease, hastened to agree. "The
cows keep them alive and they keep us alive. Bury me under
the cows in the pasture, too." Yet at a certain point Kristina
had begun to want to know exactly where the graves were.
She couldn't ask Aaron, who was gone. Andre had been an
infant and didn't know. If there was one thing Deborah would
not discuss, it was Kristina's parents and where they had been
placed in the pasture. Deborah was six at the time they died
and surely could remember, but wouldn't say. She and Kristina were not close. Something pushed them apart. Deborah
was smart, tomboyish, and bold. She had a big figure like
her mother, Grushenka. Kristina was a skinny, timid, cautious
girl with fine hands and long fingers who didn't say much
and whose beauty seemed fragile to the point of almost irritating people, forcing them to be more careful around her

than normal. If you bumped into her, she was like nothing, a feather.

She ended up picking her way across the cow pies in the pasture and studying the grasses for signs of a depression that might signify two graves. The problem was that the pasture was all rises and falls, tussocky in some places, eroded here and there where the stream along the road overflowed with water running off Mt. Tamalpais. Sometimes she stretched out on the ground and sought to feel her parents with her body and even listen for them with her ear pressed to the earth. She'd look past the cedars along the road and cultivate silence within herself as if she were picking burrs off her clothes. All the knots and whirls of extraneous thoughts and discomforts had to be pinched away so that she became a kind of human stethoscope. They were in there, Ivan and Christina, and the earth had a kind of sound, but if that sound was them, she did not know. She concluded that her parents and the earth, her parents and the pasture, her parents and the sun rising and setting on the grasses and cows and fence lines and stands of trees … all was one and the same … and all, in some hard to define sense, was beyond reach.

Deborah did explain one thing by showing Kristina a black metal box in which there was a pile of newspaper clippings: her father wrote under a *nom de plume*, John Patmos. Deborah said, "A nom de plume is a pen name. It means you can say what you want and not worry about people coming after you."

"Why would they come after him?" Kristina asked.

Deborah became mysterious. "If they don't like what you say. He was a really good writer. If he had to, he'd use other languages to make his point."

"You mean Russian?"

"No, he wasn't writing for the Russians. He'd use Latin sometimes. Doctors and lawyers know Latin. Educated people. Ab ovo? Know what that means?"

The two girls were huddled together on the floor and

Deborah was shuffling through the articles. She found ab ovo and said it meant "from the egg," or "from the very beginning." "What was he saying that for?" Kristina asked. "Because he was saying nothing is really that way, fixed from the beginning. Everything can be changed." "The way Uncle Alexei says God can change everything whenever he wants?" "No, the opposite: by man." Deborah lowered her voice: "Uncle Ivan didn't believe in God."

Hearing this upset Kristina, and she withdrew from conversations that disturbed her. She could be pointed and persistent, yet she also could be silent. She didn't rattle on when she didn't know what to say.

Over the years, she read all of John Patmos's articles; they mostly dealt with how greedy and cruel the czar of Russia was. Her reading required obtaining a Webster's dictionary and all the concentration Kristina could muster. She did not know what words like "serfdom," "imperialism," "monarchy," "backwardness," "socialism," "repression," or "imprisonment" meant, and she was fourteen before these things began to coalesce into some kind of meaningful pattern. Even then she was not sure she understood why John Patmos wrote these things … not until one night Alexei took up his Bible and began reading aloud from a book that included, almost immediately, the sentence, "I, John, your brother who share with you in Jesus the persecution and the kingdom and the patient endurance, was on the island called Patmos because of the word of God and the testimony of Jesus." And she knew that's where her father Ivan got the name and the spirit in which he wrote, which was exactly the spirit of the earthquake that had torn San Francisco apart and burnt it down and killed Ivan and Christina and from which Kristina barely escaped. The Book of Revelation, which Alexei read for the next three nights, transfixed and mortified her.

***

She feared this church-like municipal building and disliked waiting for the clerk to return. "Why do we have to use my name? Why not get married somewhere else?"

Nikandros cocked his head back to look down upon her though he wasn't that much taller than she. "I want to get rid of my father's name, and I want to marry you here and now."

"She told you they don't give the man the woman's name. Theodore wasn't even our name to begin with."

"Doesn't that prove my point? Your name can be whatever you want."

The building was making her sick; the golden hills and green corn fields and lush vineyards and Spanish missions painted on the high, vaulted ceiling were right where they could fall on her. She withdrew into her silence to deal with her nausea.

They had come to know one another at the Tiburon market, where his father sent him to sell fish, thereby getting him off the boat where they were always arguing. Kristina had been at the market for years selling milk and vegetables when he first showed up. One day he came over and helped her with a heavy can of milk, from which she filled people's containers. It was a simple favour; but he did it over and over again, and they told each other their names and began talking about their customers who barely had the money to buy anything, and how Alexei was turning more and more milk into cheese to make it last longer and Grushenka was urging Kristina to leave as many vegetables on the vine as possible so as not to cart them to the market and end up selling them for next to nothing at the end of the day just to get rid of them. Nikandros's problem with fish was that it was best fresh and needed to be sold right away. Yes, they could dry leftovers, but dried fish stank. Even sitting in peach baskets at the edge of his little stall it stank, yellow wrinkled fish with empty eye sockets he would sell for three cents apiece in the morning and a penny apiece in the afternoon.

"I think I would like to be a Molokan," he said one afternoon. "I like milk. If all I had was milk, fine."

"Here," she said and drew him a glass of milk which, though somewhat warm, did seem to please him.

"You're always so covered up," he said. "And your face, it's like you don't work on a farm at all. Look at me, I'm brown as dirt, but you're so white."

"It's because I look down at the ground when I'm in the garden and when I milk the cows, it's in the barn. I'm not in the sun as much as you might think."

"I can't escape it. For a fisherman there are three things, no, five: sun, water, wind, fog, and rain."

She knew he wanted her to like him, but he spoke disrespectfully about his father, which troubled her.

"I tell him we're Americans, not Greeks. Like you, look, what are you—Russian? Who could be more American? Just because you speak Russian, what does that mean?"

It meant a great deal. If Kristina spoke English to Alexei and Grushenka, they looked as if they were falling down a steep flight of stairs, very alarmed and uncomfortable. It had been different in the house when her cousins lived there. They spoke English all the time. Now it was nothing but Russian.

But at the same time, there was a cockiness about Nikandros she enjoyed resisting. Once he told her he had figured out how much you could sell their dairy farm for and she told him they would never sell the farm, but she wanted to know how much. He said $61,000 if they could find the right buyer. With that kind of money you could move to San Francisco and really get into things. He'd take pictures. It was his passion, not fishing, and there was not a single picture in San Francisco that was easy. The city was all hills, angles, shadows, and moods. Likewise the people, who came from everywhere. Nikandros felt free and somewhat grand among them, detecting and celebrating the unique life experiences etched into their faces and postures, solemnized forever in his crystalline images where no skin was blemished and everything within the frame seemed to float in a pearly grey haze, San Francisco's natural hue. The whole business of being married in San Francisco came from the fact that Nikandros had made a portrait of Magistrate Wycoff and his family. He had promised his influence would make it all go fast.

Now she said, "This isn't going fast."

Nikandros gave her a grin that gleamed with irresistible contrariety. He had proposed marriage to her with that grin. She never believed in it 100%, but that made him an indefinably exciting man and drew her to him. He smiled when he said he hated his father, and he smiled when he said he would triumph anyway because he could see, couldn't he? Couldn't he see how beautiful Kristina was? Wasn't that proof? "The clerk, she's a no one, so she goes back there, and the secretary makes her wait. The magistrate doesn't even know it's me out here."

Kristina felt like warm butter when he kissed her, but though he tried, she would not let him do what she knew very well was done. She had grown up on a farm and what she didn't see in animals, she heard from Grushenka, who thought it would be better if there were some other way to produce babies. Once she said, "I caused so much trouble between my legs when I was your age that it would have been a mercy for the whole world if someone shot me. Keep your legs closed until you're married."

Hearing himself say that the magistrate didn't even know he was out there suddenly made Nikandros furious. He pounded his fist on the countertop. The clerks along the line looked his way, but the clerk who had gone to see the magistrate still didn't reappear from the yellow corridor. Alexei and Grushenka looked at him in shock as he began yelling, "Hey! Hey! What's going on back there!"

The plan was that he would move onto the farm where he would focus on the cows and leave the gardening to the women and let Alexei, who had such arthritis in his knees and hands, sit on the porch and read his Bible. Once or twice a week Nikandros would go over to San Francisco and spend the night in a little room above the photography shop his friend owned and make photographs—weddings, bar mitz-vahs, christenings, confirmations, anniversaries. "But I'll be realistic," he promised. "I know the world is broke. It's going to take time before we can even think about me doing nothing but make photographs."

How much time? Alexei and Grushenka must be almost eighty or past eighty, and Kristina knew what Nikandros was thinking: soon, this farm would be theirs because the cousins in New York would never come back. Then he would want to sell the farm and move to San Francisco where he would establish his own photography shop, and the hell with the Popandroupolos clan. Let them fish. He and Kristina would make their own family, however many children came. Three? Okay. Six? Fine. But not so fine with Kristina, who did not like his rift with his family (even though she didn't know them) and could not imagine bearing child after child. Grush-enka told her the secret to controlling him. "Always remember no matter how many times the man wants to do it, you can do it more. Make him keep doing it until he has to give up. The first time that happens to him is all it will take. He'll slow down after that."

And Kristina never wanted to leave the farm, not with her parents in the pasture, and by that time, probably Alexei and Grushenka, too. On the farm, you could always eat. Through years and years of the Depression, they had eaten. And no earthquake had ever damaged a blade of its grass.

She and Nikandros had never really discussed this because he either made her laugh with wonder or drove her into silence before reaching it, but now she stood there, observing the stolid, aging couple in their seats—not aging, old—and thought of other things Grushenka said. For instance, that nothing turned out as you planned and everything was different from what you wanted and that she had never, when she, Alexei and his brother Dmitri, reached San Francisco, enjoyed the bath she had dreamt of in a grand hotel because they had to put all their money into buying the farm. "The whole time we were escaping from Russia I saw myself ending up in a great big deep white bathtub with lion's feet and all the hot water I could ever want."

Even today Grushenka and Alexei would go back to the farm while Kristina and Nikandros had their honeymoon in his darkroom above the photographic supply store. Who had money for grand hotels? Kristina would like to pay for Grushenka's dream—she thought she almost could—but Nikandros said Grushenka couldn't get out of a bathtub that big if she ever got in. Besides, they had to live cheap and keep their money for themselves.

"The magistrate probably isn't even in his office," Kristina said, knowing it would irritate Nikandros to hear her say that.

Nikandros gave her an ominous look. "He will put all this right."

"We could fix your name later."

"I want it fixed now!"

He couldn't understand why she was tormenting him, but she kept doing it. She said if he changed his name, then his father really would disown him; there would never be a reconciliation. She thought that if he had any idea what it was to lose your parents, he'd stop this. She had seen Nikandros's father once and the man frightened her. It happened in Tiburon after the market broke up. He knew it was she just as she knew it was he because of his tattered brown cap and weathered fishing boots almost to his knees. She kept walking because it would be up to a man to speak to her or ignore her. He ignored her. How could he do that when he knew Nikandros was determined to marry her and she was Alexei's niece and everyone loved Alexei for bringing them milk on his fast days? Alexei spoke to so many hungry, grateful people in his little English and said yes to whatever they asked him. They could ask if the sun would fall out of the sky and he would say yes. They could ask if they'd find buried treasure and he'd say yes. Kristina asked him about this once, sure there must be some reasoning, and there was: Alexei said that whenever people were thankful, and the milk made them thankful, telling them yes lifted their hearts even higher and made them believe that no matter what, the Lord would always provide them with milk. This was the Molokan way.

The clerk finally returned and pulled back the half-gate so that Nikandros and Kristina could walk down the yellow corridor to the magistrate's office, which was very large and impressive with high ceilings and tall windows, all of which Kristina could imagine toppling in on them. Mr Wycoff did not seem concerned about that. He was a cheery, pudgy man wearing a grey suit with a black vest and a green bow tie. On the credenza behind his desk, there was indeed a picture of him and his family signed in silver ink by Nikandros Popandropoulos just as Nikandros had told her, Michelangelo Buonarroti had been the first artist to put his name on a work of art, and where? Right on the Virgin Mary!

Magistrate Wycoff invited them to take a seat and said, "It's probably the last time you'll sit beside each other single, so enjoy it. Now, we're going to marry you, right? Shall we call in the clerk and my secretary to witness?"

"No, no," Kristina objected. "My aunt and uncle are here. They will be the witnesses and have their Bible and Nikandros's camera."

"Oh, my goodness, let's get them in here then," Magistrate Wycoff said. He called out to his secretary to do so. In a moment—a long moment, since they were old and not happy (Kristina could see this; she knew them better than she knew any cow or duck or goat on the farm, their glances, their pace, their postures, the tiny way they were moving through space as if it were full of nettles and prickers)—Alexei and Grushenka joined them.

"But first, the name question," Nikandros said.

"Name question?" Magistrate Wycoff either had not heard of this issue or preferred to overlook it, something so silly.

"You know, I take her name, not she takes mine."

"Nikandros, that's not the way we do it. The woman takes the man's name."

Kristina watched as Nikandros, who had been growing increasingly agitated, did something strange. He reached out and drew Alexei, Grushenka and Kristina to him and said, "This is my family now, not the ones who oppose this marriage."

As a big man, over six feet tall and more than 200 pounds, Nikandros could do this. Kristina wondered if it would change Magistrate Wycoff's position. It didn't. Very business-like, Magistrate Wycoff said to let these folks go and sign the papers. He said Alexei and Grushenka had joined up under their names and given Kristina her name and now Nikandros would give her a new one.

"Marriage is that way everywhere far as I know. My wife's name was George. Imagine that? George for a last name?"

"George would be a good last name," Nikandros countered. "Better than Popandroupolos. Their last name wasn't Theodore, either."

Magistrate Wycoff said, "Well, let's not get off on tangents, but what was your name?" he asked Alexei and Grushenka.

Kristina answered for them. "They don't say."

"Why don't they say?"

"I don't know. It was Russian."

"And they changed it? Legally?"

Kristina could see that Grushenka understood exactly what was being discussed and did not want it discussed. "My parents died in the earthquake. They took me in, my uncle and aunt. Whatever they are, I am."

Magistrate Wycoff spent some time pondering all this. "What proof do they have they are who they say they are? I mean ... if they're going to witness."

"They own a farm on Strawberry Point. They've been there for many years," Nikandros said. "Everyone knows them. You have a deed, don't you?" he asked Alexei. "Tell him what I said," he ordered Kristina.

"Nikandros, what does the farm have to do with it?"

"Just tell him what I said," Nikandros commanded her,

taking her by her upper arm and turning her to face Alexei.

"Well, look, this *is* a tangent, and I'm sorry I raised it," Magistrate Wycoff said. He pushed the marriage license application across his desk and tapped it with the tip of his index finger. "Miss, you sign with the name you always use, and we'll get my secretary and clerk as witnesses just to be double sure, and this is all going to be fine."

Kristina didn't know what would happen when she picked the pen out of the magistrate's pen stand to sign as instructed, but she wasn't surprised when Nikandros took the pen from her and put it back into the pen stand. More surprising by far was Alexei saying to her in Russian, "You should not marry this man. He will beat you."

"Oh," Grushenka gasped.

"What's that?" Magistrate Wycoff asked.

"Why are you saying this?" Grushenka asked Alexei, also in Russian.

Alexei was looking directly at Nikandros with his washed-out, deep-set eyes and made everyone look at Nikandros the same way, scrutinizing his pride, anger, and recklessness. "I object to this marriage," he said.

"What's he saying?" Magistrate Wycoff asked.

"My uncle said he objects to the marriage," Kristina said, feeling something swaying dangerously around her.

Magistrate Wycoff said, "Now ... we're not at that part yet."

His dark complexion notwithstanding, Nikandros had grown pale. He reached out and grabbed his large camera from Grushenka. "Object! Why does he object?"

"He's afraid you will beat me."

Nikandros faced Alexei directly. "Why would you say such a thing?"

Alexei continued to condemn him with that bottomless look. Grushenka whimpered.

Magistrate Wycoff said, "Ladies and gentlemen, I have the impression that this is an unsettled matter. Nikandros, why don't you come back tomorrow after you sort things out?"

Nikandros looked at Magistrate Wycoff as if he were a lunatic. He'd never come back here. "Did my father tell you to do this? I told him I was going to abandon his name. He knew it. I would throw it back in the water like a trash fish. And he told you!"

"Now calm down, sir. He told me nothing of the kind."

"He's like Dmitri," Grushenka said.

"Dmitri, you say? Dmitri who?" Nikandros asked.

"Karamazov."

"Kar-what? Kar—? Who is this?" Nikandros stamped his foot. He looked around wildly. "Someone answer me!"

When no one answered him, he lifted his camera up over his shoulder with one large hand as if he were going to throw it at someone. Around and around it wheeled. Gently Kristina reached up and guided his arm down. They needed to go, she said in English to Magistrate Wycoff and in Russian to Alexei and Grushenka. Go where? Grushenka asked. Kristina didn't know, but she could feel Nikandros's biceps almost bursting beneath his shirt, and the room had begun spinning and hurtling. She knew they had to go. Just go.

They walked out of the municipal building onto the street and along the footpath for several blocks before he managed to say something. She looked at him all that time as though he were a storm blowing down off the mountain; if there could be black snow, that's what he would be: black snow.

"What was your uncle thinking? Why did he say that?" he demanded.

Kristina said she didn't know. She had heard him read such things from the Bible, yes, all through the Bible there were crises like this, but not speaking in his own words and from his own heart.

Nikandros led her to the photographic supplies shop and let himself in and guided her up the narrow wooden stairwell to the first door on the left. Inside, there was a sink, many brown bottles of chemicals corked and capped shut, clotheslines strung wall to wall and a narrow cot. Nikandros sat down on the cot for several minutes and cried. When he was finished, he looked at Kristina in a way that made her wonder if he was going to send her away. His eyes were large, wild, and glistening. But he didn't send her away. He breathed deeply and raised his arm in some kind of blessing.

"We are married. I am Nikandros Theodore, and you are my wife," he said. Then he cocked the back of his hand in her direction and fought it back down into his lap. He would never, ever hit her, he promised, no matter how much sometimes he might want to.

That night they made love three times. The fourth time, he had to give up and fell into a deep, deep sleep. Around four in the morning, Kristina pulled on her clothes and slipped away. By dawn it was easy enough to find a boat crossing the bay. Then she walked from Tiburon to Strawberry Point and entered the barn and found Alexei on his three-legged stool, milking a cow. She pulled her own stool down off its hook on the wall and began doing the same.

She gave up thinking about anything that had happened except the possibility that in time she would prove to be pregnant, which she was. It was not an easy pregnancy, but it was not a lonely one. She had Grushenka to help her and Alexei to read to her.

Nikandros was too proud and afraid he would be rejected to come to the farm and beg for her return. Instead, he wrote her letters and sent her photographs that he had made in San Francisco. She chose not to reply. Every day that passed it was easier to resist the urge to give in. Of course he wasn't working at his father's fish stall in the Tiburon market anymore; his younger brother was. The younger brother made no comments about her condition, but when she was far along, he came to her stall one afternoon and tried to give her an envelope full of money, saying this was for his father's grandchild. Kristina refused it, but named the child Nikandra in feminine acknowledgement of the man who had been her father. Around the farm she called the little girl Nikki.

***

After Pearl Harbor, Nikandros enlisted in the Navy. His body was lost at sea. But Kristina did finally discover where her parents were buried. When Alexei died in 1946, Grushenka held fast to her arm and led her out to a spot and said, "Here, we will bury him next to his brother."

It wouldn't be where Kristina would have said with certainty that Ivan and Christina might be, but surely at some point she had lain atop it and listened for their silence. The earth was soft but heavy, squishy with waters from recent rains. She let Nikki spade a little, but Kristina did most of the work because she wanted to be very careful and knew exactly how to interpret Grushenka's crooked finger, pointing to the spot where she should centre the hole so as not to disturb the dead, who were alive to her and still full of the pain of a life wherein nothing that happened was what you expected and nothing that you expected came true.

birth

Somehow their marriage got caught in the car engine and it blew up. First it ground to a halt, then it smoked, then came the fire and the explosion. The explosion was a muffled thud, a sound like a sack of cement or maybe an overstuffed chair pushed out a window and landing in an alley. She felt the thud drifting into her chest as she stood on the soft shoulder and then she saw it illuminate Hal's face with a purple powdery light, a light full of recrimination.

She had made the car do this.

The first day of vacation and the car was dead and now they were in this emotional alley, scattering their stuff everywhere as they pulled it out of the car and threw it behind them and saved it from the fire which caught her long hair on the right side of her head as she was grabbing at a canvas bag of crackers and magazines. *Pouf!* Her hair just went up. Went up like tinder. Went up like a curtain.

She backed out of the car, caught her jacket on the window handle, looked at Hal for help and saw in his crushed-can face the reflection of her head half on fire and half not.

He laughed.

It was a funny thing, this deadly laugh. The laugh was full of hate, and it ended their marriage, but it was the richest, most intimate and revealing sound he had made in three years of bedrooms and bathrooms and kitchens together. If he weren't laughing at her and hating the failure of their marriage and riding this awful sound away like some kind of magic carpet, he could have had her with it all over again. She would not have succumbed to it. Nothing like that. But she would have danced with this man and squeezed him and tried to get him to make some other gorgeous, powerful wicked sounds out of sheer, perverse sexual fascination.

But her perversion was all used up.

And her head was on fire, so she stuck it in the canvas bag and fell down and rolled on the ground until the fire went out. Then she just lay there a while, gasping.

Well, she could imagine him saying, this vacation is over. He would be bitter but relieved. Not going on vacation had its advantages. There would be work he could do at home, TV programs he could watch, and money he would not spend.

And normally she would have argued just the opposite. She would have concocted some way to go on. These get-aways were crucial.

But not this time, no. Crucial, but in a different sense.

The countryside around them had collapsed into this alley. She just sat there a bit. The sounds he was making weren't really words, and she wasn't really hearing them, and she didn't really care.

The people who stopped to help loaded them up in their van and drove them deeper into the alley where they found a hotel and she found, though it was late Saturday afternoon, a hair salon where a man and a woman working together carefully put her right. It was amazing to see this soothing couple's four hands wash, cut, comb, spray, pat. They were a flight of birds. With scissors in their hands, they were storks. With spray bottles, puffins. With brushes, owls. With shampoo, cockatoos.

They nested their fat breasts on her head until it hatched.

The cracks in the shell were runny, dripping, and the being that came out was huge-eyed and soft-beaked with skin as thin as mist and down on its skull. It was her, this thing above the smock. Her.

She loved herself.

The high walls of the alley collapsed in her chest with a soft rumble of feathers. Hal and the car and the fire and the thud disappeared in this thick, weightless cataract.

Of course they wouldn't accept any money. Instead, they said she could pay them by coming to their house for dinner. And Hal should come, too. But he wouldn't. He'd stay right where he was in this dreary hotel until the insurance man called. Fact was, he said, he couldn't stand to look at her and her awful haircut, much less the people who gave it to her.

So she went alone, her wings as light as wax paper, her twiggy legs wobbling, her eyes the size of the world.

the woods

You could call anything "the woods." Lucy used the term so casually that no one noticed. Early on in New York City, she'd laugh in that easy way of hers and ask who wasn't lost in the woods. She majored in psychology because the mind reminded her of the woods that had surrounded her childhood home. The mind had no straight paths, the mind was full of shadows, the mind was a kind of hideaway beyond the fence-work of the brain. It wasn't about being smart. She knew she wasn't smart. Her mother told her that. Her mother also told her, the last child of six, to stay out of the way. So she wandered in the woods, alert to the susurrus of nature and self-noise—her breathing, her imagining, her reaction to looking up and seeing torn pieces of sky through the leaves above or peering through the trees toward traces of the grey-blue river so big it barely seemed to move.

She sometimes got poison ivy so bad it immobilized her. Her mother never dealt with it. Two of her older sisters coated her with calamine. Lucy liked Jessie and Nell dabbing her with cotton balls soaked with the thick liquid while saying, "You poor thing," and "My God, this poison ivy is terrible." Funny thing: the poison ivy was still out in the woods; what was on her skin was just the oil from the leaves; then came the weeping, itching rash. You'd say you got poison ivy, but you didn't. The woods had the poison ivy.

The first thing that alarmed her about majoring in psychology at NYU was the requirement that you see a shrink, and then the inevitable expectation that girls would discuss their mothers. Her mother was callous, but Lucy didn't blame her. This troubled her therapist more than it did Lucy.

"Everyone in the community thought my mother was a saint with six children and a husband who kept losing good jobs and drinking too much," she'd explain in that hoarse voice of hers. "Maybe she was saintly to begin with, but no wonder she lost her saintliness when I came along. She said the family's brains were used up by the time I was born. She was almost funny taking things out on me. Like never cooking enough food and giving me too little. My sisters would push some of theirs onto my plate. God, otherwise I would have starved!" Lucy really laughed at that.

One of her roommates said she didn't need psychology. This roommate had read a lot of Nietzsche and Herman Hesse. For her the key to life was achieving the laughter of the gods Lucy apparently was born with. The roommate had a boyfriend who was an English major. He came at laughter through the nonsensical wit of Laurence Sterne and Lewis Carroll. He, too, hung around Lucy to hear her laugh, a natural, oxygenating laughter, streaming in and out of everything she said. Perhaps this was why he, too, missed her variants of "in the woods," or "lost in the woods," or "you sure couldn't find that in the woods," or "what woods are these?" a reference to Robert Frost that she often posed rhetorically in response to conundrums or confessions or conflicts and unreasonable demands.

She got the degree somehow. You couldn't say NYU cared she was a mediocre graduate. The whole thing, it seemed to her, was whatever she learnt hanging out in New York and coming to understand the city the way she had understood the woods when she was a kid. She learnt to wait for things to happen, because they would. She learnt from making mistakes with people, because she would. At a point, after three so-called serious relationships, she had a not-serious relationship with a not-serious guy she actually married. They held the wedding in a loft and invited everyone, a mistake because everyone came. She looked out into the crowd and imagined them all as trees that would never grow so close together if they had any sense. Everyone wanted a party, sure, but it seemed as if they really wanted to see if you could equate marriage with the morass of how they were living in New York, communally, jammed together, all for one and one for all. Her husband Sal epitomized the proposition that one guy was as good as another. He had curly hair to his shoulders, a polka dot shirt, and a major non-future as a painter. It had been his idea they marry. Was it because she found work in J.C. Penny's human resources department and could pay their bills? No, he said it was her cheery way of passing the time.

Her sister Nell asked her the next day why she married such a doofus. "It could be annulled, couldn't it?"

"Is that a real question?"

"Lucy, he fell down drunk or stoned or I don't know what. Where is he now?"

"He's asleep. He does that all day, paints all night."

"Where's the honeymoon? What's the plan? I just don't get you."

Lucy accepted their mother in Nell, criticizing her. "There is no plan, but at least you're worried for me. I'm grateful for that."

"You don't realize it, but you're such a catch. Guys think you're a sweet squeeze."

Lucy really laughed at that one.

"At least don't have a baby with him," Nell said. "Promise me that?"

They were in a Chelsea café with beaucoup mirrors, so it was easy to see they were sisters, the long upper lip, the nice hair, the builds that would hold up as they aged, boobs not too big, hips not too wide. Nell had been married and divorced and remarried. Lucy would never throw this in her face, yet that fact gave her a helpful insight. People close to you spoke as if they were inside you, which they weren't, and knew all about you, which they didn't. She had married Sal more out of a sense of mystery than anything else. She didn't know him. But telling Nell this wouldn't improve their conversation, so she didn't say it.

She stayed married to Sal for seven months. He didn't protest the divorce. Couldn't—he slept through the court date, proving her point they were laughably out of touch.

Another year passed in the granite, concrete, steel, brick and glass woods of New York City. She lived in a shitty Lower East Side building whose gloomy hallways with their heavily locked doors resembled a very old penitentiary. That year she practiced Tae Kwon Do five nights a week and recovered in bed alone on Saturdays and Sundays. Then, according to her sisters' predictions and urging, she would give up Tae Kwon Do and marry a second time, hopefully getting it right. She'd be mature, approaching thirty, professionally solid.

She resisted. Everyone should be happy, she knew. As a little girl she'd watched the whole family twist and writhe and carry on in spasms of happiness, or what passed for it, but instead of joining in, she'd gone across the lawn, jumped the sagging snow fence, and wandered in the woods.

I'll go to forestry school, she thought. Nell and Lucy's one brother, Johnny, told her she was too old and not prepared. It amazed her that they wanted to save her from this mistake, as if living the way she was living wasn't a mistake. Johnny tended to walk around when he lectured her. Of course this had to happen in the family house, which he had acquired, because you couldn't walk around in her place on the Lower East Side. He also gave her the unknowing look he'd given her all her life. She had the distinct feeling that each time he encountered her, he had to be reminded of who she was. He was like their mother in this way, but her mother had had to work at it a bit because Lucy had emerged from her womb, whereas it came naturally to him, eleven years older than she.

Like their father, he was an alcoholic. Maybe the booze haze he stared through explained his pattern-recognition difficulties, making it hard for him to see that something shaped like Lucy was, in fact, Lucy.

"See those woods?" he said, pointing out the window past the swimming pool and the snow fence now flat on the ground. "You left them behind. You live in the city. What do you know about woods?"

She laughed for the first time in a long time. Johnny got angry the way their father got angry. Became really violent and abusive. Lucy had done some work on alcoholism at NYU and in J.C. Penny's human resources department. What she found meaningful was the way in which alcohol abuse lowered all standards of speech and behaviour. An alcoholic tended to see himself as a low-life loser or a Napoleonic figure of all-knowing grandeur. Johnny's decision was to be a ranking officer in the Grande Armée. He told her she should climb the corporate ladder, get herself a decent place to live, and grow up.

He concluded by ranting, "You know who got the trees! I did! Those woods were my woods before you were born, and now I really own 'em. Just forget about forestry school and live your goddamned life."

Her goddamned life. Such a forest dark.

She started with long walks in Central Park, then visits to the New York Botanical Garden in the Bronx, and then hikes in state forests up the Hudson, field books and notebooks in hand. Setting Tae Kwon Do aside, this was her new passion. She overdid her preparation, in fact. The Yale School of Forestry accepted her more because of her social science background than her home-schooled mastery of Linnaean taxonomy, the life cycles of forests, and acid rain. Yale was a disappointing experience—policy pulp—but after six years, by now in her thirties, she landed an actual forestry management job in Oregon, a job and life in the woods contemplating black and white oaks, quaking aspens and ponderosa pines. It did take a while to internalize the size of the Oregon woods versus the Jersey woods where she had wandered as a child. Trees of a certain height or girth eluded her sense of intimacy until she found ways to think into their silence, the way they wrapped time within their rings and pushed it skyward. The West was spiritual in a broader sense than the East, beyond laughter, poetry, alcohol, and of course, her family, which never visited but sometimes expected her back East for graduations, weddings, and funerals.

After those trips home, she scheduled detoxifying back-country treks. Once a man named Pat was assigned to walk a sixty mile circuit with her. She did not fear or dislike men. The question this man presented, however, was how much she might like him. Walk ahead or behind someone for eight hours a day. Build fires together. Pitch tents near one another. Wake up soaking in the cool bath of morning air. Evaluate the man and the depth of his absorption in what absorbs you. Then you will begin to know him.

She had some difficulties with Pat for a while. He'd been at this longer than she had. Normally the male-female relationship development phase expressed itself in sharing experiences, exploring memories, telling stories. But Pat was past that, way past. Pat had never lived in a city and walked with his feet, not his mouth. He silently crouched to study root systems as if they were ancient runes, which of course they were, for five or ten minutes. When he finished, he kept what he'd seen and thought to himself. Didn't share, or, to use another verb, didn't warble, hoping the female of the species walking behind him would suddenly declare it was time to mate.

He was like a walking tree, she decided. There was no such thing, or she'd never thought there was such a thing, but he was. They trekked along. The terrain nagged and pulled at them. Sometimes her toes, her thighs, and her walking sticks were the only thing involved in steep ascents. Sometimes to keep the rest of her body from falling down the canyon trail she'd just hiked, she literally had to hug a tree, face wet with sweat, and hold on tight.

Then she realized she was a walking tree, too, and what she'd always been, and why she'd always wanted to be in the woods. She was possessed by the natural silence of the woods that wasn't silence at all. It was breathing, it was boot scrabble and loose stones kicked back down the trail that was no trail, just a dry rut in the wilderness. She seldom felt compelled to say more than, "Look." Pat seldom replied by parting his lips. He just looked and saw what she saw and finally saw her, too. Perhaps not the greatest pattern recognition but good enough: That tree following me around is Lucy. Her own tree. Her own woods. Bark as soft as velvet to the touch.

So they got married and lived as foresters until their knees and hips gave out. Then they spent much of their time on their cabin's porch, contemplating the trees gathered around them to bear witness to the burls and lightning strikes of their old age.

what now, widow?

How could Nero in Rome have given orders in time to save me? That's just his self-serving, false claim. Everything happened in an instant. Thanks to Nero, Seneca was dying, I cut myself to join him, and it was Seneca himself, not Nero, who commanded, "No! Bandage her, she must live!"

"Please, let me go with you!" I cried. But our slaves obeyed him even as he lay bleeding in his steaming bath. In those wispy tendrils of vapour, I saw his spirit finally find release.

I cremated him in private with no eulogy, his oft-stated wish: "When I am dead, I will not hear a thing. I shall be out of earshot, I assure you, though where, I know not." Death, death, death, how he rattled on about it. Yet his cremation was alive, so like our marriage, a combustion of his fire and my air.

Afterward I faced the fact that our estate was an imperial jest. Nero confiscated most of Seneca's money and left me property I could not afford to maintain. He clearly wanted me stranded in opulent poverty. He certainly did not want me hosting dinners for two hundred people, as was our custom. To think that so many Romans might hear from my mouth what they had never heard from Seneca's—Seneca who had been Nero's tutor when he poisoned his half brother, Seneca who had been Nero's advisor when he murdered his mother— surely made worms writhe in Nero's bowels.

Now our patios and grounds and the great hall of which Seneca was so proud are smeared with the grime of disuse and neglect. To walk from one end of our villa to the other would entail several minutes spent with no sign of actual life. I have three slaves left—a cook, a groundsman, and a maid. I once had 130. So many sold, so many freed, so many terrified to hear me say that they must go as far from Rome as possible lest they be identified as someone else who might know what Nero would not wish them to know.

So our dwelling is barren. I hear the rattle of my heels on the marble and thump of my brass-tipped walking stick. I see the glints of cobwebs. I occupy my mind with computations of how long my money will last to buy food or pay a doctor. A year? Two? And I look at my face and figure in mirrors and wonder the same about me. My face is crepe. My shoulders are sunken and stooped. When was my hair last washed? How could my hands have become such dry, gnarly roots? So naturally I have asked myself many times why Seneca forbade my committing suicide with him.

He would dictate to his scribe in his study, and then he would come tell me why he insisted on propounding views in which he did not really believe. Most of what he wrote (excepting the tragedies) contradicted his experience. He insisted he considered this his civic duty.

"To lie?" I asked.

"Someone has to praise friendship, mercy, generosity, dispassion, or where else would these things be found? Not here. Not in Rome."

He was not as rich as Nero wanted people to think, but after he left Nero's service, Nero desperately wanted him known as a hypocrite, a man who praised abstemiousness and embraced excess. Of course, this made seizing Seneca's so-called riches all the more justified.

Had he lived, he might have chuckled. His true view was that one should be indifferent to wealth and poverty alike; neither was morally worse than the other. He compared silver and gold and jewels to an illusory patina. "I feel I could poke my finger through all the world's riches; they're thin as ash. Here, not here. Present, gone. Why not enjoy what never mattered in the first place?" Thus he would observe preparations for a feast and enjoy how savory the roasting meat smelled to him, but then he would give me one of his educational pats on the rump to get my attention before saying that all sensual pleasure was transient. "That is why pleasure is to be accepted where it is found. We sense its death in its birth."

For him the same was true of pain, however. The first time he met Nero, he told me, gall burnt in his throat. But rather than wretch, he defended himself with his proposition that one must never base one's evaluation of someone else on a first encounter. A newly-met person could be manifestly supercilious and vicious but change, said he. A person could have tortured slaves for sport but change, said he. A person could have hidden, beneficent powers yet to emerge, said he. He doubted all this. Who wouldn't? "But that's what I told myself on entering the salon where Agrippina introduced me to her son, whom she meant to succeed Claudius, even though he was not Claudius's son. She wanted this complaisant, mysteriously cooperative boy groomed as though he were a future Solon. Impossible. I instantly saw he meant otherwise. This remote child would grow spikes down his back, he would spit venom, his fingernails would become talons." "You literally saw this in the theatre of your mind?" I asked. "I literally did. All my horrors were bundled in this boy, although I do confess that almost any boy unfettered in his desires and authority would turn out as bad, if not worse."

These were his confessions to me. Seneca would smile his toothless smile—he did have teeth, all of them, but you couldn't see them when he smiled—and expatiate wickedly, possessing my imagination as if it were my body. He married me when I was young, and even as I aged, I always was young to him. Whatever he wanted, he got. I never believed he had the affair with Livilla which led to Claudius exiling us to Corsica because I knew him to be exhausted in my own bed.

Those eight years on Corsica deepened him. He embraced the depths and invisible contradictions of the chaotic sea—sea on all sides, formless and chaotic—and ever after was a phlegmatic philosopher on the outside and a choleric cynic within. He became his own double, much to our mutual amusement. We weren't so unhappy in exile. We certainly did not believe in Rome. Rome after Tiberius and Caligula? Rome in the times of Claudius, a fiend for following his own weaknesses wherever they led him? And then Agrippina married Claudius and had us brought back so that Seneca would teach her little monster rhetoric, history, mathematics, and eventually what he could understand of philosophy, which was not much because he already believed that *he* was philosophy, the world's meaning, what others should study and revere.

It could almost be said I lived for those talks of ours, but now Seneca was dead, and I was a widow, and I did not understand why he had wanted me to live without him. To escape my consternation I had a favourite grove where the ground was bare and the towering trees gave me solace. I could be alone there, although no one visited me anyway. If Seneca's nephew Lucan had not been forced to commit suicide for plotting against Nero, he would have come, of course, and we would have enjoyed one another, flirting over what amused us, though naturally Seneca disapproved of him.

"Why should a *poet* save us? He's the worst of conspirators. A poet cannot rescue Rome any more than I can reach into the sky and grab a bird with my bare hand."

"But you wrote your tragedies," I objected. "They were a form of poetry."

"My tragedies dramatized the futility of struggling against the unconquerable disorder of things."

"Lucan's poetry does not do that, too?"

Seneca's face went aquiver, soft and sensitive as a horse's nose. "You're the one who urged me to withdraw from the court, plead age and infirmity, have nothing to do with public life. Is Lucan's dangerous agitation something you now encourage? You know what the fool is up to."

"I simply do not condemn him."

"He needs to be condemned by someone before he ends up dead. And then," he predicted correctly, "you will have him dead for his youthful activity and me dead for my elderly inactivity. Death by association. Death by refusing to help ensure Nero's death."

I asked him if he was fearful of that.

"It's decades since I have not lived in fear."

"Fear of the unknown goes against reason," I said to provoke him to unmask himself, the other Seneca, the one I loved most, the one who was ours, ours alone.

"All right, but I have reasoned my way to the reasonable conclusion that soon I will be dead, and at that point it will be *you* who have to answer the question: What now, widow?"

For some reason he wanted me to outlive him. Why, if his life and mine had long since become the same?

The truth is that I had no great interest in poetry or politics. What I liked was my grove and the solemn way in which it imitated a recessional march, glorious in its somber shadows. What I disliked was that these trees had come before me and I would not live long enough to add to them. I certainly could not convert the surrounding valleys and uplands to join them as temples of forest not polluted by priests or spoilt by the ambitions of powerful men who think that a certain ritual or prayer or libation will suborn the sacred to their cause.

I had, after all, no children, and never would. Another mystery. He was sterile or I was infertile. Who knew? My lack of family, others to pass the burden of answering his question—*What now? What now?*—was not for want of coupling. He might say things to me like, "I do not suppose you were so pretty at dinner this evening only for the other men," and I would like it, patting the bed beside me, inviting him to join me. Or he would say, "There is no way to spill everything in me out of my mouth or stylus," and I would say, "Spill what's left into me then." More often than not, he prematurely spilt himself onto me, not into me, but still these were the moments when my air fed his fire and we were watery wet and earthy, too. He made up poems in the aftermath of satisfying me. He could do that, though of course he would not record his descriptions of our lovemaking, where he placed his kisses and fingers and rubbed his tender, equine face.

Need I emphasize, then, that I would call what we shared love? Surely it requires love to want to die when your husband dies. Loyalty of that depth does not emerge from nothing. Even mutual interest requires love. The fact is that when you love, you become interested in things that are not interesting at all. No one else would care, only the two of you. For instance, the public Seneca, a kind of insistent, loyal soldier, and the private Seneca, my Seneca, a hissing satirist of the spirit.

More than anything, my grove made me well. Its scents were healing fragrances. The wind in its leaves sounded almost as intelligible as words. What was it trying to tell me? Why Seneca had wanted me to live? If so, I could not make it out, and I confess that frustrated me to the point that one day I imagined one of these trees being arbitrarily chopped down and carted away. This violent fantasy shocked me. There is a rhythm to the way one looks at stands of trees, after all; they make a rolling impression in one's mind. And then I thought of Seneca, who wrote as a beloved sequence of trees grew, one self-contained observation after another, each on the same theme but each original. Yes, his writing was exactly like a grove, so it was in the midst of my comforting grove that I realized that what truly unsettled me was the ruined rhythm between the trees in my own mind, the gap, the stumble in the cadence. That's what I had been imagining. *He* was the tree who had been removed. I had seen him become ashes. I had breathed his smoke.

I began to fear my grove. All I could see in it was what was not there. Finally one day I felt a terrible shiver as if a jagged splinter had been driven into my breast, and I knew why I still lived. I sit here now because I know it. It is all I know. I cannot resist it. But am I up to it? I have never done what I do now, but this is why he told me about the pain of his life in such great detail, while only writing about it as conclusions, forever hiding behind his philosophy and the figures of his tragedies, never letting anyone really see and know him as he suffered. He despised living so much; he devoted himself to overcoming it, disdaining the shame of exile, the rise and fall of his influence, the barbs of criticism that he was such a hypocrite, despising wealth rhetorically while accumulating it in actuality. Nothing mattered, he countered. But it did matter, all of it, and now I was skewered by how much it mattered. He wanted me to live so I could write his life.

I left my grove and went to his study where I sit now and tried to swallow my disbelief. What woman has ever written a biography of her husband? I can't think of one, yet here I must write my husband's life in order to finish living mine. What a trick Seneca had played on me. I so much rather would have died than say the things he never had the courage to say himself. But at least … at least I have begun.

the deal

As they listened to the prayer, Diane glanced at Will, towering and gnarled as a weathered volcanic plug. She could see that he had lost track of their quarrel. He was pumped-up, proud. In a few minutes, she would take over—her turn to kite the fickle, shifting winds of the presidency. The day's sullen, rainy gusts were the perfect prelude to this struggle, but the umbrellas stretching far, far out onto the mall deepened her sense of solitude, and that was a blessing. Time spent alone strengthened her.

"Our Father, who art …"

Justesse was weeping.

"Stop that," Diane whispered to her.

"I don't want to."

"You'll make me cry."

"So?"

Justesse kept weeping. With wavy red hair and ultra-fair skin, she was more than a pretty woman. Reserved like her mother. Electric like her father. Stubborn like him, too.

The preacher pleaded with the Lord for guidance, grace, mercy and compassion, a good vocabulary list. Look them all up. Use them in a sentence. But the person Diane fixed on was the frail poet who would speak next. If nothing was new in religion's rhetoric, everything was new in his spare verse. How did he make his poems so lean? So elemental? Asking herself that question burst an aneurysm of memory. That steam room of a summer in Texas, where they had a single bed, she mostly to herself, Will prowling, gabbing, phoning people, drumming up volunteers for work and pleasure even as the McGovern thing went south of south. "Thank God, it's not me on this ticket," he'd say, and she would get angry and take the bed, leaving him the couch, the phone, and the front door. McGovern wasn't going to win, but she refused to laugh about it. She wanted Nixon gone.

Then Kitty Noguchi let herself in to use their one-person kitchen, peeked in the bedroom door, saw Diane by herself, and asked, "You asleep?"

"I wish."

"Where's Will?"

"No idea."

"Why do you put up with it, Diane? I just don't understand."

"Because he makes me happier than he makes me miserable. I don't know what else to say."

"What if you behaved the same?"

"I might if someone more interesting than Will came along."

"But why does Will do this stuff?"

She propped herself on her elbows, angry, succinct. "Because they're his mother. Loose like her. Laugh like her. That's why he can't keep his hands off them."

"Have you told him that?"

"Of course. He always lies to me, and I always tell him the truth."

For forty years right up to this morning when their tectonic plates had collided again.

"Dammit, Diane, I hate what we've done. It's a great big fucking mistake."

What she hated was cramped Blair House and him crowding her when she dressed.

"Too late, Will. You took your oath last week. Today's my turn."

"We should have shut everyone else out and dug into each other on this. Really thought. I should have told you no."

She did her best to ignore him. She liked a jacket that felt like it wasn't there. This jacket didn't feel that way. Too tight. How did that happen?

"Shoulda, woulda, coulda. I've got a speech to give. That's what I need to be thinking about right now."

Will touched her cheek. She flinched, not wanting her makeup mussed.

"I never gave a speech word for word in my life."

"That's your style, not mine."

The frail poet rose, casting Diane a good-humoured but chiding look. He had protested he was the least oratorical poet in history. He would be done in a minute. Then read two poems, she had suggested. No, one was all he could manage, he had said, but he would stand there for a long moment before and after he read. That might make a single piece seem like two. Now, right after the preacher had beseeched God for help, he countered that all the help anyone needed lay in heeding nature's beauty. Do that and ride the divinity of things into eternity. A perfect poem learned as Emerson, quick as Dickinson. What needed to be said was said. That's why she had wanted him standing there, looking out at the rain as if he loved it. A man in the present tense.

She took the oath. Her amplified voice ricocheted off the west face of the Capitol. "… so help me God."

The chief justice had the reassuring face of a small town doctor despite his hideous views. He congratulated her. Justesse kissed her. Then Will embraced her with awe in the lightness of his touch. She stepped to the lectern and took her own moment to stare out into the whipping rain. Suddenly words came to her that weren't in the teleprompter.

"My fellow Americans, this wind and rain will pass," she said, letting go. "We'll see our Capitol and our country in the sunshine again. We'll see great mountains, beautiful plains and rocky coasts that belong to every one of us because none of us is born rich enough to deny where our riches come from—from all of us, from the freedoms passed down to us through the generations—and none of us is born poor enough not to own America, too. Today, as I stand before you, we have had a black president, and now we have a female president, so we can say, rain or shine, that our ambitions and dreams are alive and well. We are one country, we are whole, and we are blessed."

A roar shook the weather-cave in which everyone stood, exactly what she wanted for the pure, unfettered joy of it. When at last she focused on the teleprompter, the prepared speech tumbled out of her. She had practiced it to the point of barely knowing what she was saying. There were cadences, there were inflections, and there were pauses. Those were her targets. She let the words take care of themselves; they all added up to what she said at the outset anyway and resonated fully in her final phrase, "… because we can only be free together, and that's why God has blessed America and we pray She always will."

The delayed response—had she actually said that?—outdid the first explosion all along the mall, more the jubilation of a convention than an inauguration, 250 years of inequality howled into retreat.

She stepped down from the rostrum and after the ritual courtesy of waving goodbye to her tall, thin, exhausted predecessor on the east side of the Capitol was led inside by the Inaugural Committee. Justesse sat beside her in the spouse's seat. She would be family member number two. Will, at his own table, would be number three. Everyone in the marmoreal hall glanced his way to see how he was taking it. He might feel as dead as the encircling statues of legislative legends, but he had the same rapt look on his time-trampled face that he had talking to shoeless children in Africa or tsunami victims in Indonesia. Diane overheard him parsing her speech's meaning for the nation, the world, and his own state now, the Empire State, where he'd told the biggest lie of his life—that this was what he wanted.

When it was time to go, she sent an agent to pull him away. He brushed her emissary off like a pigeon that had flown down from the domed ceiling and landed on his shoulder. So his own agent leant in.

"Mr President, the President is going now."

He looked toward her. Held up a single finger. One more minute?

Diane simply stared. Negative. No.

Eventually they reached the reviewing stand. For three hours Diane laughed and waved and pitied the marchers in the rain. Thumping drums, wailing trombones, flying batons, quivering braids, shiny black shoes, high white boots, the overhead heaters warming the dry stand while out there on the street it was in the mid-thirties, every state having its moment, dispatching National Guard units, fire departments, mounted police squads, university bands, polka clubs and dragon dancers.

When that was done, Charles and Madeleine were in the front hall to take their coats. By design, only them. Diane wanted it that way.

Will cocked his head back, taking things in. "Chapter one again. Can't believe it. Want to walk around? See if you've got any buyer's remorse?"

"Nope, I'm keeping it. Not going into the Oval to cry with you."

"I've been there enough since not to cry about it anymore." His voice was soft and sad, though.

"I'll be upstairs lying down."

"I'll go with you, Dad," Justesse said.

"You always have, darling. Except now I'm just visiting, and you'll be back in your old room." He took Justesse's hand and headed toward the West Wing.

Diane said to Charles and Madeleine, "My Lord, it's been sixteen years. You don't get tired of this?"

Madeleine answered for both of them. "No, Ma'am. Welcome home."

Upstairs every detail was the same as before. A mistake to ask for that. The brightness of the upholstery and carpeting did not stand up well against the rain-lashed windows. She'd have to have the place redone. And get someone to pay.

Easing onto the bed, she pushed off her pumps. A new maid timidly knocked on the door and brought in tea.

"Madeleine thought you might like some," she said.

"Thank you. What's your name?"

"Eleanor."

"For Eleanor Roosevelt?"

"No, for my grandma. She was the one named for Mrs Roosevelt, Mrs President."

"Madame President, I think."

"Yes, Madame President. I wasn't sure."

"Close the door, please."

"Yes, Madame President."

Alone again in a bedroom where she had slept for eight years, she experienced a soupçon of vertigo. Time and space turned upside down. What on earth had she done?

What she had done was call Will before her campaign was a month old and said, "Look, I can't see how I can lose, so we've got to go over a few things."

"Like what?"

"Next week Chuck will announce he's not running for re-election and I'll have it leaked he'll be my Treasury Secretary."

"Chuck agreed to give up the Senate before you're elected? Jesus, that man's ambitious."

"It's his dream job. So this means you can run for his seat."

"What? You've got to be joking. Have Andy run for his seat."

"No, I want you to do it. Andy will be Attorney General. But he won't step down until after the election. He's holding back just like his father."

"Then someone else, not me! Where'd you get this?"

"Will, listen to me. I've thought this through. I want you

out of The White House but close and helpful with your own separate operation."

"I already have my own separate operation."

"I mean a distinct, active political identity people can focus on apart from me."

"That's impossible. You know it."

"Not if you're at a distance from The White House. As a senator, you can move yourself, your voice, and your shadow to the Larson Circle house. Make it yours. Justesse will be my hostess, but you can pitch in when you're free."

Will had exploded. Who said New York would elect him senator? He didn't want to be a frigging senator. Use him some other way—all the ways they had already discussed, in the background, on the edges. Again, who the hell had thought this up?

"Will, it's my idea because it's going to be my presidency, and you've got to have your own job, your own constituency, and your own agenda. You can't hang around The White House like the ghost of Christmas past."

"Please, don't talk to me like a goddamn child."

"Senators aren't children. In the senate you'll be on top of things on you own."

"I'd be on top of things if you invited me to help with what you're doing."

"But I'm not inviting you to do that. Chuck will be good at Treasury, Andy will be good at Justice, you'll be a lion in the senate."

"I'll be a cub eating scraps under committee tables."

"You're a former president. It won't be that bad."

"Really? I'll tell you how bad it will be. They'll say we're a mixed-doubles powerhouse planning to take over the whole country. Put me on the Supreme Court. I'll wait for one of them to die."

"You'd never get through the Republicans."

"Well, the foundation. I can just—"

"—Justesse will take over as chair. You and I have to be out of it."

"She's going to do that between giving house tours to the First Lady of the Philippines and having tea with the First Lady of Burundi?"

"Do you want to have tea with the First Lady of Burundi?"

"Diane, you never said anything like this. You said we'd work it out. I said I'd be there for you whenever you needed. Nothing I wouldn't help with. That was the deal."

"Well, this is how we're working it out, this is the deal. I run and I win. You run and you win."

"So I can live by myself in that crypt of yours?"

"It's two miles from The White House, three from the Hill, and you'll have the place in New York, too."

"Diane, this isn't going to work. I'm campaigning for you, not for me."

She had responded with a silence that meant they could talk about how to make this work or they could not talk at all, and in his unique way, Will had begun doing the talking for both of them, the words frothing out of his mouth, white-water hissing and whirling. He didn't want to be a senator, but all right, Fulbright had been a senator, and he loved working for Fulbright. McGovern had been a senator, and he loved McGovern. And Bobby Kennedy, he loved Bobby, and he could staff himself the way Teddy had with people smarter than smart, and he'd still be ex-president and would keep the office in Harlem, and a couple more upstate, all that, sure, sure (his monologue began souring, sticking to his tongue), along with side trips to Buffalo, Albany, and Syracuse—doing all the politicking he always had hated beforehand, loved during, and hated afterward.

Diane had said the good would outweigh the bad. She had told him to use his imagination. "Don't think about how Fulbright and Bobby and Teddy did it. Think about how you'll do it. Take something I'm pushing and help make it happen. Be me there. But not in The White House. One president there is enough, two is too many."

It had been terrible, the first time she had done anything as bad to him as he had done to her.

"I mean, we don't live together," he had yielded at last, his anger faded, his spirit gone. "Nothing to do with love, nothing do with commitment, just fact. Always as close as a phone. Always as far away as the north pole from the south. And ice in between. Rock solid, mile deep ice."

"Oh, please, I'm talking about tomorrow, not yesterday."

"All right, but I have to research this."

"There's precedent."

"I know. J.Q. Adams in the House. But Taft went on the Court."

"Maybe if you helped get the Senate back, you could be confirmed. But that's a big if."

"Can I at least sell that Larson Circle house and live in the old president's club? I could walk across Lafayette Park and be at The White House in five minutes."

"No, it's a terrific house. Redecorate it if you want. Put a corn crib in the living room. Make yourself at home."

He had laughed his most hollow, most defeated laugh, and hung up. And just as she said, both of them had run, both of them won. How about that.

When she woke up, he was sitting in a chair, looking out the window at the rain and nightfall merging.

"I get to dance with you at thirteen balls tonight," he said.

"You get to hold me up so I don't fall down at thirteen balls tonight," she said.

"Justesse and I walked all over the place. It's sure not like visiting again. This is different."

"Sad or happy?"

"Sad and happy at once."

"Isn't that the way things always are?"

She didn't mean to be callous but waking up and seeing him there, so thin, ancient and dreary, alarmed her. Would he even survive a senate term? She looked out the window herself at the tree limbs receiving the night. Mothers without children. She always thought that looking at trees in winter.

He came over to the bed and kneeled on it, staring straight

down at her. "Maybe everything's all mixed up, but sad winning is still better than sad losing. I have to admit that."

She pulled herself up against the headboard to let him know they wouldn't kiss. No more of that. Just looks, by now the only thing they had left.

a life

We begin with a girl and end with an old woman. The challenge will be to make her a story, although, in truth, we have our doubts about stories, which underplay so many interesting details because they tend not to be recursive, don't double back to pick up things that fall out of their pockets and ought to be known, things we would pause to recount parenthetically in conversations, or as footnotes, or as surprise additions to the dramatis personae who somehow don't "fit." This could be the strength of novels and deficiency of short stories. But who has time for novels anymore? Two thousand words and done. Subway ride over. Bath cold. Battery running low.

Laura Hudson Chatterjee is seventeen, American, raised in New York, her father a Bengali-born and Oxford-trained proctologist, her mother a descendent of Henry Hudson the explorer, and her brother the one who will have the controversial and still unique sex change in order to banish the testosterone feeding his advanced prostate cancer. Henry Hudson Chatterjee is his name—before he becomes Henrietta, Etta, for short—a plumpish savant who gets jobs in politics and museums through connections and then romantically partners with the ex-wife of one of his powerful political bosses. They will take their lesbianism seriously when he joins her as a woman. It will be like pouring half a glass of water into another half a glass of water. Very full.

But that's all in the future and this is about Laura, a girl who always seems to be looking over her shoulder, not in fear but in expectation. She's going to be on the tall side like her father. But then he dies when she is eighteen, so this is a fact about Laura. Fatherlessness opens things up for many girls. In her case there are a number of volunteer substitutes, all of whom she manages to elude because she dislikes the very idea of a father. Hers was imperious, stiff, rude, and not a sexist with a heart of gold. At his funeral the loneliness and vulnerability she feels is having lost the opportunity to look forward to him dying some day. "People can be shits," he told her once, having taken a drop too many, "and I know I'm one of them because I didn't have the courage to be myself. If I were you, I'd consider dropping Chatterjee as a last name and go with Hudson, Laura Hudson. It sounds better, don't you think? I mean here in New York. If you went to Calcutta, you'd never survive. People would expect you to know something about the Chatterjees, and you wouldn't know a thing. Here, okay, I know it's fashionable to be half from somewhere else, but not there, and even here it gets old fast. Don't make up some story about your ancestors and peddle it around, how they haunt and speak to you, and you must make a pilgrimage. Rubbish. That's what I like about V.S. Naipaul, he gets the rubbish right. Read him? No, I didn't suppose so."

She goes to Cornell, unlike the rest of the family who attended Columbia/Barnard or Oxford, and already is so attracted to birds that she becomes an ornithologist. Birds have come into her life on Block Island, where she has one set of friends. Another set of friends belongs to the Athletic Club. And there are school friends and rogue intruders. One is supposedly an Australian trucker taking a break in the States. She is convinced he is "the one" until she goes with a friend to Waterville, Maine one summer and meets her goofy, charming brother. His naked body when he is doing pull-ups in the barn turns her inside out. She sheds her clothes and grabs the beam beside him. When they drop down, she gives him her virginity. The horses understand. They've seen him pull this one before.

No matter. Her body, five ten, broad shouldered, slender breasted, capped by a healthy grin of a smile and thick brown hair, attracts others. But she values her inquisitive, retentive mind more than her looks and is disappointed when she realizes men generally do not like women who expect interesting things of them.

We know, by the time she is twenty-four, that Laura may never marry. We know she has a cabin in the Adirondacks and a beach house she can freely use on Block Island and that there are relatively few interesting birds in New York City, and the ones there are have largely been "taken," as it were. They're documentary stars. They think they're human. The five borough African grey parrot count has already been established. It's 2100. They live in lofts, condos, grocery stores and car repair garages.

Inevitably Laura is going to become physically tough from hiking and climbing, and she is going to be permanently sun- and wind-burnished, and she adapts well to spells of solitude. Research grants and a part-time teaching job in a college close to the lower Connecticut River estuary keep her going. She becomes an excellent painter of birds. Her work sells. She is twenty-nine now, and there is a flurry about her work which is a distinctive mixture of the naturalistic and the expressive.

But then she does marry. This is a mistake from the first week. Of all people, Laura makes him feel trapped. Wandering, self-directed Laura.

Three years later she has a baby named Zack and no husband. Carries Zack everywhere as long as she can and eats sweet potatoes, beans, pasta, and eggs to save money while making the decision to raise him in the Adirondacks, although putting up with elementary school in the Adirondacks is grim. She compensates by working hard with him on reading and drawing and starting him on the curriculum of an undergraduate naturalist at age four.

It is not a nonissue that she never marries again. Zack comes first, but there are men she has learnt how to calibrate to her needs and expectations. Not looking over her shoulder anymore. Looking straight ahead.

When Zack takes to hunting, it's a shock. He shoots squirrels, fox, deer, and bear, eschewing birds in deference to her, but no man ever disappoints Laura more than Zack, not even her father. He's deliberately obtuse around her. Plays dumber the smarter he becomes. Once he has a truck, he's impossible to keep watch over. Army bound. Killed in Afghanistan. Thereafter hunting season blasts in the woods twist in her bones like screws. He is buried in a place only she knows, having dug the grave herself.

When Etta's lover dies, she becomes Laura's cabin mate. Etta has known a lot of people, many more than Laura, and they will visit, and there will be the element of disbelief that such intelligent, well-educated and even worldly people would live in a cabin that isn't, despite what people expect and want for them, really a lodge. Didn't their mother leave them anything? No, she did not. Nothing fell out of her pocket. It was empty when she expired.

Laura is fifty-seven now. Her hips have spread but she still wears jeans well. She sits on the edge of her single bed and yanks them on from where she dropped them the night before. These days she's illustrating books. There's a market for books that capture feelings most people have but cannot express. Laura's illustrations do that for them. She works a good part of the day on the second floor, which is a loft studio with two sky lights.

After she's studied photographs of a bird, she makes sketches, and after the sketches, she paints. Through the day, dumpy Etta brings her snacks and looks at her work and murmurs both approval and disapproval. Etta is almost twenty years older than Laura, and there is no ignoring her reactions. She may know more than anyone on earth because she will admit to remembering what she thought as a man.

Eventually Etta slips on the rocks while going down to the creek where she likes to meditate. She hits her head and dies, and Laura faces the fact that she cannot invite all of Etta's friends to the cabin for a memorial.

Manhattan becomes the place, then. Laura is no stranger there—she has a following in the publishing and art worlds—and Etta never lost the cachet of her sex transformation or significant jobs in politics and museums, so people, all kinds of people, more than two hundred come to the memorial and want to console Laura and invite her for a meal or a walk in the park and generally be kind.

Laura has inherited Etta's semi-abandoned apartment and is 64 and uses it because she can't otherwise keep up with the work thrown her way in New York. Even back in the city, she retains that nature girl way about her, the sun- and wind-parched skin, the strong hands, the habit of seeing scenes in people's eyes that they want her to paint: dunes, a riverscape, a red-tailed hawk on a power line surveying a purplish field of dry grass for quarry. They tell her it's poetry. She must write it down. She makes a face. What is it about people who can't think without words? This weekend she is going up to the cabin. That's poetry. Liberating Zack's truck from the city and parking it forever by his hidden grave, that's poetry.

But she looks at her fingers and wonders about splitting wood. They've grown soft. And she thinks about her energy level. Does she really want to drive that far? What about an early dinner, a little too much wine, and maybe a man who diffidently will let her know what men want woman to know?

She finds that last thought trite, but it is precisely her indifference to men in their sixties that keeps them coming. Now, after all these years, they dare to be interesting. That's not easy, but she lets them try, and tonight this man recites passages from Thomas Hardy's poetry, and it works.

So we are going to see a late in life affair blossom and burn for a dozen years and then his death in Sloan Kettering.

We are going to see Laura come out on the sidewalk and

choose to amble a few blocks by herself before hailing a cab, and then we are going to see Laura begin to cry and the driver look at her in the rear view mirror and not mistake her for a mental case.

She's a beautiful old woman, her white hair thick and braided, her face partially covered by her tree root fingers, but only partially because she is unabashed about meeting the cabbie's eyes in the rear view mirror with her own. She wants to see him see what appalls her: she is not through yet. She will live on. And eventually she will tell him where she wants to go.

the door

Dennis proposed he be Natalie's first client in the skinny brownstone on East 63rd her father had converted to offices and left her when he died.

"That's impossible. You're my cousin."

"Second cousin," he corrected. He stared across the street at the scalloped slate roof of a church backed by a receding pilgrimage of Manhattan skyscrapers, shepherded along by the vicar-like Chrysler building with its gleaming silver crown. "This is a nice spot. Great view but private, hidden."

"I thought seeing it is why you came." She surveyed the furniture she'd bought, chairs and a sofa in variants of beige, the carpet with its mixed weaves of tans, and the off-white paint—restful but not soporific. Then she came to her father's drafting table in the corner, overhung by a black architect's lamp clamped to its side. "I only question using that for a desk. I can see him hovering there in the lamp." None of her images of her father, who had his first heart attack when she was five, were terribly clear. She knew he didn't have a praying mantis physique, but she also knew that he was an attentive, observant man, so the symbol of the lamp worked. An architect would look like that inside.

"No one's going to come in here and think, 'Ooh, that must be where her father was working when he died. You really didn't think I'd propose seeing you?"

She smiled at him. Handsome, husky Dennis, they'd been through so much. He used to say they were like Russian nesting dolls—Matryoshka dolls.

"Out of the question."

"You said you were drawn to Gestalt because there are no rules."

"I never said it has no rules. What's going on with you?"

He tried a different line: "My Baby Bear becomes a therapist, the most interesting thing that ever happens in our family, but I'm excluded."

"What could you say that we haven't already discussed?"

"I still don't feel realized."

"You're mocking me."

He heaved himself onto the sofa. "I just have the sense that there's an outside-New York in which I live—" he gestured toward the window "—and an inside-New York like this." He raised his massive arms as if pulling the office down around him, blanket-like. "Just let me tell you things and see what you make of them."

"We can go to dinner whenever you want. Splurge on me."

"Dinner's outside where everything's hidden. A place like this is where it comes out."

"Where *what* comes out?"

That broad Slavic face of his, built to hold up against high winds and sleet, seemed to tremble a bit, though you could never really tell because his eyes were such slits. "Oh, failing in life. Nothing big."

"The divorce?"

"No, the divorce was a bunch of this and that. More serious things. What you've been studying, leaving me behind."

"Leaving you behind? What do you think I've been studying anyway?"

"I don't know. Soul things? Self things? That's what interests me."

"Really? I never noticed."

"Oh, fuck you."

"See, that's why this wouldn't work. I know you too well."
They had lived in the same apartment through most of their
childhood until he moved out for good, having graduated
from Cornell and gone to NYU for law school.

"How can you say that when I don't even know myself?" He
stood up, unfastened his belt, unbuttoned his pants, unzipped
his fly, resettled his shirttails and put himself all back together
again.

Whoa, she thought, after they had hugged goodbye.

***

"Even if this isn't therapy and we're only talking, you'll have to
sign a liability waiver since this is a licensed place of business.
You know that. You're the lawyer."

"You think I'd ever sue you?"

"No, but I want to do things right, and the first thing you
have me doing is something wrong."

Dennis swooshed out a Mount Blanc and signed the waiver.
"Okay, I'll start right here. Your Uncle Michael would not
have signed that thing, but if he had, he would have done so
knowing he still could beat you in court. "

"Dennis, I know the man."

"You never worked for him."

"Working for him is all that different?"

"Working for him is *everything*, which is why I never wanted
to do it." Dennis drew back his big shoulders and took a deep
breath. In so many ways, his body was his message, words
to follow. "A few months ago I let a woman spread a map
of Byelorussia on my desk and talk to me a half hour about
where her family comes from, how this is connected to that—
fucking this and that again. I don't understand half of what
she's saying, but some of these gorgeous Russian women with
the white skin, the red hair, you think they must be making
some kind of sense. The fact is she knows zip about Byelorussia even with the map spread out in front of her, but I'm

165

soft-hearted, and I sit there until my father walks into the office for the first time in literally years and takes a picture of the Statue of Liberty off the wall and puts it on top of the map and says to the lady, 'Madame, when your former sister-in-law gets out of the Soviet Union and can see this, we can see her, but until that time comes, we cannot assist her.'"

"And he showed her the door?"

"He certainly did."

"Did he put the picture of the Statue of Liberty back on the wall before he left?"

"Very funny."

At least part of the reason for not counselling your cousin, Natalie thought, had to do with not being brought to your knees by a psychic hailstorm in the first session. Time would have to be spent on learning a few things about this domineering father—his age (sixty-four), his profession (all-but-retired immigration attorney, specializing in Soviets seeking safety), and his background (followed his own father into practice, lived in New York all his life)—before focusing on the fact that he thought his son would wreck the family business after his calamitous forays into real estate and marriage.

"With parents you talk about them until your being exceeds their being," she said. "Once your life is full enough and theirs, by virtue of age, is diminished enough, you move on."

"Easy for you to say with no parents. Is this something they taught at your institute?"

She disregarded his swipe at her parents. "They taught me that people in parental pain experience a deficit greater than their quotient of being can fill. Which is to say that you will not find your being in the black hole of Uncle Michael's being, and if you keep trying, you're never coming out."

They laughed. The proposition that Dennis would could ever possess sufficient being to escape Uncle Michael's negative attraction suggested that when he, Dennis, walked into a room, the windows would blow out and the walls would crack and crumble. Dennis would be Superman.

robert earle

***

Michael Theodore, Dennis's father, wasn't Natalie's uncle—he was her father's cousin—but she called him that because when her father died, her neurotic mother turned to Michael for help with Natalie and her older brother Ellis, six and nine years old respectively.

"What do you mean by help, Margaret?" he'd asked.

"I'm so confused, Michael. Pavel did everything. I did nothing. I'm so impractical."

Michael pressed his broad flat lips together in a frown before he spoke. "How about now that he's dead we stick with his legal name, Paul?"

"I called him Pavel because I felt it spoke to his Russian past."

"How could it when he didn't speak to his Russian past himself? In fact, I would think he found it irritating hearing you call him Pavel." Having said this, Michael released the weighty energy in a frown.

"All right, if you insist."

"Thank you. Now what do you want from me?"

He asked this question knowing what Margaret wanted: that he take in her children while she adjusted to widowhood. What would two more lost souls matter to him in a life overflowing with them? Several nights a week his enormous apartment teemed with clients, their relatives and friends. Getting at him in the office wasn't enough for these people. Having helped settle them in New York, he was a community paterfamilias, enduring off-hours consultations and petitions that grew more and more plentiful as the city swelled with Soviet runaways, fleeing all things Stalin, then Khrushchev, then Brezhnev: persecution, exile and death. He opened his door in service to Mother Russia, but this activity wasn't without compensations. The side deals it turned up made him wealthier than ever. Now, however, he was going to be asked to take two immigrants into his home quasi-permanently.

"Let the kids stay with you for a little while until I pull myself together. I feel that if I don't get away …"

Ellis sat on one side of his mother as this conversation took place in Michael's large den with its array of Russian gimcracks (brass samovars, gilded icons, borzoi prints, crystal troikas and antique ivory chess sets yellowed and splintered like an old man's teeth) while Natalie sat on the other. They'd both seen Michael handle everything about the funeral while enduring his wife Jeannette's anger at him for responding so patiently to their mother's inability to manage anything except dressing well. The theme of his eulogy was unsentimentally accurate yet eloquent, given the integrity and wilfulness of the deceased: Paul Alexander Theodore was an architect who lived the life of his deepest desires; he died too young but happy; nothing that belonged within him was excluded, nothing that was extraneous was included; he was a complete, self-invented, self-enclosed New Yorker who lamentably did not care about his family's homeland, but made the most of its new land and was responsible for dozens of exquisite renovations throughout the five boroughs and the birth of two wonderful children, Ellis Alexander and Natalie Sofia.

"If you don't get away, you'll what?" Michael asked.

"I don't know what. I just …"

Michael couldn't bear playing this out. He knew (Natalie eventually would realize) that his wife viewed their arrival as the end of her dream of having another child beyond Dennis, but he could not admit that any task, even a task levied on him by a cousin he didn't like, exceeded him. So he said, "What do you think, kids? Do you want to come stay with me and Aunt Jeannette a while?"

Natalie knew this was something her mother wanted and said, "Yes, I'd like that," the first big lie she'd ever told in her life. What she wanted was for things to be as they were, for her father to reappear in her bedroom doorway late at night, coming to tuck her in and let her feel the smooth, cool back of his hand on her cheek.

"Ellis?" Michael asked.

Nine-year-olds are exponentially older than five-year-olds, and Ellis was a precocious nine-year-old who worried about the risks of intruding into another family. "I don't know. What does Dennis think?"

"What does Dennis think?" Michael asked, laughing at the shrewdness of this question.

Jeannette said, "Sometimes the adults have to decide these things, Ellis."

"No, no," Michael said. "Let me go get Dennis. He's in his room."

In a moment Michael returned with twelve-year-old Dennis. Had he been told to be happy and say, "Great! Please, come live with us!" or was he really that happy? Afterward Ellis contended that he had been told, his exuberant welcome was a big act; Natalie never thought so. Whatever the case, he said yes, leaving the three children smiling tentatively at one another while the women began to weep and Michael already had begun looking at his new wards with an expression of concern that would never leave his face.

Within a few days, Ellis and Natalie were installed in bedrooms just beyond Dennis's room on the opposite side of the large salon, den, dining room and kitchen from the suite where Michael had his little home office and Jeannette had her dressing room and the two of them shared their immense bedroom with its view of Central Park.

Their mother? Not clear. She was in the city at a hotel, then out of the city; then back staying with "a friend," then gone; then sending letters and presents, then not; then calling, then not; then saying come see me in Phoenix, then apologizing because she was moving to San Francisco. Meanwhile Ellis and Natalie had a mysterious new cosmos to confront, meaning the high-ceilinged, formal, very quiet apartment that was virtually unoccupied during the day and then alive with guests night after night between six and eight. Some of them were funny, like Mr Lagunov, and the animals he could make with his fingers. Some were quirky, like Mr Maximov, who only sipped his tea when someone else sipped tea, never before or after. Or there was Madame Dubasov and her daughter Inez Dubasov, who dressed for a visit to the Theodores as if they were going to the opera, both of them sporting what could only be called peacocky hairstyles with jewels dotting the long thick curls that draped down over their shoulders. The idea, Natalie quickly discerned, was that Madame Dubasov thought Inez would be exactly the right match for Dennis. Dennis wasn't buying it, however. He did his duty passing around caviar and crackers and refilling teacups, but he had no inclination to accept Inez as his pubescent fiancée. The girl he liked, this was obvious from the start, was Natalie. First he called her Little Bear, then Baby Bear, and he welcomed her tailing him, handing out damask cocktail napkins. He could make her giggle by spotting things like Mr Maximov's monkey-see, monkey-do teacup or the speed and dexterity with which a certain Mr Litnivov helped himself to multiple snacks by using both hands and pinching his take between his fingers.

Ellis would have nothing to do with these evenings. He'd eat alone in the kitchen before people arrived and then hide in his room, but he still understood what was going on out there before either Dennis or Natalie did.

"Uncle Michael wants Dennis to become a lawyer like him and take the whole mess off his hands so he can retire."

"Would that be the worst thing?" Natalie asked.

"It's like he doesn't even have a choice," Ellis said, staking out his claim to their father's legacy of doing only what you want to do when you want to do it.

In fact, Dennis had the bonhomie for such a role and the lifelong experience of distinguishing between Russians, Estonians, Ukrainians, Georgians and the like, but still, as Ellis would say, it was numbing to see your life laid out for you in such detail that looking at the future was like looking at the past. Natalie worried for Dennis. Aunt Jeannette, she came to realize, was well informed, a great manipulator and steely partner in Uncle Michael's practice. Uncle Michael knew everything there was to know about immigration law, the immigrant experience, Cold War politics, Russia's tragic history, and how to get rich. They weren't warm and personal, and hearing his parents tell him where he stood with them all the time—halfway up some kind of family Olympus, heading in the right direction but with a long way to go—unnerved Dennis. He wasn't a straight-A student. For a few years his acne was barely sub-bubonic. His passion for ice hockey collided with his parents' social schedule. But at least it ensured his acceptance at Cornell, which his father referred to as "sort of a farm school," and Aunt Jeannette described as "not Yale."

The one person Dennis could always count on, Natalie felt, was her. He could count on her to take a walk with him, ice skate in the park or at Rockefeller Center with him (she wasn't bad), giggle with him watching Saturday morning cartoons, drink hot chocolate with him, and celebrate the disappearance of his acne with him, which left him peculiarly fresh looking, almost brand new.

***

All that was fine when she nine or ten, but by the time she was fourteen and Dennis was twenty, she was full of new desires and urgencies, and they settled hard on Dennis. He was big, muscular, clear-skinned, dark-haired, still goofy, still warm, still her Papa Bear, but more than that. He'd come home from Cornell and kill her with his older guy looks and ways of throwing himself around and riding out the family rituals and demands, knowing that in a few days or weeks he'd be back on campus, free of what he now called the *ancien regime*, Moscow in Manhattan.

"Farm school?" he teased his father. "Did you know we had Nabokov at Cornell?"

"You mean Mr Lolita?"

"One and the same."

"Well, I'm glad you had him there and not here in the city," Uncle Michael said. "42nd Street's overcrowded as it is."

Nabokov? *Lolita*? Natalie got her hands on this book. Reading it did her in.

One morning when Dennis was home, she left the door to her room open a crack, sat down on her bed in just her jeans, no top, started painting her toenails, and voilá, there he was.

"Dennis!" she protested, covering herself up with crossed arms.

He smiled that endearing smile of his with the centre of his upper lip pressing down while the corners of his lips rose. "Wow, you're all grown up. Come on, let me see."

They bantered a few moments. Then she removed her arms and gave him his look. Breasts. Excellent plump breasts.

With Ellis at the library or the movies or just walking, endlessly walking—anywhere but Uncle Michael and Aunt Jeannette's lugubrious (one of Ellis's new words) apartment—Natalie and Dennis had time for mischief. He would come into her room and push and plead and she'd let him look, then let him touch, and after that the making out really raged although she kept it all above the belt. Above his belt, too. With which he archly agreed. "Right," he'd whisper, "don't you dare size me up." He'd wag his finger at her playfully, making her laugh.

What jolted her almost like an electric shock when he touched her breasts? The taboo of his particular hands? Maybe, but she had researched it. Biologically and legally, second cousins were okay. FDR and Eleanor were second cousins.

"In that case, maybe you and my father would be all right, too," Dennis suggested. "Wouldn't stretch things too far."

"Oh, that's rotten. Shut up!"

"You're the one who wants to talk. Why not just enjoy doing it?"

She said she was beginning to sense that thinking was part of her sex drive, too. Even when you went all the way, she suspected, you would be tumbling and squealing throughout your mind as much as your body.

He told her about the various girls he'd slept with—six, so far. "With a couple of them, frankly I'd say things get more intimate in a subway car."

"Even if you were having *sex*?"

"They lay there like logs."

"Did you say anything?"

"Of course! You know me. Nothing worked. I tried it all."

"Like …?"

"Like this," he said, touching her nipple with the tip of his tongue and then surrounding it with his lips. "What's that feel like?"

"It feels good."

"Real good?"

She wouldn't tell him how good; it was too private. She asked when he had first "noticed" her. Sooner than she thought, he told her. She was twelve, exactly Lolita's age.

"But you didn't want to do anything?"

"No, come on. It was just … nice. Looking at you."

"I didn't know that."

"Yes, you did."

"I didn't!"

"Did."

More kissing and fondling and decoupling and holding Dennis back and wondering why. Who would she rather give her virginity to? Who did she trust so much? Who else did she make so happy? He *was* happy. And his happiness made *her* happy, obliviously happy … dangerously happy.

One morning a few weeks into their activity, she made herself a cup of coffee and decided to take it into Uncle Michael's study where he was reading the *Wall Street Journal* as he did religiously front to back Monday through Friday. She never went into his study like this with nothing special to say. She and Uncle Michael weren't talkers, ever. Sometimes he might smile and have a laugh with her about something,

173

but he had no pet name for her or interest in her interests. The issue of whether she would ever leave the apartment was long settled by deep, deep silence. She and Ellis maintained separate relations with their mother who sent them ample spending money and sometimes tickets to visit her in Boston or Atlanta or wherever, which they did travelling by train or plane together, somewhat like an adolescent married couple, very adult and self-sufficient, and then returning with no message for Uncle Michael and Aunt Jeannette, no explanation from Margaret or desire on their part to state the obvious conclusion: we are going to be with you until college because our mother is usually drunk by noon and slept through half our visit and made no sense when she was awake.

Imagine telling her mother about fooling around with Dennis. No more likely than saying anything to Uncle Michael, for obviously different reasons, but it definitely was her relationship with Dennis that made her feel she was a person who, on that particular morning, might sit on the green leather sofa and be somehow content and justified. She just had this good feeling; she loved Dennis and who knew? Who really knew?

Uncle Michael knew. He lowered his *Wall Street Journal* and looked at Natalie for quite some little while. At first it was a look she didn't get, a look she mistook for dissatisfaction with some tidbit of market news he'd just absorbed. He was sitting there in his perfectly laundered white shirt and gold and blue rep tie, and she was sitting there in her green plaid tartan jumper, ready for school, so they were not dressed for drama. But the longer he looked at her, the more dramatic the situation became. He lowered the paper even farther so that she could see his well-shaven face and lips as he made his voluminous, one-sentence speech.

"I want it over," he said.

That was all. No need to go on about what "it" was, no intention of elaborating on what "over" meant. He simply pulled his newspaper back over his face and she sat there with her cheeks burning and then got up, took her coffee cup back to the kitchen, and felt, as she headed out the front door, a kind of second punch in the stomach, realizing that he could have said that just as easily to Dennis, but he didn't. He said it to her because she was the one whose feelings meant nothing to him.

***

Their adolescent dalliance being fourteen years ago—and in Dennis's case a marriage ago—Natalie wouldn't have connected it to Dennis's current sense of doom and befuddlement, whose justification seemed clear. Working under his father was humiliating. Uncle Michael took him into the firm after his real estate debacle and divorce, giving him a below-market salary and forcing to him to rely on the immigrant/exile community for supplemental deals.

"The debts I ran up in real estate are my problem, he says. When he dies, I'll be worth millions. For now I'm hustling out in the streets. You would never know from his princely life at home how grubby his business is downtown. New York and I spend a lot of time looking each other in the eye, wondering what's next. It's unbelievable what comes up next. Thank God for the gifts."

The gifts! Grateful newcomers and reunited families gave him food baskets, tickets to Knicks' games, Swiss watches, carte blanche at Russian restaurants, rent free use of one apartment after another, no charge bodywork on his Porsche, cases of vodka … and three sessions into what she had decided they would call their "conversations" as opposed to therapy, the most unusual gift he'd ever received.

"Look at these!" They were ice hockey boots to which he had a shoemaker rivet a kind of rail that was in turn connected to four hard rubber wheels that ran straight from the heel to the toe. He had two pairs, one for him, one for her. "I mentioned I was a hockey player in college, and a guy gave me these wheel thingies. The Ruskies use them for training on the streets when there's no ice around. Remember when you and I used to go over to the skate in the park and down to Rockefeller Center over Christmas?"

Remember? The excitement of just being with Dennis when she was a tubby eight-year-old? The frosty scent of the gleaming ice? All the pretty girls? Watching Dennis chop-chop-chopping his turns with overlapping strides, his hands clasped behind his back?

"I've never seen anything like them. You don't fall over?"

"Do you fall over on ice skates?"

"And you had this pair made for me?"

He smiled that cute smile of his. "The guy gave me two sets of wheels. Naturally I thought of you. Who else?"

"Dennis, are you lonely? Is that what this is all about?"

The smile went away, answering the question with its absence and a severity of expression suggestive of his father's undeniable force, alarming Natalie. For a moment that look hung there, threatening to consume her, then veered away. "Do you think I have real friends in the Moscow Menagerie? You can feel it drying up. The Commies are extorting people for exit visas. No one's coming out. I told my father maybe we should start focusing on Central Americans or the Chinese. Vietnam's almost over, what about them? What if I took a few trips, made some connections? He told me that's not our mission. What we do is outsmart the Kremlin first and Washington second."

"But it's your feelings you want to talk about, not the Kremlin or Washington, right?"

He banged the side of his large head with the butt of his hand. "If I could figure out how. What's in here? I feel steered away from myself—no time to think and nothing to think with."

"There are different personality types. Maybe you're not the thinking type."

"But that's so incomplete."

"I suppose it is," she agreed, perhaps too honestly. "But how many people can skate like you?" she asked, wanting to make him happier. "When do you want to try these things?"

To have relatively free streets, he would come to her apartment at six in the morning, and they would cross 78th to Central Park and then for an hour pump up past Harlem Meer and down along the reservoir and the Metropolitan and over to the zoo. Bikers slowed to ask what those things were; runners couldn't keep up; the air in the park was cool, settled, clean; the city's squawks and clanking and grinding and whooshing were random and distinct, not the clamorous din of Gotham in gear. Even thirty pounds heavier than when he was at Cornell, Dennis still had that powerful stride, legs like two horses upon which he was mounted in perfect equilibrium, his head and shoulders steady, not a thing moving above his waist.

Afterward, they'd have coffee at Charlie's down the street from her place, and then their hug and goodbye, each off into their day except Wednesdays when he continued to come to the office, exactly like a client. It was hard not to let him go on about a Soviet Union that was all Siberia now, all Gulag, teeming with oppressed Christians, Jews, refuseniks, dissidents, Muslims, whatever, but she couldn't get sucked into how sad and interesting they all were. Despite insisting she wasn't offering him therapy, she felt her job was to help Dennis become less sad and more interesting himself.

"If you have to, Dennis, talk more directly about your father. These stories you're telling me are diversions."

"I thought you said he's not the me in me."

"He isn't, but these people you're describing are even less so."

"I like helping them. They move me."

"Your father doesn't move you?"

"You want to know the truth? I hate my father. I'd like to kill him."

Clearly he expected this declaration to have a great effect on Natalie, and it did, but she concealed her dismay by clapping her hands and using the technique of welcoming grisly revelations as good news. "Great. We can skate around that like we do runners in the park or we can go inside it and say hello."

This tripped Dennis up. He had begun perspiring, just a light patina of sweat dampening his temples, but after staring glumly down into his lap a moment to steady himself, he went on. "I'm not saying I literally would kill him, but I see him lying there dead in my mind, and I feel responsible and don't know what to do. It's paralyzing."

So he was blocked, couldn't get through. An image came to her, one of the most fundamental images in life, energized by her own trepidations and sense of psychic confinement: do not ever make a mistake. "Trying thinking of him as a door. What would you say to him if he were a door?"

"Open up. Get out of my way. Let me through."

"And what would the door say to you?"

Dennis looked at the door to Natalie's office. Then he looked at her. There was a spell of silence as his associations brewed. "Doors don't talk. Doors say, 'We are here to keep certain things in and other things out.'"

"Is that what your father door says?"

"My father door says, 'Barge through if you want to. Go ahead and try.'"

These, Natalie recognized, were real words in the sense of being felt words. She could hear in Dennis's voice how it fatigued him to say them. He veered away almost instantly, spewing lighter, less meaningful words, assaulting his father for enslaving him, for abandoning the office to him while still calling himself the rainmaker, which Dennis found more than appropriate. His voice got heavy again as he talked about his father as rain drenching his life, making it soggy, hard to trek through while tantalizing him with the promise of sun somewhere in the future when he was finished pissing on him.

"And you know what? It goes further back. I didn't know my grandfather, old Andre, but what he did making my father the way he is makes me dislike him, too. These Russians! Were they nuts? Here was a man who was born in California and moves to New York. Who does that? Blue skies for this? Great weather for this? But to Grandpa Andre and his brother and sister it was a reverse gold rush, the immigrants were pouring into New York, so this is where they came to mine them, and now here I am."

"But you love New York."

"I love the New York in the sense I can't get into. Every free minute I have I head for it—the inner New York, the one I told you about. Maybe your father really had it, maybe Ellis has it—talk about someone who's a shut door!—but not me. I don't get there carrying on with all my Ruskie sycophant cronies. Or maybe I just don't know how to eat and drink and carry on right. Maybe there's a secret. In fact, I think there is. It's this: I need to have what my father doesn't want me to have. I want the money I make for me, not seventy percent to him, who does absolutely zilch for it. I want my old man dead."

"Figuratively," she reminded him.

He nodded. "Sure, sure." Then out something popped, some door somewhere having flipped open for a second. "Did he ever make a move on you?"

"What?"

"Did he ever make a move on you?"

She said no but felt she was lying. He'd made a move on her when he forced her to pull away from Dennis and then explain to Dennis why and almost perish when Dennis gave a hollow, fearful laugh and capitulated. "Okay, then we won't do it anymore," he'd said. That's all. What a coward! He didn't love her at all! "Of course not," she agreed, stunned that Uncle Michael had been able to wedge himself between them like the blade of an axe, severing their intimacy. But what could she do? She worried that Uncle Michael would send Ellis and her back to their mother, who by then was soon-to-die, drowning in champagne.

Dennis said, "Well, I'm glad to hear it. That means he's no good getting into the inner New York, either."

"If I'm the inner New York, I don't think I impress him enough to buy a ticket."

"He's a closed door to you, too?"

She had to get away from the subject of her and Uncle Michael. If she didn't, Dennis would sense something. "He's not my father. That's my father." She pointed to the praying mantis-style drafting lamp, which hovered in place, not turned on.

***

From that point, she recognized a burgeoning energy in Dennis. Physically he was more alive. His eyes were more alive. His voice was more alive. She had actual clients who sputtered along erasing everything they just said, every little sign of progress, as soon as they let it sneak out and stare them in the face. Dennis, she felt, was no less troubled than they, but he seemed to be in an altogether different phase of self-revelation. Could it be the crazy skating they did in Central Park more than their Wednesday conversations? Should she get more of these roller blades and hand them out to her clients?

One Wednesday he said, "I told my old man no about something today."

"Really? How did he take it?"

"He went off like a cannon."

"And how did you take that?"

He patted his belly with both hands, as if indicating where the cannon ball had hit. "Didn't bother me."

She wondered if he was trying to impress her with the invisible development that was going on inside of him, or perhaps, who knew, reclaim something, restore something they'd both lost to Uncle Michael long ago. They'd never processed that. Everything they had left they put into acting as if nothing happened—it was just puppy love, only that—so that the relationship closed over the wound without healing it, Uncle

Michael still embedded between them. Forgotten, but now emerging, working his way out.

Another Wednesday he told her, "When he said he wanted me in the office earlier in the mornings, I said how the hell did he know when I got to the office since he never shows up and how was I supposed to be there at nine if I didn't finish working until nine or ten the night before."

"What was his reaction?"

"He didn't have a reaction."

Dennis was so gravely satisfied by this that he seemed almost Michael-like himself. She was more dutiful than Ellis, but other than holiday visits, she had avoided the man and that apartment for years. She once described her childhood as ending when she became a permanent hotel guest at age five. And ever after she'd had the fear that one day she'd be presented a very large bill.

"Have you had some kind of general conversation about your relationship, or is it just these various incidents you're telling me about?"

"I told him I've been talking to you, and it's helping me."

"What did he say to that?"

"He asked if I was paying you. I said, 'How could I with the money I earn?' He said he was giving me a raise, ten grand, it was time. 'Just don't give it to Natalie,' he said."

"What a mean thing to say!"

Dennis gave her a very odd look, his face uncomfortably moulding itself to something stirring inside. "He never forgave you. It's one of the reasons I dislike him so much. You were a kid. I never forgave myself, either."

She ignored her own feelings and seized on his painful honesty as she would if this were really therapy. "Hey, you were just a kid, too."

"I was twenty, old enough to be drafted and sent to Vietnam."

She grew very uncomfortable. There was too much to parse. The sudden $10,000 raise ... but don't give it to Natalie for seeing you! She knew full well that Uncle Michael disliked her father and despised her mother. Was that what made her unacceptable for his very special son? Was he telling her, through Dennis, that he was still watching, accusing and exiling her, this time for good? She said she wished they could go to dinner instead of doing these Wednesdays. And she wished they could involve Ellis once in a while, become a generation of their own on their own, not constantly looking over their shoulders at the phantoms of the past.

But Dennis wasn't having it. He began telling her stuff that he said he would never tell Uncle Michael, things connected with container ships, the docks, the airports, Canada, and people being smuggled in "paperless." He said one time he was given a small bag of diamonds that proved to be worth $21,000 on 47th Street. He said another time he found a mysterious buyer for one of his lingering real estate debacles who plunked down $425,000, enabling Dennis to settle a lien and pocket forty grand for himself. He described a party in an apartment in Brighton Beach, where he wasn't playacting God as far as these Russian fugitives were concerned, he *was* God, God eating and drinking with them, no end to what they sacrificed to him—*God!*

"I'm in some doors," he said one day. "Places that are fun, places that make me nervous, places where my father must have been himself when he was starting out with his old man. We can't just get by on the law."

Dennis was excited when he said this, as if in sharing his questionable dealings with her, he had liberated himself once and for all from his father and barged into his own life as furiously and fast as he skated. She was so disconcerted that she had the impulse to blurt, "Great! Wonderful! We don't need to keep up these conversations anymore. You're in!" But she didn't. The stuff he was doing sounded wrong.

"You say you're doing things your father must have done—don't you see what that means? It means you're turning your back on what we've been exploring."

Dennis became angry. "What are you talking about? My turn is now, I can feel it."

"Feel what?"

"I don't know. This energy … this …" He gave a look that hovered in front of her like a scary dragonfly.

"Dennis, you can't let this happen to you. You're too good and wonderful and nice."

"I am not," he said. "Yesterday my father started in on me about something I have to do for him now because of the raise and I told him he could forget the raise. I don't need it."

"What did he say?"

"He said if I didn't stop hanging out with you, I'd make more boneheaded mistakes than that."

"Me?"

"He thinks I'm falling in love with you."

"What?"

"Maybe he's right. Maybe I am."

The dragonfly flew away. The space between them grew vacant. They couldn't look at one another.

"Let me understand," she said quietly. "Did he actually say that, or are you interpreting what he thinks?"

Dennis licked his lips with his tongue. Now they were looking at one another again. "He said it, and I said what if I were, and he said you and your brother and your mother and father were four different faces of the same problem. You're all wrapped up in yourselves."

Natalie didn't know which line of what she was hearing to pursue—Uncle Michael's judgment or the possibility that Dennis was falling in love with her.

"Look, this is getting out of hand. I'm asking you again: are you actually talking to him the way you and I talk, or is it just these eruptions?"

Dennis puffed out his large cheeks. "We're talking," he admitted sourly. "He asks me to stick around after people leave his open house things. He tells me he wants me to be thinking about when I'll be the one hosting these soirées myself. He says he's gotten tired of it, doesn't need it, the hell with it."

"Is what he's saying something new or has he been saying it for a while?"

"Relatively new. And relatively unbelievable. His whole life is built on being paid court. My mother's, too."

"You sit in the den and what, have another drink?"

Dennis nodded. "It's like he doesn't want me to leave. It goes from taunting me to treating me."

"And I am discussed?"

Dennis looked at her as if she were dimwitted. "You don't feel anything for me?"

"Who wants to know—you or your father?"

He laughed, as if he took her genuine question as flirting, but there was a pained change in his voice; it groaned a little under the weight of his words. "I ran." He meant back then, fourteen years ago. "You told me what he said and I ran."

Back to this again? "Dennis, we're beyond that. It's ancient history."

"No, I ran. I'm still running. What did you think of me for doing that? Don't lie. Tell me the truth."

"Do you think I lie to you?"

"Yes, I do."

The memory of Uncle Michael grilling her mother about wanting to abandon her children surged through her. How could her mother have done that? How could Uncle Michael have been so clinical? And then yes, Natalie lied. She lied, she lied, she lied. "I was hurt."

"Really hurt?"

"Dennis, please, what do you want me to say?" Tears filled her eyes. "I was really, really hurt."

Dennis smacked himself on the side of the head. "I knew it. How could I *be* that way? Don't you see—I veered away, I bounced off. And what about now? Do you feel anything for me now?"

"Of course, I feel something for you, but not that, it can't be that."

"Why not—the cousin thing?"

"No, no, it's not biology, it's that you're my family, you and Ellis, and look at what is happening. Something like this is why I didn't want you coming here in the first place. We're too intimate. It's too powerful."

"It is powerful," Dennis said quite soberly. "I am out there in the city doing things and all the time I'm thinking, 'I am totally on the wrong path. I should be with Natalie.' That's what brought me here. What happened back *then*."

She tapped the arms of her chair with all of her fingers, her mind racing past things so fast that she didn't know what to grab onto. "Dennis, *then* was something else. *Then* was finding out about sexuality. Are you saying that's what you're here for?"

Dennis gave a start; it was almost a small convulsion. "Sometimes I do think about you sexually. But we never got there. And then I went through a marriage not getting there, and I'm still not there. I just flopped when he pushed at us. I was scared."

"I was too."

"Well, are you still scared?"

She thought of herself floating into Uncle Michael's study with her cup of coffee, flaunting her feelings, and she thought of herself leaving, her feelings meaning nothing. "Yes, I'm scared."

"Too scared?"

"Dennis, please, stop …"

"I don't want to stop. I don't know how to stop.

They were sitting across the glass-topped coffee table from one another, she in her chair, he on the sofa. What would be the truth? Should she just let what happened be the truth? How else could she find out? She didn't know.

"Dennis, if you really want to have sex with me, say so and let's do it."

He paled. "You mean here?"

"Why not?"

"Now?"

"Now."

"Because that's what you want, too?"

"No, because it's what you want. I'll do it for you and we'll see. I just can't promise you anything."

"Natalie, Jesus Christ."

He covered his face with his hands. She wondered whether, when they came down, they would reach out for her ... take her by the shoulders ... try to pull her out of herself. But his hands fell to his thighs and he sat there squeezing them. He couldn't do it; it wasn't in him; he was too deep on the other side of where she was, too afraid.

"Maybe what we should do is just go out and have a drink," he said.

"No, I don't think so," she said. "What I want ... I want you to go."

"All right. I understand. Are you mad at me?"

Natalie shook her head, not meaning no, not meaning yes. "I want you to go. Just go."

Dennis went to the door, opened it very gently and left. Natalie went over to her desk, sat on her father's stool, turned on his lamp and focused it on the door. It was smooth and without blemish and blank, the way doors are. It had a large mouth, if you wanted to think of it that way, but the mouth was closed.

on being a woman

"What do you do, Mr Chatterjee?"

"Evidently I produce prostatic cancer cells at an alarming rate."

The doctor suppressed a smile. "I mean professionally."

"Until my illness, I was a museum director."

"Interesting work?"

"Very interesting. I'd like to return to it in some fashion."

Now Dr Blair did smile. 40s. Pretty. Thin. Impressive long nose. Excellent posture. Beautiful clothes. "That's our objective. We develop an effective treatment plan, and you survive for many years."

"But you don't treat me yourself."

"I advise some patients who come to our group and treat others who have been advised by one of my colleagues. That way you receive a quick second opinion. Or you can get your second opinion elsewhere. So," she continued, leaning forward, her fine black hair drifting toward her jawline, "tell me more about yourself."

Henry understood that Dr Blair worked with the whole person, but Henry wasn't interested in the whole Henry. He was focused on the cancerous Henry and after a brief autobiographical recitation turned the conversation in that direction.

"I am fifty-six, a tad overweight, but cancer aside, I'm fine. My mother is a Hudson who endowed me with my first and middle name, Henry Hudson. My father, surnamed Chatterjee, was a London-trained Bengali proctologist who practiced here in New York. I have degrees from Choate, the University of Pennsylvania, and Columbia. Initially I planned to obscure myself as a classicist, but I was drawn into sociology by Professor Thomas Sudbury who became Senator Thomas Sudbury. So ... politics, of which fifteen years proved a surfeit. I then moved into the directorship of the American Museum of Folklife and Social History and was happy there until last January when I had my prostate gland removed because my Gleason score was seven. But unfortunately the subsequent velocity of my PSA readings suggested there had been a jail break; the cancer had tunnelled out of the prostate capsule. Now I'm told we ought to radiate the prostatic bed. Then we ought to retest my PSA levels. If they continue upward, we go after the vagrant prostatic cancer cells before they get into the lymphatic system one of two ways: either we suppress my testosterone production through hormones because testosterone has a nourishing effect on prostate cancer cells, or we—I say 'we' with reservations—chemically or physically castrate me."

Dr Blair had a long look at the olive-skinned Henry Hudson Chatterjee. He was a short, paunchy, highly intelligent, witty man who deserved old age.

"Has someone been going through all this with you?"

"Senator Sudbury's former wife, Patricia, is a dear friend of mine."

"She lives here in New York?"

"She does."

"And you?"

"I've left Washington and taken refuge with her. May I add that I don't think any of this is going to work?"

"Oh, but we're far down the road in treating prostate cancer," Dr Blair protested.

"I'm afraid my prostate cancer is far down the road, too. I picture it having a cup of coffee somewhere along the Route

66 that courses through my troubled body. Let's think of it as a character in a Cormac McCarthy novel out there, up to no good."

Dr Blair couldn't help laughing. "Okay, given your skepticism, what are your thoughts?"

Henry's voice tightened as he struggled to retain his sense of irony. "My principal thought is that women don't die of prostate cancer."

"No, women don't have prostate glands."

"Nor testicles. Nor testosterone."

"Meaning?"

"Meaning I foresee a period in my life that is dramatically miserable and prematurely terminal. I already have ceased to function as a man."

"You've only had your prostatectomy seven months ago."

"I know it's early, but in the midst of my likely hormonal treatments, radiation, and chemotherapy, I fear I shall have a sick, discouraged Henry Hudson Chatterjee on my hands. It therefore occurs to me that if the idea is to prevent my masculinity from killing me, I might rather experience my final years not as a eunuch but as a woman. Don't just castrate me. Commit to that antiseptic phrase I've come upon: reassign my gender. Give me the Tiresias experience so that I, too, will experience life from both sides, male and female."

Dr Blair had never heard anyone say what Henry had just said. "Are you homosexual?"

"I am not."

"Have you felt you should have been born a woman?"

"I have not."

"Those are prerequisites for what you're suggesting. Gender reassignment isn't an accepted treatment for prostate cancer."

"This may be true, but if I end up merely castrated, I'll be a selfless self. By going further, I'll be a woman. Is that such a hideous fate?"

Once again, Dr Blair had to laugh, "I haven't found it so."

But Henry knew he'd have to push hard. "I won't say I'm

indifferent to sex as a man, but I will say that I'm a cerebral/ aesthetic sort, and as I think of all the women I've known, with the exception of my ex-wife, I have sensed that being male isn't necessarily the better lot in life. Woman take things in that men miss. If this were a Kafka story and I woke up tomorrow morning not as an insect but as a woman, I think it would be interesting."

It had been a long time since Wellesley, but Dr Blair had read Kafka's story, "The Metamorphosis." She also knew that the prophet Tiresias had come upon two copulating snakes, struck them, irritated the goddess Hera, and as a consequence been transformed into a woman. For the next seven years, Tiresias had been a notorious prostitute. At this point she came upon another pair of copulating snakes and either struck them again or passed them by. Whatever she did was sufficient to release her from her femininity and make Tiresias a man again. This qualified him to settle an argument Zeus and Hera had about who enjoyed sex the most: men or women. Tiresias said women.

But Dr Blair stuck to medicine. "Again, gender reassignment is not a prostate cancer treatment."

Henry smoothed the thighs of his grey flannel trousers. The two of them were talking in the doctor's office, not an examining room, and he was a master of one-on-one negotiations that didn't involve digital rectal examinations.

"Perhaps not yet, but as I see it, step one is a simple procedure. I am castrated, an outpatient operation. *Voilà!* I instantly stop producing the testosterone that will hasten my death. Naturally most men don't like this option, but why stop there? Why not make the balance of my life an adventure? I've found no evidence that someone who has had a gender reassignment has lost her personal memories, legal status as an American citizen, access to her bank and investment accounts, or acuity of mind."

"Mr Chatterjee, women are different from men," Dr Blair objected. "If you had a vagina and a clitoris and amplified breasts and buttocks and altered facial features and possibly an altered voice, none of that would matter as much as the female hormones you'd receive. They'd change the psychic ground upon which your existence rests."

"You put that beautifully. I shall remember your phrasing."

"What do you want from me, Mr Chatterjee?"

"I want you to refer me to a sex change physician with a 'please expedite' sticker on my forehead."

She wanted to say that would be unethical, but was it? "You'd have trouble getting any insurance company to pay for this."

"In the valley of the shadow of death, money isn't an issue."

"All I can say is that you'll have to let me think about this."

"Okay, but please remember our friend is going to finish his cup of coffee any minute and as in a McCarthy novel, he may be hard to track."

***

Patricia had seen him in her study with piles of Greek and Latin books from his days at Choate and Penn. He was fixated on Tiresias. There was the story of Tiresias being both a man and a woman. Then there was Tiresias in *Oedipus Rex*, reluctantly revealing that Oedipus had killed his father and married his mother. Oedipus wasn't pleased. Tiresias was thrown out of the palace. Along the way he'd also become blind, some said as retribution for having spotted Athena naked while she was bathing. But his mother, the nymph Chariclo, persuaded Athena to wash out his ears (the blinding being irreversible) so he was able to understand birdsong, enhancing his prophetic gifts (birds know what's up in the world). And then there was Tiresias in *Antigone*, where he told Creon, the king of Thebes, that the city was sick because of him. Tiresias apparently had a habit of annoying gods, goddesses and kings on a fairly regular basis.

Patricia loved Henry for many reasons, one of which was

that he reminded her of the restlessly inquisitive Thomas Sudbury. They cared about things; they wanted to understand. Tiresias for instance.

"So many things happened to him that he's obviously a composite, more than just a prophet, almost a prophecy in himself," Henry said. "Isn't he, in fact, an emblem of mankind's quest for total knowledge?"

"What are you getting at?"

"I'm considering dealing with my testosterone-fuelled prostate cancer by becoming a woman."

Patricia sometimes said she lived to be bowled over. Thomas had bowled her over. She knew New York's best writers, publishers, artists, lawyers, bankers, and architects. They bowled her over all the time. No one, however, had bowled her over like this. She couldn't help her reaction.

"But what about us!"

"You have never had relations with a woman?"

She'd had a crush on a girl in boarding school. They did each other's hair. Sometimes they looked at one another sternly in the morning (they were roommates) and said, almost at the same time, "Now I'm going to kiss you so you have a great start to your day." And they would kiss, but no tongues, and part with protracted secret looks binding them eye-to-eye.

"Not really. Have you with a man?"

"Mason suggested it in college. I declined, but we're still best friends."

"It's different. Mason is gay. You wouldn't be gay."

"No, I'd be embodying the Tiresian prophecy in a way that goes beyond gay." Henry was looking at her with Euripides's *Bacchae*—in which Tiresias cross-dresses to have an intimate encounter with the Theban women—open in his lap. "As things stand, I have ceased to be a man and soon may cease to be a human being. Alternatively, I might live and explore dimensions of life that hitherto have been walled off from me."

Patricia involuntarily plumped down on a hassock. She was

reeling. "Henry, you could do anything you wanted at the museum, but this isn't curating an exhibition."

"No, we're definitely not talking about exhibitions, we're talking about life. What would I be like as a woman? Can you picture me?"

"What I can picture is that we might not have any sex at all."

"Presently the case."

"It could change."

"Not as things are going. I wish I'd had SAT scores as high as my PSA scores. Would have made Harvard."

"What if you became a woman and fell in love with a man instead of me?"

Henry said he would always love her; they had been secret soul mates from the beginning. "You know that. And I mean holding you, kissing you, being yours."

Patricia wasn't sure she'd like being held and kissed by a woman, even if the woman were Henry. She said this softly, supposing he must be in incredible pain despite his frightening composure. To think such a thing! But he went on thinking it:

"Ask yourself, is it better to be dead than to be a woman? Wouldn't Tiresias look around him now and see his prophetic example fulfillable? Be a man, be a woman, have it all? If I can kill myself, which I don't want to do, why can't I become a woman? How could I possibly become so disagreeable as a woman that you would want nothing to do with me?"

"You may lose your view of things, your personality, your irony, which I hope is on display at the moment."

"Or I may fascinate you with new insights. I may take us places where we've never been. I may write a book that is dual in its gender perspective, or I may just keep poking at Tiresias, returning to my undergraduate studies in the classics."

She tried to imagine Henry's body transformed. Who hadn't looked at cross-dressers and marvelled at their ability to appear as they were not? But this would go further. "A sex change operation wouldn't give you the sense of what it is to have been a woman all your life, the memories and disappointments and hopes and resignation … and what about giving birth?"

"Don't you see, I *would* be giving birth precisely because I don't want to die."

"I don't want you to die, either."

"Or live as a eunuch."

"Castration isn't inevitable."

"Perhaps not, but the fact remains that my testicles are killing me. Everything that will be done to me over the next few years will be aimed at neutralizing their effects."

Patricia didn't know how you went from Tiresias to reshaping a penis into labia, a clitoris, and a vagina. Henry wouldn't be Henry, but how could she stop loving him for that?

***

Dr Blair discussed Henry's case with Dr Hart, a gender reassignment specialist. Dr Hart first wanted to know whether this really would deal with Henry's prostate cancer. Dr Blair said that his body scans were clean; the issue was confined to the prostatic bed.

"Which, yes, I would remove in a sex-change operation," Dr Hart said. "But here's the problem: he's not proposing this because he's convinced he's a woman in a man's body."

"Apparently not. I talked to his urologist and his internist, though. They said what is obvious: he's bright, clear-headed, and quite rational."

"Were they surprised to hear he'd come up with this idea?"

"The urologist, yes, but the internist laughed. In any case he's definitely a normal heterosexual male. He has a female lover, Thomas Sudbury's ex-wife. He went into the prostatectomy eager to maintain his relationship with her. Instead, he ended up with more cancer."

"How long would he last absent this radical measure?"

"Two years, three?"

"But this way?"

"How can I say? This has never been done before."

***

Thomas Sudbury had vowed to get back to New York from California to see Patricia every two months. Didn't happen. The demise of their marriage provoked him to invent an odious new word: it *peripheralized* Patricia while centring him in his new West Coast life, not the easiest of transitions. People in California thought of the Atlantic seaboard as though it were somewhere under the national bed, littered with dust bunnies, porn magazines, and long lost slippers. Thomas had to scramble, network like crazy, spend more weekends on elaborate patios and in overdecorated hunting lodges than he wanted to, and learn not to annoy people in Seattle by talking about the people he knew in L.A. Everything was the future, and the future had an irresistible honeyed taste accompanied by relationships with women who had a lot more money than he did, but at seventy-three, he was choosy and often fouled things up with memories going all the way back to Nixon. So what if Thomas had worked for him? No one cared. People hadn't read Thomas's books, either. This made him wonder if he should write a new one. He hadn't done so in fifteen years, but then he'd had Henry's help. And now? My God, news of Henry's operations—plural—motivated him eastward. He sat in business class brooding about whether he always knew Henry coveted Patricia. Further, he asked himself what his reasons for leaving her were. In short, he couldn't bear what she obviously had come to think of him. Once upon a time he was a gorgeous academic steed, then politics turned him into a sway-backed nag who never stopped casting his eyes around for the next bag of oats, or, if you will, donors. He raised money until he wanted to scream. When he entered the senate he had to raise $5,000 a week. When he left, $100,000 a week. Every week for six years. She didn't like the man he became; he didn't like the man he became, and the peripheralization set in. He had transferred his erotic energies from his wife to other people's wallets. That's where he wanted to put his prick … plus the occasional fling … but this … this …

He sipped his bourbon and remembered both Patricia and Henry when they were young. He used to say Patricia was so slender you could slip her into a cigar tube. He used to say that Henry had the most uselessly interesting mind on the planet. And Patricia was more fun than anyone else in New York City, certainly in Columbia faculty circles. Who pulled off pot luck dinners with that stuffy crowd? Patricia. Who arranged picnics for thirty people in Central Park? Patricia. Skating parties? Patricia.

He had to get back to New York and see her, though he was leery of seeing Henry.

"What does he call himself?" he'd asked on the phone. "Etta, you say? Henrietta Chatterjee, is that it? Listen to me: I can say it without stuttering. I've been shocked into a cure. What's he look like? This is real, not just cross-dressing?"

He listened to Patricia describe Etta's weight loss, her surgically sculpted figure, the miracle of cosmetic surgery on her face that shrank her nose, gave her brown Indian eyes greater play, strengthened her weak chin (inherited from old Chatterjee, the proctologist) and then the vocal cord modification. She still had a deep voice, but it was a mature woman's voice, and her hair was jet black.

"Isn't this sort of thing supposed to happen in California, where I'm six steps behind all the time, and not New York? I'm not sure I want to see her."

"You won't have a choice. She's left the museum. She lives with me."

"And you two … how do I ask this?"

"If it's none of your business, *don't* ask it."

He got nowhere. You are married to someone for so long and then realize your relationship has dwindled to an encounter at a high school reunion. But he missed her. She was so real, so consistent, so grounded. All those years while he was politicking around New York, she'd escaped to estate sales, barns and basements and attics, buying and shipping curiously intriguing artefacts to her own little warehouse in Brooklyn. Why? Pure love, fascination, simply to escape from Thomas's endless barbecues, clam bakes and pig roasts, but now by God, she'd used her scavenging of signs, furniture, picture frames, andirons, glassware, doors, mantelpieces and so forth to jump-start an interior design business that mattered to her … and the buildings and neighbourhoods where she worked meant something to him, too. She was deeply involved in the city where he was born and he wasn't. That hurt.

He twisted his big body around to retrieve his smart phone and look at the picture Patricia sent him—an elegant South Asian woman with Henry's restrained, knowing smile only smaller, Mona Lisa-like. You would not think this was once a man.

A chill passed through him. The little woman scared him. What must she know given what she already knew before she did this to herself? Was that Tiresias stuff Patricia had relayed to him real? And during all those years the three of them had spent together, Henry the ingenious diplomat had been his aide-in-chief while Henry the folkloristic sociologist had been Patricia's stoutest moral support and admirer. That hurt, too.

**

Patricia had come through spectacularly when Henry had his prostatectomy. More spectacular still was her love seeing Etta through her sex-change operations. When her penis was inverted and reconfigured, Etta found herself in turmoil; for quite some time she couldn't look, dreading the mass of red swollen tissue between her legs. Meanwhile Patricia sat with her and read aloud the new Fagles translation of the *Odyssey*. The Oxycontin made Etta woozy; she'd drop off repeatedly.

Nonetheless, when she wakened, she found Patricia still reading, holding the book with one hand and Etta's hand with the other.

At last the hormones began to comfort her as much as the painkillers. She developed a new sense of self, kindred to birth or having given birth, she wasn't certain which, but a new beginning. She asked if there wasn't something she could do that would help Patricia in her business. Patricia said of course she could; she let Etta examine her financial statements and marketing schemes and project plans. As an interior designer, Patricia was, in a sense, just like Etta: a make-over artist. They joked about that. One day a dreary apartment or townhouse became a new one without losing its connection to the past.

Patricia was out when Etta had her first look at her groin. She sat on the closed toilet seat deploying a little pocketbook mirror. Her nethers remained swollen and confused; she could barely touch them to wipe—only pat—but the fundamental statement was clear: no penis, no scrotum. Was there, in fact, something beyond her puffy labia, as Dr Hart promised? Would she use it? There could only be one reason—sex—but she was so feeble that the thought of sex wasn't much of a thought. She pushed her knees farther apart and used her fingers to expose her new clitoris. It was swollen into a kind of tiny tulip bulb.

What about her breasts? The nipples and areolas were darker than they'd been, larger than they'd been, angled some-what downward and away from her breastbone. She thought of her bosomy mother and her scrawny father, who'd lost weight year by year as he aged. Mixed physical role models at best, who had a pact that when Henry was ten, they would separate, and when he was twelve, they would divorce. Henry would live with his mother, and they would live well because his father was affluent and his mother got a ton of his money and first dibs on the estate if his father died first, which he conveniently did.

The work on her face wasn't terribly painful, but any operation saps you. The human body rushes its phalanxes of recuperative powers to the site of what doctors sometimes called "the insult." What part of her hadn't been insulted? She went back to Dr Blair for an assessment. Dr Blair couldn't find a speck of prostate cancer anywhere.

"So your idea apparently worked," she said.

Etta was dressed in clothing Patricia had bought her, a white cashmere sweater and a black skirt with an interesting weave. Not too girlie. She hadn't had her vocal chords adjusted yet, so her voice was exactly the voice Dr Blair had heard the first time they met.

"And now I shall live, you see."

The two women contemplated one another, seemingly inquiring what the other might consider living to be, what being a woman meant.

Dr Blair asked, "What will you do with your life?"

"I'm helping Patricia with her interior design business at the moment. Eventually I may do some museum consulting."

Dr Blair asked if she would consider writing about her experiences.

Etta didn't know. "I don't have enough perspective yet. You'll recall Tiresias became a notorious whore during his period of femininity, but frankly, I'm feeling rather timid. Dr Hart didn't give me a literal hymen, but I'm a virgin, wouldn't you agree?"

Dr Blair agreed. Who knew where this demure Indian-American's new anatomy and hormones would take her? Beyond that, when Dr Blair took the trouble to look into the Tiresias myth, one thing struck her: his gnomic utterances were consistently rejected, just like Cassandra's, the prophetess doomed to be always right and never paid heed.

***

Patricia observed Etta's transformation with wonder. Etta

walked, sat, talked, minced celery, chided herself for forgetting something, and held her tongue like a woman … a certain kind of woman, a very good kind of woman. She retained her exceptional mind and knowledge, yet managed to probe her own thoughts and observations with even more discrimination than before. She confessed she was wary of men not only because she feared the moment of discovery but because, like many women, she found men could be awkwardly disruptive or mulishly reserved. In other words, they forced their opinions on you or played dumber than they were.

Thomas fell into the disruptive category as both Patricia and Etta knew.

"I think you ought to see him alone, without me," Etta said before his visit. "I could go to Boston for the weekend and get out of the way."

Patricia said, "No, if he's going to see me, he's going to see you. We're a pair."

"He won't like me," Etta said.

"Have you considered that it might be *you* who doesn't want to see *him*?"

"But I do want to see him. I'm curious about what he's like not being in academe or politics anymore."

"And older."

"Do you think that's a factor?"

Patricia said, "With men you never know. Some hang around in a state of formaldehyde-like preservation from their sixties to their eighties, and then, zip, they die. Others wizen to the point you can scarcely believe they are who they were. Women generally fight the aging process. Men either are lucky to escape it or give up without knowing that's what they've done."

When Thomas reached the apartment he and Patricia had shared for twenty-two years, he was the same tall, silver-haired, red-cheeked, haughty Thomas.

Right off he teased Etta, "I am pleased to meet you, Ms Chatterjee. Don't think we've met before, have we?"

He said this quickly, defensively, wanted it on the record that he didn't know what he was dealing with. Etta clearly didn't take what he said especially well, having worked with him through her doctoral dissertation and most of his three terms in the senate.

"I wanted to live," she said to him quietly. "That's all."

"Of course, of course," Thomas said, sitting down and asking for a bourbon, which Patricia already was pouring. "Of course," he said a third time, at a loss.

The facial reconstruction had made Etta look at least ten years younger; her voice now was that of a woman. Her hair, surely it was dyed, was as black as a Bengali's, and it appeared to be hers, not a wig. So much for looks, which Thomas could barely take in, stopping somewhere around her throat.

"But let's not talk about me," Etta said. "Let's hear about you."

Then came the questions about his life, what he did at the Rand Corporation, his visiting lectureship at Stanford, his board membership at Microsoft, and how he found the West—the kinds of questions an old female friend might put to him and he might half-answer or fend off with a chuckle or turn into a disquisition on the effects of immigration on California (immigration was his scholarly speciality), ignoring the fact that the woman with whom he was speaking wasn't interested. But Etta was Henry, and Henry was Etta, and there wasn't anything Thomas could say, however detailed or abstruse, that Henrietta couldn't follow.

Indeed, now this pretty woman took him to task for criticizing California's high personal income tax rates.

"So I'm rich and want to get richer," Thomas laughed. "The people I know constantly put me on the spot to repay their hospitality, and I don't have their kind of private palaces and have to do it commercially—fancy restaurants, that sort of thing. The whole bloody West Coast costs a goddamn fortune."

"New York doesn't?" Patricia asked.

Thomas appeared ready to continue his eruption on tax policy but suddenly stopped. "Okay, filibuster's over," he said seriously. "When last I saw you two, you were heading toward coupledom. Does that remain the case? Which of you, if either, is gay? I mean ... "

"We know what you mean," Patricia said.

"Well, for Christ's sake, Patricia, what do you want me to say? We were married a long time. Henry was my right hand man for a long time. Henry, I mean, Etta, were you gay then? Is that why your marriage didn't work out?"

Etta had married a redheaded folklorist from Kentucky who was fierce, smart, and thought Thomas Sudbury was a big-time phony for whom Henry shouldn't work. Her name was Bernice. She thought even worse of Henry's mother and father. In fact, the punishing attitude she took toward Henry's entire life mystified and repelled everyone except Henry, and there was general relief when she marched back to Louisville.

Now Etta said she wasn't gay as a man but might be as a woman. Thomas said not even in California had he heard someone say something so screwy. Etta said she had been told she was more unique than screwy. Thomas said she could assume her uniqueness to be a fact until proven otherwise.

Just like that, they were fighting. Patricia remembered them fighting all the time during the senate years, and then afterward, once Thomas got Henry the museum and foisted a big political donor onto his board, but this was unmistakably a sexually tinged fight. Patricia saw that despite himself Thomas found Etta attractive.

She *was* attractive. Initially they'd begun lying side by side, Etta under the sheets, Patricia on top of them, so that Patricia didn't disrupt things too much getting up and down to give Etta her pills, a sip of water, even help her turn over. Eventually she said, "Etta, we've been under the sheets together a hundred times, I don't see why we shouldn't be there again. We'll both sleep better, won't we?" Sleep? People sleep together precisely when they are not sleeping. But again, given Etta's condition, they actually did sleep at the outset. Then came a point when her condition no longer mandated regular assistance and the old soulfulness between them drew them together for a true embrace, an unrestrained kiss, an explicit movement of hands. Patricia told herself, "Well, I'm not getting any sex with men, am I?" Etta spoke to herself a bit differently, "My dear Patricia," she would think, over and over again, remembering her so well and yet experiencing her so differently.

The fight between Thomas and Etta continued. Patricia could see that Etta, too, was stirred. Thomas was best when he was nettled; his brain cells crackled; his eyes grew fiery; he still had some Pegasus in him. To put a stop to this curious flirtation, she fed them the kind of dinner they had shared so often when Etta was Henry and Thomas was Patricia's husband. Then there were after-dinner drinks. More calm, some chuckling, a kind of normalization and acceptance. Inevitably, though, Thomas began to grow restless. He had his luggage with him, but would he spend the night? If he spent the night, where would he sleep? In the guest room? In his old study, now the focal point of Patricia's interior design business? Did he think, had he thought, that Patricia would let him sleep with her?

He surprised both Patricia and Etta by talking frankly about sex. He admitted he used to be a fiend, but now he had the devil's own time escaping California's numerous divorcées, some of them half his age. He wasn't bragging, or only a little bit. In fact he said he was lonely, he had no one out west with whom he could be candid. Saying these things in front of Etta—they'd never discussed sexual matters, Henry had just overlooked Thomas's philandering as did Patricia—embarrassed Thomas a wee bit, but not enough to stop him from saying that he had always wanted what *he* wanted and still doubted he understood what a woman wanted.

"What is it like being a woman?" he asked Etta. "Maybe you can tell me that in a way that a—what should we say, 'a woman of origin'?——might not. Speak Tiresia. Tell Hera and Zeus your tale."

Etta looked at him like a woman who understood the rule of secrecy that bound her to her femininity from within, but she forced herself to speak. "As a latecomer to the club, there's only one thing I really know about women, and it's not whether they enjoy sex more than men. That's a stupid question."

"Is it really?" Thomas asked.

"Very stupid."

"Then what is it that you've discovered that's more important?"

"I think no woman would ever do what I did for the reason I did it. No woman would become a man to escape death. We'd rather die, we'd rather accept death and let it have its way than become you."

"Is that an indictment of men?"

"I think it's simply sense we have, perhaps because women give birth, that life will go on without us. In that regard we're much more alive while we live than men. Death is not our enemy. We are more free than men, and having learnt that, I'd never go back."

Thomas listened as carefully as he'd done many times when Henry was his aide—that's why Henry had been his aide for so long—but never on a subject like this.

"I hear you speaking from somewhere beyond my ken," he said. "I suppose I'd say that as a man I'm on this earth to wrestle my troubles to the ground. And if I succeed, I go looking for some new set of troubles. It's in my nature, it's who I am."

Patricia said, "Then you've certainly been true to your nature. Now where do you plan to sleep? Here or in a hotel?"

Thomas said he thought he'd spend the night there, with them. "Is the guest room free?"

"Yes, it is."

"And you two will …?"

"Don't worry about us," Patricia said. "We'll work things out."

The three of them shared in the cleaning up, and then there was the sound of doors opening and closing on bedrooms and bathrooms and water sluicing through sinks and toilets and the rustling of bedspreads and sheets and the soft background wash of New York's nocturnal tides—elevators whining up and down their shafts, street traffic mildly cranky ten floors below, rooftop HVAC systems hissing, and the cries and moans of people sleeping together who weren't asleep.

pivot point

Annie arrived at the crowded, smoky, cackling party and saw no one she knew, including herself in a mirror. She wore frameless glasses, cheapest she could buy. She hadn't put on makeup, not for work, from which she had walked across the bridge. Her *University of Louisville* sweatshirt was smeared with potter's clay. Looked awful. How she felt.

"No, no, no," a girl was saying, voice authoritative, describing snorkelling in Montego Bay. She'd dove down to swim along a reef's mesmerizing street-like passageways and there wasn't anyone with her. She'd gone way too far out, she realized on surfacing. "I totally lost track. The sea had me and getting back wasn't easy, but things that happen are better than things you plan."

Annie thought of joining the group but had no idea how to pursue the girl's point. She had never planned anything in her life, and she was tired. Shouldn't have told Rich she'd come. Where was he, anyway? Hadn't come himself. But going home seemed beyond her. She'd trudged over from the pottery, and now she'd have to trudge back the same way to get her car and drive to Asheville just to sleep a few hours before returning to the pottery, which was a false name for it. It was a ceramic production factory in a failed hydroponic vegetable greenhouse Rich and his partner Greg had bought from a friend who had given up. They had motorized shades, large fans, and more plumbing than they needed except when it came to the bathroom, which was an outhouse on the fringe of the slope down to the river. "Or we could shit here and fire it," Greg said. "Might sell better than what we're doing." Rich didn't like that.

Annie sank into a chair. Within a minute a guy sat on the chair's arm with his back to her. Next he'd turn and speak, but there would be *nothing* he could say as important as her own thoughts because she'd spent the day working so hard she hadn't thought anything, wearing a rubber respirator mask and concentrating on producing flawless plates and cups as samples of what Rich hoped to sell *Simple Homes* for their twenty stores throughout the US. And she didn't think with her mind when she worked, she thought with her hands. She mixed mud—that's what they called it, not shit—poured it, glazed it, fired it, and cooled it. Just the three of them. She wanted to think about that. She wanted to think about why she had picked Asheville and scanned Craig's List for jobs in Asheville and liked this one—join the team of one of the fastest growing potteries in the Southeast—without realizing it wasn't really in Asheville and how bad minimum wage sucked, but for a while she was happy not to be in Louisville working as a day-care assistant.

When the guy turned, she got up, found her way through the kitchen to the back steps, went around the house to the top of the hill and paused, listening to the rocky river's susurrus under the bridge. To their credit, Rich and Greg sometimes declared time off for tubing, and they'd scramble down to where the cool water blessed them and the unmediated sunlight freed them. Nothing as risky as Jamaican reefs albeit semi-unplanned. Annie liked floating along the bank, studying exposed roots and the sight of true greyish brown, muskrat-scratched mud.

She passed the hamlet's three-store commercial cluster—grocery store, bar, and post office—and then the expensive new condos tucked into the rusting old mill and recrossed the bridge and climbed the hill a quarter mile to the gravel road that led to the pottery. She liked crunching along in the overhanging hardwoods' deep darkness and considered again what she'd considered before. She could sleep in some unused corner of the building and save rent money. In the winter, the kilns would keep the place warm. In the summer, she could crank open the windows and run the fans for ventilation.

She had a blanket in the trunk of her Echo. She got it, thought about not being able to brush her teeth—so what, she'd wear the mask all day tomorrow—but would have to pee and couldn't bear the thought of the slap of the outhouse door and the updraft of the waste below. So she went in the woods where she heard two owls hooting and then the crying scream of a fox. She peed and remained squatting a long time, just thinking. About the coolness of the air along the forest floor. About the fox. About the river and what it would be like at night.

Pivot point, she would have said if she'd had the energy to enter the conversation at the party and talk about what happened versus what you planned. But now she had the energy for some reason, and she wasn't dumb, she knew what the girl was talking about even if she had never planned anything and just waited for what happened to smack her in the face.

She took off her clothes except for her boots and carried them with her to the river. When the leaves stopped rustling under foot, she removed her boots and padded barefoot into the mud, slipping right into the water. The frogs plopped away in urgent succession, abandoning their insect hunting on the river bank until this large white creature went away.

The river chuckled and whispered. Up close it was its many sounds, not the unitary susurrus of the distance. She listened a while, half floating, half standing, sometimes dropping down to cover her shoulders because the water was warmer than the air. She looked up at the stars and pondered her mean-ingless education, which had included courses in literature and economics and US history as well as sculpture, pottery-making, drawing, water-colours and oils. None of it had the cool passion of the river water, the mud, and the light of the stars in the heavens raining fire into the night. She loved this, all of it. Anyone else would ruin it, man or woman. But that was only a passing thought. She wiped away anyone else and was alone again. She used her toes to dig into the mud the way she used her fingers in the daytime and climbed back up the slippery embankment where she stood on one foot while wiping the other before putting on her socks and boots. Then she threaded back through the forest to her blanket and pile of clay-smeared clothes and went into the pottery to make her provisional bed.

She fell asleep wanting to dream what she had been living just now, driving this pivot point deeper into her, making it fast and sturdy, but her dreams were of fugitive mud. As she sank into them, they slipped away. What stuck was patchy and crumbly and indecipherable, and then the rising sun congealed everything, took away its excitement as well as its frustration, created reality as though light were glue. Even looking at the pipes and tables and wiring and vents and kilns and shelves and boxes from down on the floor did not help. Planned or not, daytime is what stayed in place.

my name is libby

Hi, my name is Libby. I'm an alcoholic. Thank you for letting me join you. It's hard for me to say I'm an alcoholic. No one else says I am. I just drink to calm myself and make the day go away. My husband doesn't complain even though he has every reason to. I'm forty pounds over what I was when we married. It's the vodka. I start with it in my orange juice in the morning, the bitter frozen kind that goops out of the can and you have to beat to make it mix with the water. Then I make my husband and kids breakfast. They all like different things. He has scrambled eggs and toast, which he only half eats, I finish the rest. My boy would eat Wheaties three times a day. My little girl will take oatmeal, box cereal, frozen waffles, anything I give her.

I know I'm supposed to talk about being an alcoholic, but this is my first time, so I have to listen to what you say to know how to do it. I don't know what else to say right now except I drink too much. This morning I told myself to stop, but I don't feel too good. I have to admit it. Thanks for listening.

***

Hi, I'm Libby. I'm an alcoholic. I had to drink after the last meeting. It's nobody's fault except mine. My husband sees it. My son does, too. I don't know about my little girl. Maybe she just takes me as I am. She's like that, the sweetest, easiest child. Nothing like me, I'm afraid. The truth is drinking helps me stand up straight. I'm not quite there when I haven't had something. After my son was born, that's when drinking began to feel different, not like it was before, not a party, more like a wake. I would be exhausted and didn't know how to take care of a baby and I would think, *I'll have something*, which could happen at any time because day and night got all mixed up. I needed to have a drink and pull myself together and stop being so anxious, and then my husband would come home and see how things were, and he would take the baby in this little chest papoose, and he would go out at night and walk. He walked at night before the baby, but even more after. He didn't want to confront me. I'm sure that's it. His mother was an alcoholic. I sometimes think that's why he fell for me. It's supposed to drive people off, running into a drinker when one of your parents was a drinker. But for him it worked the other way. It's terrible to say, but he got what he was after. His mother died when she was in her forties, and now when he looks at me it's like I'm something he's seen before and expects and can just ignore. The kids aren't babies anymore. He doesn't have the same excuse of taking them off my hands, but he works harder than he did when we were first married, and he doesn't drink hardly at all. He couldn't. He's got a heart condition. He breaks out in sweats and shakes because it beats so fast. He takes nitroglycerin pills. Frankly, I don't think they give him much relief. He's only 31. I'm only 29. But look at us. He's thin as a rail and I feel like a railway train, a runaway train, I get up and it's my first thought: the vodka in my orange juice. Finish one and start another. We don't go anywhere because he's so busy and I really don't care, but coming here, I'll tell you, it's harder than labour, the hardest thing I've ever done. When I leave today, I'll tell myself, well, that's done, I did it, I feel so much better, I'm not alone with this. But then you know what I'm afraid I'll do? It's years since I could walk past a bar or a liquor store. It's like there's this force pulling me inside. And when I get in a bar, I'll have one and then tell myself I'll top off and go, but I top off again, or if I'm in a liquor store, I buy two bottles and then I see another store, and I buy a third, and they all know, the ones who sell me the stuff. She's fat because she drinks and she drinks because she's fat and she keeps buying clothes so she has something she can get into. I'm so sad about this sometimes I sit in my room and cry and tell myself not to go to the kitchen, not to check on the kids, just sit there on the bed and put the knitting on my lap to cover the bottle and then I pull it out and take a swig and put it back and cry and it's been the same piece of knitting for months. Supposedly a scarf. I feel like using it to hang myself with. Thanks for listening. If I'm going to turn things around, it's going to be here.

***

Hello, my name is Libby. I'm an alcoholic. When I got pregnant the second time, four years after my first, I told myself I couldn't drink for the baby's sake, and I stopped. I didn't want the baby drunk along with me, simple as that. Same blood, same oxygen, same booze. I did not want that. In a way the baby was like my first meeting, like being with you, before she was even born. I would talk to her and say, "If you're going to live and grow in me, I'm going to keep you safe there." How did I do it? That's not something I exactly know. This big realization, I guess, that when it came to a second baby if I wasn't careful, I'd lose her in the strange way I lost my first. I don't mean a miscarriage. I mean my husband would take the baby away from me when he came home. I don't know if I can explain how he does it—he still does it if he has time—but he walks the children through the city, and I gather he tells them all sorts of things. I ask them what he said when they come home. My boy won't really say. It's like his secret, he has to keep it from me. My girl isn't that way. She tells me it was something about the history of New York or a building or why so many different looking people live here. Sometimes they sit. It could be on a bench or a wall. And my husband will ask them what they are thinking and what they see, and when he brings them home, he's all talked out, and just like after the first baby, bam, I took up drinking again, and I have kept on drinking. I'm an alcoholic. It's sort of what I am, and what would I be if I wasn't? I'm not sure anymore. I came here from Syracuse one weekend, and all these years have passed, and I'm not anybody except a drinker. I have a name, but that's not what makes me me. The vodka, the gin, whatever I can latch onto, then I'm me. I broke my pledge two hours after I left here on Tuesday. I kept breaking it until last night and this morning. I had to stop because I couldn't come here and talk to you when I was loaded. It would humiliate me. Okay, so I made it, but I feel really uncomfortable. I'm not right. Thank you for listening.

***

Hello, my name is Libby. I'm an alcoholic. My husband isn't interested in me. My kids love me, I know they do, but they're kids, and each of them has the kind of distance and independence their father has. They live for him to come home at night and give them a walk almost like they're dogs, or on a weekend he'll take them on a subway up town or to Brooklyn or somewhere and go to a museum and have lunch and then walk home. I can't do that. My feet won't take it. Once he asked me to go along when he planned a picnic in Central Park, and I could see how sad the children would be if I didn't say yes. But I hid a bottle in the basket and fell asleep almost right away. It was humiliating; I had a chance to be with them, and I blew it. I don't know how to say how bad that hurt me. I don't talk much anyway, I mean other than here. My husband and son are naturally quiet, too, so the apartment is almost as quiet when they're there as when I'm alone. Even my little girl is a better listener than talker. My own family, when we go to Syracuse, I panic with them. It's not panic like going crazy. It's panic that gives me the sense that they're sorry for me, and yet they blame me. My husband has a worn out look to him. How long will he last? That's what they blame me for. He has to deal with me, and that must be terrible, they think. So absolutely the worst time I ever had was when I drank too much up there in Syracuse and they put me in the car for the trip home, and I didn't even know it until we were almost in Manhattan. I just sat there crying. Why would I ever want to go back? My mother calls and asks how I am, and you know what she means. She means am I drunk. She means am I ever going to be fit to have in her house again. It's terrible to say, but what about her? What about the rest of my family? Are they all perfect? I won't go on. This is supposed to be about me, not them. Thanks for listening.

***

Hello, my name is Libby. I'm an alcoholic. Alf is my sponsor, and he encouraged me to come here, but I sometimes think he should give up on me. I go to the store and watch my hand move and I've got the bottle. Okay, am I going to put it back? But what could it hurt, a drink or two? No, I don't put it back. By the time the kids are home from school, I'm kind of cruising, and I know I can make it the next few hours through their homework and getting dinner on the table and my husband coming home if he doesn't work late. But if he does come home, he'll sit at the table and I'll feel so guilty about what he goes through, all I want is to sneak a drink, pour it in my coffee if I have to. Why does he work so hard? Sometimes all night? I know what you think, but I don't think it's a woman, not that I could blame him. Nothing is like what it was for us when we first met. Then it was the big city and my new guy and I loved it, we both loved it, and I would hike everywhere with him, owning the place. But then you get pregnant and there's a point where for some of us, that's almost it for walking. I had a phobia that the varicose veins would stay, and after the baby, they did, so I would not walk. I read magazines, I turned life into alcohol, I made it foggy and sad and hard. That's what I did. Now I sit at home thinking I'm coming here and what will I say? Should I say what I say to Alf? Is that all right? It is? He's such a nice guy who lives across the way in Peter Cooper Village, and he could see what I was going through because he had been through it himself. We would be a better couple than me and my husband if just saying what was on your mind is what made you a couple, but please, I'm not saying what you might think I'm saying. My husband's had a hard time, too. You live with a man long enough, and even if he doesn't tell you everything all at once, he tells you everything one way or another in bits and pieces, sometimes only with his face. A face of a certain kind can only come from a certain kind of life. My father, he had a machinist's face. My brothers have it, too. They've made everything: ball bearings, bushings, washing machines, pipes, transmissions. And as time passes the metal worker gets a kind of hard burn. That's the best way I can put it. The drinker? I look at myself and I see I'm out of it and I want to learn to let my panic out. I don't want to keep drowning it. Three days now I haven't had a drink. The hardest days of my life. Anyway, my husband, he's got a thin face, and a telling face, a face that says he works too hard and isn't sure he'll get where he wants to go. He has this wealthy cousin he grew up with for a while, and he does things for him so he can be on his cousin's level. I don't know what the arrangement is, but if he gets anywhere, it won't be at his day job, it will be with his cousin, who gives him this other work which he won't discuss. Things, he says. I ask what money it brings in. He won't say that, either. All he'll say, he said this once, was that what he does for his cousin is really for Ralph and Cynthia, our kids. Ralph is lanky like him, and Cynthia is more full, like me, although with girls pears can become champagne glasses, if you know what I mean. And what is my contribution? Get on the wagon, stay on the wagon, don't make things worse, but what I see in the morning is the puffiness, and what mortifies me is what I see when I think of the pictures Alf showed me of cirrhosis of the liver, how it gets hard, twisted, and ugly with scars. My nurse after I had Cynthia, when I hadn't even been drinking, I didn't know right away why she said it, but she turned talking about how painful giving birth is to the most painful of deaths, and finally I realized she was on to me. The most painful death is dying of cirrhosis of the liver, she said, and she wanted me to know that because she could see my past in my face. She said those patients had to be in private rooms whether they could afford it or not. The doors needed closing. There's no scary movie like cirrhosis of the liver. I remember her putting it just like that, but what good did it do? I went back to drinking as soon as I stopped nursing. Cynthia got the bottle, and I got the bottle, too. Thanks for listening.

***

Hello, my name is Libby. Yesterday, I went into a bar because I didn't want vodka in the house, and I had kept it out for five days, but then I thought, *Well, this would be easy. One and out.* How could I think that knowing I should go to a phone booth, and Alf would come get me and stop me? But I went in and had a vodka martini, and another and another. A man bought me the last one. We do not want to focus on sex, I know. We want to focus on alcohol, but I had not had a man look at me that way in a long time, and as part of what I've been trying to do, I'd been to the beauty parlour and there I was, listening to *his* story. He said he was a diehard Yankees fan. Now what would I say to that? I don't know anything about baseball. All I could think was he needed someone to win for him because he was a loser, but I have not been intimate with my husband in almost two years, and this man put his hand on top of mine, and I almost went for it. I just barely got away and wasn't sure I could make it home. But I did. And when I got there, somehow there was a pint of vodka in my purse, and I drank it. After that I called Alf. He said I should come here for the 7 o'clock meeting. I said I wasn't fit. He said okay, come today then, which I have, because he knows, he really knows. If you were in a little boat and there was a giant iceberg next to you all the time, wouldn't you know? Thank you for listening.

**

Hello, I'm Libby. I'm an alcoholic. It's a week now, the longest without a drink since I've been coming here, but I'm still an alcoholic. I always will be an alcoholic. I accept that, and I have said it to you, but I have not said it to my husband, and I knew I had to tell him I come here, so I did the other night and it went badly. When we were alone in the living room, I said that everyone has problems in their life, and I certainly had, and I could not solve them with alcohol anymore. I could never solve them that way, so I had to face the fact that the first problem was the alcohol. I told him I am an alcoholic and come here and will have to keep coming here and maybe if I did, I could get at other problems. Like what problems, he asked. Like my weight, I said. Like our marriage, our family. As soon as I said family, his expression changed. He's so thin and lined and worn out that it's almost impossible for his expression to grow hard, but it did. Like a stone. He said we had beautiful, wonderful children. I said yes, and it was a miracle, given what has happened to me, and he said what has happened to me had nothing to do with them. Just stop drinking and stop talking about it. I said I had to talk about it. I couldn't get better if I didn't talk about it. Well, it upset him terribly, and then I made my worst mistake of all. I asked if refusing to discuss this was because his mother was an alcoholic who never admitted it and died from it. I asked if he felt guilty about his mother and about me. I wanted to know what he felt about it, or if he didn't feel anything at all, was it that bad? He isn't well himself. I've told you that—his heart. And me talking about this, it was like looking at him dying. He wasn't, but that was how he looked to me, just like he was dying right there before my eyes. Are you all right? I asked him. Do you need your pills? And he said no. What he needed was for me to do what he told me. Stop drinking and stop talking about it and never mention his mother again. And that was the end of the conversation, and you know all I wanted was a drink, but I didn't have any in the apartment, I'm trying so hard I really didn't, so I went into the bedroom and put my head under the pillow and cried and wished I were as dead as his mother. All the time I ask myself, Am I ever going to find my way back? How am I going to climb glass walls and squirm through the neck of the bottle? I mean, people can see me in there, can't they? Don't they know that's where I'm trapped? Thank you for listening. Right now it feels like you're all I've got.

the only good thing about getting older

When she was a little girl, Sheila wished she lived alone, happier to settle whatever she had on her mind by herself as opposed to letting someone else into her thoughts and feelings. Nothing was ever settled with her family, and understanding why not was impossible. One thing always crashed into another. It was safer to fight and dislike than to get along and love. Being at fault almost seemed right. She was eight when she had it spelled out for her: fair didn't matter. She hated that. If they couldn't love each other, couldn't they at least be fair? She wished everyone else would just disappear. Let her fix her own breakfast, put Band-Aids on her own cuts, forgive life for what it did to her, and make her own mistakes.

Upstairs her parents slept in the largest bedroom, Ted slept in a smaller bedroom, and she slept in a very small bedroom with a slanted ceiling. They had bare wood floors everywhere because her father didn't want a vacuum cleaner. To the extent he could help it, he didn't want any machines in the house. At his gas station he spent all day leaning over fenders or down in the pit messing with nuts and screws and wrenches and grease. So he wanted a quiet, simple, well-swept and dusted house that had to have plumbing and electricity and a refrigerator and an oven, but he never gave in to a dishwasher or a dryer, just a washing machine. He didn't want pets, either. He'd grown up on a farm to the west, near the border with

Bluefield County, that had every kind of animal, and he had to take care of them all—pigs, chickens, cows, mules, goats, guinea hens—and he wanted nothing to do with them and their appetites and wastes, as he put it, reducing an animal to that phrase, not a mule but an appetite and its wastes, not a kitty but an appetite and its wastes. He had lugged feed pails through the squish of their wastes, and he had shovelled their wastes and smelled them and hauled them in a hand-pulled cart and wanted no more. When he was old enough to drive, ten, he got into the family truck, pushed his legs out as far as they could go and navigated by looking under the top of the steering wheel and just over the horizon of the dashboard, so trucks and later cars did make sense to him. He could squirm in the truck's innards and fix things no one else could reach. He had an ear for what was broken and went right to the spot. He did not like to touch an animal, but he would steel wool a rust speckled chrome bumper until you couldn't tell it wasn't new.

At the dinner table his hands bespoke his mechanical life. He had two fingernails that were permanently blue underneath. He had a missing fingertip and a finger that stayed crooked all the time. His skin was always a little pink, almost raw, from the way he scrubbed his hands with something called Mione soap, a rough, sandy kind of grit that hardened as its can rusted on the shelf beside the faucet near the kitchen stairs out back.

Her mother was afraid of her father. If they began fighting, her mother got a screech in her voice, as though she had a baby owl in her throat. Her father detested that sound and would order her to go to their bedroom. Her mother would have to stay there while her father settled into his rocking chair in the parlour and fished out a *Nettles Neat* that he would light with a match cupped inside his hand as if there were a wind in the parlour, though the only wind in the parlour was him, and the only clouds were his exhalations of smoke, and the only smell, after he had been to the sideboard, was the bite of his moonshine mixed with what he called a dab of water.

When Sheila was little and crawled onto his lap to be read to, he made her do the fitting of their bodies, never adjusting to her needs. After he read for a few minutes, he said, "Okay, that's it. Go help your mother in the kitchen. Learn your cooking." But in the kitchen Sheila did not get to do much because her mother prepared meals with cautious precision in line with her father's liking and a little girl either would get the amount of flour wrong or not get all the silk out of the rows of corn on the cob or be spattered with hot grease or spill milk or put her hands in things where they did not belong. She would eat cookie dough before the cookies were baked. She would stick a finger in the ice cream maker when she was supposed to just keep cranking. She would ruin a piece of aluminium foil that could be used again. So she kept out of her mother's way, pretending to be efficient in sweeping up dirt Ted tracked in after football or baseball practice.

Even when Ted wasn't that big, he seemed big to her. His clothes were what they called husky, but he was springy. In baseball he was a catcher who could leap up and throw a base stealer out when he was nine years old. In the county football league he played guard and would drive defensive linemen up into the air before knocking them to the ground. He only was allowed two sports because his father said he would look ridiculous on a basketball court. Instead he had to help at the gas station after school in the winter and in the late summer when the baseball season was over. His job was to hand his father things and pump gas. When the children were both in school, their mother did those things, plus managing the cash register and the crackers and peanuts and sodas they sold in the office. After dinner she would tote up the cash, match it to the receipts, and enter everything into her long green ledger book while her father sat in his rocker, smoking *Nettles Neats* and sipping his moonshine with its dab of water.

He hated television because Ted and Sheila squabbled over what to watch and the reception was a snow storm unless he got up and adjusted the rabbit ears all the time. They lived in a crease in the woods that fouled up the signals coming from Nettles. The houses nearest them were a pretty good walk. Sheila liked walks for various reasons. She had friends to see along the main road and up gravel side roads where their mothers served milk and cookies or pie because she had a certain status. Her father was a Burke, not the kind of Burke who was rich, but at least he had his own business. Other fathers didn't. Almost all of them worked for the rich Burkes' dying tobacco business in Nettles and certainly would lose their jobs, or had lost them, whereas Sheila's father only had been a mechanic for *Nettles Neats* ("Rolled Right, Wrapped Tight") long enough to accumulate the money he needed to buy the gas station and get away from the government's attacks on tobacco, tobacco farming, tobacco advertising, and tobacco smoking, so the theory was that he could never be put out of work like her friends' fathers.

Greentail Falls County was not, strictly speaking, tobacco country, only a point of assembling, packaging, marketing, and distributing tobacco, all of which was concentrated in Nettles, the county seat. Thanks to the rich Burkes, or the right Burkes, or the lucky Burkes or whatever you wanted to call them, Nettles had the auction and warehouse facilities and exclusive use of the wondrous cigarette-making machine that transformed the industry. So the other fathers in Greentail Falls County would drive to work in Nettles, leaving behind the thickly forested piedmont hamlets where they lived. In turn Sheila's father sold them gas and kept their cars and trucks running. But even early on he deduced, and therefore the entire family deduced, that his little station was in a precarious position. Changes affecting other families had to affect his family and not for the better.

The rich Burkes were so rich that they probably did not even realize they were cutting and running. They probably thought that Lemuel Burke's creation of the university named for him kept them where they'd made their fortune even after they left. They understood Nettles would wrinkle, rot and shrivel, but the university would keep it on the map even after new Burke fortunes were made in power companies and banks and insurance and drug companies in places like Charlotte and Atlanta. What did they care about the folk they left behind in Nettles, much less Greentail Falls County?

Sheila didn't have to be very old to grasp the fact that the only safe place near at hand lay within Burke University's seven mile stone wall, wrapping snake-like around its wondrous campus with its giant trees and ponds and meadows and lawns and manicured quadrangles and winding walkways among the grey granite castles that served as school buildings and dormitories and dining halls and libraries and gymnasiums. She was smart and always got A's. Tests were like stopping a moment to tie her shoelace. Ted and her father did not seem to like that any more than they seemed to like her in general. Her mother was the one who signed the report card.

Increasingly home life revolved around Exxon making noises about cutting ties with her father and Ted hogging the bathroom. When he came out, he would bring his latest pimples to their mother who would tell him they would go away and stop popping them, but then he would go right back into the bathroom, lock the door, and stare at his face, apparently. Not pooping that long, certainly not peeing. Just messing with his speckled face, for which Sheila felt sorry and which she also feared. Ted said that if he had acne this bad, her face would look like a baboon's ass when she was thirteen.

The only thing good about getting older, he confided, was sex. He knew some girls who were getting ready, and so was he. Before long, he said, some boy would try to show her what he meant; but that boy better watch it. Ted wasn't having anyone getting all over his sister, much less inside her. How exactly would that happen, she asked. He showed her his penis when it was erect once and told her that's what would get inside her, right up her pussy. He chased her out of his bedroom with it and almost caught her.

The person who did catch her was the Sunday school teacher,

Miss Hartness, a thin, gentle single woman with a long face, large smile and soft voice who lived with her widowed old father down one of those gravel roads. The girls and boys had separate classes in the basement so they would not fuss with each other, and of course there was a Boys' bathroom and a Girls' bathroom. That's where it happened. Miss Hartness had a rule that no girl could go down the hall in the middle of the class to tinkle unless she went along to make sure everything was all right. The girl would sit on the toilet and pee, and then Miss Hartness would hand her some toilet paper to dry herself off. "Good and dry now?" she would ask, insisting the girl spread her legs so she could see that the task had been performed properly. Sometimes she would reach down to the girl's ankles and pull up her panties for her when she stood up. But other times Miss Hartness would tell the girl, told Sheila once, "Now, honeybee, that's still damp," and she would take a few pieces of fresh toilet paper and pat the girl, patted Sheila, and rub back and forth and ask if that felt good.

Sheila suspected that Miss Hartness had no business down there, but she liked Miss Hartness gently making her feel warm and buzzy between her legs. She said yes, it felt good.

One Sunday after Miss Hartness took care of Sheila in the Girls bathroom, she said she had to pee, too, and asked if Sheila would help her get dry. Sheila knew women were hairy because her mother was hairy. She was surprised at how hairy Miss Hartness was, though. Miss Hartness said this was exactly the problem for her, how wet it all got. She stood, and Sheila pressed the toilet paper up between her spread legs, and Miss Hartness said no, she had to rub a little, not just pat, and get in past the hair into the crack because that's where she sometimes dripped even after she was finished. Sheila rubbed a little, exactly as Miss Hartness had just rubbed her, and Miss Hartness's hips began to move back and forth toward Sheila and then suddenly Miss Hartness began trembling like a quivering arrow that had hit its mark. At the same time she made a choked kind of moan. Sheila thought she must have hurt

Miss Hartness, but Miss Hartness pulled Sheila's head to her belly and held it there, and after a bit she said she was all right. "Now let's hurry back to class," Miss Hartness said, because the other girls were waiting.

Sheila told a girl about this new part of going to the Girls' bathroom with Miss Hartness, and the girl told her mother who told Sheila's mother who told Sheila's father. This was on a Monday night, right after he came home. She told him in their bedroom where he was changing out of his work clothes, and there was yelling, and then her mother came out of the bedroom having been pushed, hard, calling for Ted to go see his father while she went into Sheila's room with her and shut the door.

Her mother called her a name she'd never heard before and grabbed her by the hair, hurting her, and then pulled her to her waist, almost the way Ms Hartness had done, and began crying.

Finally she kneeled down to look Sheila right in the face and said, "You don't ever let anyone touch you like that again, do you understand? Never, never, never."

Sheila began crying, too. She promised she wouldn't. Then she heard her father and Ted come out of her parents' bedroom and bang down the stairs and out the front door. She asked her mother where they were going. Her mother hissed that the devil had gotten into their church, but the devil wouldn't get away with it.

She grabbed at her mother to get closer. They tumbled on Sheila's bed and lay there, holding each other, Sheila saying that she was sorry, and her mother saying Sheila wouldn't be the one who paid, and Sheila feeling that she had done something Jesus would never forgive.

They fell asleep. When they woke, it was dark, and her father and Ted were coming back into the house. Ted's footsteps were the ones they heard running up the stairs. Her father's footsteps didn't come for an hour or more. He must have been sitting downstairs in his rocking chair, drinking moonshine and smoking *Neats*. Sheila and her mother were too frightened to go see.

They got under the covers fully clothed. Sheila lay there smelling her mother's hair and her breath and the laundry soap smell on her blouse. It seemed like the night would never end. Ted coming out of the bathroom didn't end it. Her father heavily and slowly climbing the stairs didn't end it. That night was the longest night of her life. She lay there praying and pleading and listening to the rasping of her mother's breathing and being afraid to go out and pee. So in the grey light of dawn, she ending up wetting the bed.

When her mother realized what had happened, she snapped, "What have you done? Are we going back to *this*?"

Sheila had no idea what to say. She felt like a green leaf turning yellow in the autumn, drying up and falling. Her mother pushed her out of bed. There Sheila stood, soaked with pee, just like the sheets.

"You've got to grow up!" her mother whispered. "No more of this, you hear?"

At school that day she heard that Miss Hartness and her father had died—their house burnt down, they couldn't get out—and she felt terrible, especially when the girl she had told about the last time she went to the bathroom with Miss Hartness said they couldn't be friends anymore. "I'm not allowed. I have to forget the awful things you said. You tell too many lies. I hate you!" The girl began crying and ran across the playground to get away. Sheila did not try to follow. She stood by herself and watched some other girls jump rope without asking to join in. They counted to a hundred and fell in a pile, laughing because they'd made it. No one bothered about her standing there, not doing anything, just standing there.

The next Sunday when the family squeezed into the car and drove to church, she would not get out. She fought and struggled and held on. Ted grabbed one leg, her father the other. Her mother cried at them to stop. Whenever they got one of Sheila's hands loose, she tightened harder with the other. She pulled her foot right out of her shoe. She twisted onto the ground when she couldn't hold on any longer and made such a mess of herself she could not possibly go into the church. So they left her in the car. Every Sunday for the next month she sat through the service out there. After that her father and mother just gave up. They went to church with Ted and left her behind, which was how she liked the house best, having it empty and all to herself.

Ted began to hate her, too. He called her a troublemaker. He said maybe she couldn't tell the difference between a boy and a girl, so maybe he ought to show her again. He pushed her into her room and closed the door and said what if they both got naked, how would she like that?

She told him she wouldn't like it. He pulled her hair and grabbed her in a hammerlock and knuckled her head. He put his hand over her mouth so no one could hear her crying. She was just so dirty, he told her. Now he'd have to wash with Mione soap, too. But first he forced her on her bed and lay on her, twice as big as she was, so that she could not move and felt his boner right through his jeans.

He was so angry at her that it happened again and again. All she could do was get out of the house, go off alone, avoid him and other people, too. She stopped raising her hand in school and sometimes tried to spend a whole day without saying a word or, if it was a weekend, hearing anyone else say a word. She thought about what happened in the Girls' bathroom so much she wore holes in it and it wasn't there to think about anymore. Her problem was Ted. Was he upstairs or downstairs? Had he come home from wherever he'd been? Had he gone to wherever he was going? Why was he doing these things to her? Why did he hate her so much? That's what she thought about, not Miss Hartness. What did Miss Hartness look like? Sheila couldn't picture her. All she knew was that she was at fault, her, staring at herself in the mirror.

Then one day when she was eleven, Ted said Miss Hartness's name as he began grabbing her wrist and pushing her fingers back over double, and it was like the fault had a new face, his, because he was the reason why Miss Hartness and her father were dead, not her.

She remembered him and her father going out and coming back that night and knew where they went and what they did. She said so. Ted became really upset. He smacked her face and said the person he would kill would be her if she ever said that again. But then he offered to make her a deal. He would lay off if she would shut up. She asked how long he would lay off. He said he would lay off forever. She didn't believe him, but she could see how scared he was so she agreed to his deal. If she said anything, Ted and her father would go to jail. Sometimes she pictured them that way, her father in a jail for men, Ted in a jail for boys. It helped her live in the same house with them. When they smacked or punched her, she knew she could tell and hurt them worse.

She began to have feelings about boys, and boys who had ignored or stayed away from her began to notice her and talk to her. She liked that. She used peroxide on her hair, creating trouble at home but a stir away from home, part of her reputation. She didn't just want a bra, she needed one. Her mother and father and Ted didn't want to see her without one. She wasn't welcome at the breakfast table in her nightgown. Dress first.

She earned A's, but if a teacher who needed at least one person to answer a question turned her way, she lowered her face or looked out a window. To an extent she gained in popularity for this. She could not help being smart but tried hard to be normal. That's what she focused on, not things that had happened to her, not being part of her family or Ted's sister, who was really tough, just being herself. It took years, but it worked.

She kissed boys in the sequence of her attractions, only one boyfriend at a time, and let them touch her breasts but nothing lower even if she went lower herself in her bedroom and realized what Miss Hartness had been after. She didn't envision Miss Hartness or other women, though. She imagined boys. Guys in higher grades, not Ted's age, but older than Sheila, paid attention to her. There were firehouse and school dances, walks home, kissing in cars, French kissing, and the hostility toward her at home as increasingly they saw that she might need a bra but she didn't need her family.

Her mother warned her sex could hurt you even if you weren't a little girl being fondled by a sick woman. She said her father insisted on sex even when she had her period and the more he pushed and grabbed, the less she felt. Men didn't know when to stop. "And I can't say anything or he'll slap me just like he slaps you. It's his one pleasure in life, but it's certainly not mine."

She knew it wasn't his one pleasure in life. He also liked to smoke and drink and boss everyone else, Ted the most. Someone had told him Ted could get a sports scholarship to college, and he would belittle the idea or turn it around to demand that it happen so someone else could take up feeding him. If Ted reached for another pork chop or more mashed potatoes, he'd flinch halfway and glance toward their father and say, "Well, someone's got to eat it. You want it?" And their father might say yes even if he wasn't hungry and their mother would get up and find something else to bring to the table for Ted, more bread, more milk, the scrapings from the mashed potato pot, a slice of pie that was almost half the pie because, she said, she wasn't having any, Ted could have her share.

When she was fourteen, Ted told her to stop messing with boys if she didn't want to get them hurt. So he was back at it, trying to bully her, and made her angry, and she asked him what it felt like knowing what he'd done. She thought that would stop him, but it didn't. He said, "If I was Dad, I would have thrown you in the fire with them. So stop giving it to guys, or I'll do it on my own."

"I'm not giving anything to guys."

"That's not what I hear."

"Because guys like you lie about what they can't get."

Ted laughed and said his girlfriend Dixie gave him everything she had. "And her tits are twice the size of yours."

When she was fifteen, a university medical centre doctor and some nurses started a free clinic once a week. They held it in the school gym and set up pleated cloth screens on stands and needed volunteers to help some of the older people get inside or to sign their names or to sit with them after they had stitches or a boil lanced and needed time to compose themselves and get the blood back up into their heads. She signed up.

The university medical centre was in Nettles proper, then came the university on the western edge of the city, and then the county, which was bigger and more spread out and poorer than the doctor and nurses understood. There was no good way to get around except on foot or a bike if you were a kid or in a truck or a car if you were an adult, but many older folks and sicker folks did not have a truck or car and couldn't walk or bike like a kid.

Sheila knew about these people and approached a nurse and suggested that just coming to the high school gym wasn't enough. There were people who needed house visits. The nurse talked to the young doctor in charge. He invited Sheila to figure out where they should go and how they should notify people they would be coming. Sheila loved setting this up. She collected information, helped create circulars, got them distributed and was asked to go along with a nurse and the doctor, a second-year resident named Robert Heilbronn, for a weekly afternoon ride in a medical centre van stocked with supplies. They started with assessments in shacks and trailers and often came upon situations that required immediate treatment—bandaging, antibiotics, sometimes stronger drugs or giving someone a new cane or a foam toilet seat. Many cases were worsened by the conditions in which a person lived. As Robert (Sheila called him that) and the nurse, who sometimes was Nancy and sometimes Betty, tended the patient, Sheila scrubbed sinks and cleared out trash and fixed jammed windows and carried in wood. She also was given chances to administer ear drops, take temperatures and things like that.

One day the clinic staff brought her a uniform like the nurses wore with a name tag that said *Sheila Burke, Volunteer*, of which she was quite proud. She'd dress in the girl's locker room and spend two hours out in the gym and then head into the county with Robert and one of the nurses. Robert may have just become a doctor, but he already had a way about him that settled people. As he talked with patients for a few minutes to get to know them, he conducted a visual examination. When she asked about this, he told her all the basic indicators: skin colour and tone, health of eyes, lips, teeth, even fingernails, and posture, very important. And of course there always was the weight question: too fat, too thin. And mood, spirit, energy level, enthusiasm or depression. Affect, he called that, a person's feelings.

After Robert looked a patient over, he investigated with his ophthalmoscope, stethoscope, otoscope, pressure cuff, and patella hammer. Sheila memorized the names of all these instruments and asked questions about them as she, Robert, and the nurse drove from place to place in the van. Robert liked talking and was good at it, just as he was good with patients. His plan was to go overseas and work for a relief agency once he had finished his residency. The nurses sometimes teasingly would return to a question that had been discussed before: did he intend to do this alone, not marry? Robert would say he would have to put that off. When he came home, there would be time for a wife and a family. For now he just wanted to do things like what they were doing in Greentail Falls County, getting out of the hospital, going to the illness, not waiting for the illness to come to him.

Before overtime expenses kept the nurses from automatically travelling on these extra rounds, Robert's dove grey eyes would flicker up into the rear-view mirror so that he could see Sheila in the back seat when he was speaking to her. He told her more than once that this outreach program never would have happened were it not for her and that he hoped she'd think about applying to Burke University when the time came. Was she related to the Burkes? Oh, no, definitely not, she said, and she could never afford it. He said she'd be offered a scholarship. He'd bet on it. In fact, one day he brought a letter of recommendation for her. She had never read anything more flattering, especially the last line where he said that for every opportunity the world gave Sheila to learn and grow, she'd return the gift many times over.

If they went to a place where the person didn't have heat, or enough to eat, or the rain came through the roof, Robert would ask Sheila if she could prepare a note and send it to the County Department of Social Services. He gave her stationery and said she could sign for him. The notes would begin: "On an outreach medical visit in Greentail Falls County, I noticed a few non-medical issues I would like to bring to your attention." Then Sheila would list the issues and sign the note and give it to the women in the high school's front office who would get it over to Social Services.

Eventually Sheila told herself that she either had a crush that wouldn't go away or she actually loved Robert Heilbronn because she could not stop thinking about him. All she wanted was some sign that he understood, though she told herself— and imagined—that if he gave her more than a little sign, she would take it. She'd like to lose her virginity for real this time and leave poor Miss Hartness behind forever. She definitely was not a lesbian. She'd proved that with boy after boy.

One spring day she and Robert went to see an old man with an ingrown toenail. It was a long ride out there, and Sheila talked the whole way about how she definitely wanted to be a nurse. The clinic had convinced her this was her calling. Robert endorsed what she was saying and laughed with her about some of the grisly maladies that they had seen together. "Morgue humour," he told her. On the way back he drove slowly, and they had the windows down, and she put her hand beside her on the seat, and as she wanted, he put his hand on top of it. She didn't pull away.

In the most natural way he said, "I suppose you've had classes in sex education?"

She said, "I've had classes, not much practice."

"I like the way you put that."

"To be perfectly honest, I'm a virgin. Not that I'm proud of it. Just born that way."

They laughed. He squeezed her hand and held on to it. They were in the woodlands, passing notches beside the road every now and then where hunters would pull over and follow trails during hunting season. But it wasn't hunting season. The understory of the woods displayed patches of colour—a redbud, a dogwood, smaller trees largely out of place among the pines and oaks and ironwood and poplars.

He asked her if she'd like to pull over and take a walk and have a look at things. She didn't even have to answer. She wanted to take a walk with Robert more than she'd ever wanted anything in her life. That was obvious.

He had a condom and was as gentle as any virgin could hope—probably because he knew exactly what he was pushing through—until he began to have his orgasm. There was no escaping him. She was pinned on the forest floor, but thrilled to be witnessing a Robert beyond any Robert she'd ever seen before.

They did this on three outreach trips in a row, but when what would have been the fourth time came, Robert didn't show up. Instead the nurse named Betty came alone and when they had finished the clinic in the gym, she said to Sheila, "Now I want you to come to the Girls room with me before we go off in the van."

Sheila hesitated and said she didn't need to go to the bathroom, but what Betty had in mind was not that. She wanted to give her a pregnancy test, and she wanted to look her over for any signs of venereal disease or lice. Sheila pretended she didn't understand and then dropped that and began to weep as a real examination took place.

Betty removed her latex gloves and took a step back. She was a woman in her forties whose elbows were dimples in the fat.

"Sheila, here is how it is: I've been watching, I've been seeing, I told him to stop it, he didn't stop it, so now he's not coming back. You both have too much at stake for this to get out of hand. You've got to understand you're a woman now. Any time you want a man to do it with you, you certainly can figure out how to get him to play along, but first you'd better think long and hard about whether it's really right and worth it."

Betty didn't humiliate her at all. She said Sheila could still volunteer and do outreach, but she could never be alone with a doctor again.

"We could lose the whole clinic. You don't want that, do you?"

"No, I don't."

"Then keep your legs closed when we're out here, all right?

"All right."

"And don't forget that we all have sex, nothing wrong with it and nobody's fault. It's just not your time yet, but it will be soon, I promise. Now let's get on with treating people who are really sick."

Betty put her arm over Sheila's shoulder in a friendly way and walked with her out to the van. The strangest thing was how soft she was when Sheila took a misstep and kind of bounced against her. They both laughed at that. So for the simple pleasure of it Sheila did it again. She didn't know when in her life she'd ever felt anything that soft, and it made her start to cry like a little girl.

do you even know i exist?

A message appeared on Alison's smartphone accompanied by a photo of a woman who looked like what she'd look like in a few years. The message read: "Do you even know I exist?" Sender: Margot Morton.

Alison called her mother who said it must be some prank.

The next morning, another message: "I'm your half-sister."

Alison called her mother again. "What *is* this?"

"Delete it, dear. These social media are dangerous."

"But what do you think?"

"We've been thinking about visiting. Charlottesville's getting dreary. Are you free for dinner tonight? We can discuss it if you want."

It was getting cold in DC, too, the dark red brick townhouses across the street were patched with dying, yellowed vines. People on the footpath wore hats and gloves. "Yeah, I'm free. I just sent you the message and her picture. You'll see what I mean."

Down in Charlottesville Eve looked at the photo. Her husband Mark was out back, raking leaves. Margot Morton looked like him, the straight nose, the colouring, trust-inspiring temples and rounded forehead.

For dinner they asked Alison's brother Tom to come down from Baltimore. The four of them regarded one another quizzically.

Eve said to the children, who weren't children anymore, "I'll let your father talk. Just keep in mind I know everything he'll tell you."

Mark told Tom and Alison that he had a relationship in Florida that ended when he came to DC to go into the Navy. He'd already met and married Eve when the woman showed up, eight months pregnant. She wanted child support until the child was eighteen. She also wanted Mark to never contact the child.

"So for eighteen years we paid child support and never heard from them," Mark said. "Biologically, she's your half-sister. Biologically, she's my daughter. But that's where it ends."

"Her name is Margot, and she uses your last name. That's not biological." Alison began to cry.

"Don't make a scene," Eve said.

"Tom?" Mark asked. "What do you think?"

Tom looked more like his mother, fair-haired, ears small, his shoulders on the broad side because he still was an obsessive swimmer. "What's done is done. It's more than eighteen years now. It's like …"

"Twenty-eight," Mark said.

Alison asked about Margot's mother. Mark said he was in the graduate program in biology at the University of Florida before he went into the Navy and started his business. She was a lab assistant who took care of the animals: frogs, snakes, alligators, Florida crocs.

Alison pressed for more details about the mother. "And her name?"

"Her name was Paula."

"What else?"

"What do you mean, what else? Have I ever asked you about your relationships?"

"Have I ever had a child I didn't tell you about?"

Eve intervened, "Alison, your brother's right: it's before your father and I even met."

"She's reaching out to me. I'm trying to figure out who she is."

Mark said, "All right, all right," calming things. He sipped his wine and made a few gestures with his hands, apparently toward his past—the guy he was, the girl he'd pursued. "It seemed to me she had a more intense relationship with the animals than me. Amphibians interested me, but I couldn't turn the corner from being an undergraduate in Gainesville to being a graduate. I had no idea she was pregnant when I told her about the Navy. Maybe she didn't, either. Anyway, she stayed in Gainesville and your mother and I were married when she showed up with her news."

"That was fast," Alison said.

"We were in love," Eve said sharply. She grasped Mark's forearm.

"Didn't you want to see the baby?" Alison asked.

"I told you, that was out," Mark said. "Her terms."

"But *now* wouldn't you want to see her?"

Eve said, "The answer is no. He doesn't."

"I was asking Daddy. She's got nothing to do with you."

Tom said, "Yes, she does. She and Dad both put a lot of money into her."

"I wasn't referring to money."

"Maybe that's ultimately what *she's* referring to, this Margot Morton," Eve said.

Alison said, "I don't think it's money. 'Do you even know I exist?' is like an accusation. I feel as though she's looking for some admission of guilt. Like I took her place. Daddy, you don't say anything."

Mark said he didn't know what to say.

***

Alison messaged Margot back. No, she hadn't known, but now she did. For her part she said was single, a lawyer, lived in DC, had a brother, Tom, a financial advisor in Baltimore, and her parents were retired in Charlottesville. What about you? Margot wrote that she was married, had three young children,

239

had worked in the same lab where her mother worked until Margot's second child—a girl—was born, and her husband insisted she stop working. And that brought up an issue. The children had three grandparents and a phantom. Margot didn't know anything about her father. For years her mother's answer had been it was just some man they didn't need to talk about. Their only contact was monthly support checks, which is how Margot discovered his last name and adopted it herself when she legally could.

Margot's husband Philip took her mother's side. He said the kids were fine, she should forget her father the way he forgot Margot. But once she began searching for this man surnamed Morton, it wasn't that difficult, first Google, then Facebook, then Alison's page, and the shock of seeing their resemblance to one another. It felt as though she'd never looked in a mirror until that moment, never been able to link her face to what must to resemble her father's face because Alison had it, too.

Alison sent Margot a picture of Mark. Now there were three who looked alike. A few days passed. Margot explained that she'd gone numb. She looked at Mark a hundred times. Finally she showed him to Philip. Philip grew angry. He seemed to feel he had a rival, someone more important to her than he.

They lived in a garden townhouse in Gainesville, one of three complexes Philip managed. The battle over Mark's picture raged wherever they could fight out of the children's hearing. He wanted a family meeting with his parents and her mother so that they could agree *they* were the ones committed to Margot, not this stranger. Margot shouldn't disturb the happiness they'd found with each other.

Margot said, "Happiness? I *was* happy until this. Happy with my life, with you, and with the children, but I'm not happy with your reaction. He can't take your place, Philip. That's not what this is about."

Philip was a large man. He'd been a football lineman at the University of Florida, playing in the stadium they called "The Swamp." He couldn't give up that connection, which was why he took over managing the townhouse complex he and his teammates had lived in. Then he took over a second student complex, and now a third, for adults. He picked her off her feet—they were in the laundry room—and held her as if demonstrating that nothing supported her in life except him.

"Put me down!"

"Tell me you're forgetting this first."

"I don't know what I'm doing except I do know you're being an idiot. Why can't I send messages to my half-sister?"

"Because you don't even know her."

"I'm getting to know her. We have the same father."

"You don't know him, either. I don't think your mother even knows him."

He put her down. The windowless room smelled of pine-scented soap.

"Don't do that to me again," Margot said. "Ever!"

That was what caused her to drive to the lab where her mother had been promoted to "curator," though the titles used behind her back were "The Snake Handler," or "The Snake Charmer," or "The Frog Woman," or "Curator Croc." But she enjoyed the researchers and their teasing. Like her they were at ease with amphibians, the most transitional beings in the evolutionary chain, not all one thing, not all another, ancient messengers in the air and in the water, rapacious and fugitive, timid and fierce.

Having worked there, Margot knew her way around the lab. The faecal scents, the rotted food stink, the skin slime odour, and the interspersed smells of medicines and heat lamps made a familiar world for her, duplicating the smells of collecting expeditions, time spent in boats, in turbid waters, in mud, in the breathtaking heat, helping her mother and the researchers bring in specimens: oak toads, spectacled caimans, snapping turtles, crocs, gopher frogs, blacksnakes, cotton-mouths, coachwhips …

Now here was this man, an image she pulled up on her mother's computer screen. "Is that my father?"

Paula Greenwood had a bundle of grey brown hair piled on top of her head to keep it out of the way. She lowered her glasses and stared at Mark for some time, examining his baldness, the wrinkles under his eyes, the boldness of his eyebrows. "I might say so if you asked me."

"I'm asking you."

"Where did find him?"

"Through his daughter Alison on Facebook."

Paula smiled. "But I got you and he didn't. I won." She patted Margot's wrist.

"You saw it as a competition?"

"When you've been left, it's nice to get something more valuable in return. Do we have to keep looking at him?" She turned off the computer screen and looked at Margot seated on the little plastic chair squeezed between her desk and the grey metal bookshelves in her tiny office. "I never said you didn't have a father."

"You never said I had a half-brother and a half-sister."

"Do you?"

"You didn't know?"

"No."

Margot was leaning forward, her forearms pressed between her thighs, the intimacy of a single mother and only daughter unshakeable. Only this one breach.

Paula said, "All I knew was he made the payments and I wasn't letting anyone else get me pregnant."

"He went into the Navy, then ship construction."

"Did he?"

"And he has three grandchildren."

"Really?"

"Yes, mine."

"Oh, I get it."

Paula flicked on the screen again. She looked at Mark as she might look at a new creature in the lab. What did you feed him? How much room did he need? What temperature? Mist him or give him a pool?

"I didn't want anything more from him than the child support."

"You *never* wondered about him?"

"I'd see things in you sometimes."

"Like what?"

"Your good teeth. Your nose and eyebrows."

"I feel like one of your things here, half this, half that."

"You do?"

Margot showed Paula a picture of Alison. "Yes, until I saw her. We're both obviously full of each other's genetic material. Philip's upset, but I want her to visit. I want him to visit, too."

Paula looked at the image of a daughter another woman had produced who matched the one she'd produced, feature for feature. "Maybe it would be easier if you went up there."

"You don't want to meet him?"

"I've met him, and I gather Philip doesn't want to."

"He's jealous and won't admit how ridiculous that is."

Paula studied Margot carefully. "Tell me again: why did you do this?"

Margot said, "I did it because there's a ghost in the family, and I don't want the kids to be scared of it. He's their grandfather."

Everyone liked Paula because she was quiet yet sometimes summed things up in a way that could lead to a dissertation or a complete book. "Biology takes care of itself automatically. It's human relations that lag behind."

"Isn't that reason to work on them, help them evolve?"

"You may not be evolved but I am. I went through that phase."

"If they came, would you see them?"

"I don't know. I just know your own family is more important than that one."

***

Gainesville had spread out, inflated by the expanding university the way a python is inflated when it swallows a white-tailed deer, yet Florida's relentless vegetation seized every gap, its natural green vividness contrasting with the tinted blue windows of buildings sealed against the heat and suggesting that this baking city had become rich by sucking nutrients from the deep, moist soil. Getting out of their rental car at the hotel, Alison and Mark felt sweat breaking out on their almost identical foreheads.

"Lord, it's hot," Alison said.

"Often is," Mark said.

"You lived here almost six years. It didn't drive you bananas?"

"Of course, and I've been bananas ever since."

She saw how nervous he was and asked if he wanted to rest before they did anything, and in a few minutes, he found himself lying on the bed in his room, the curtains drawn, staring at the stuccoed ceiling. Margot was his daughter, but Margot was a stranger, and he wasn't good with strangers.

Alison came to see him. "I just talked to her. She said anytime. It's three miles. Look at my phone map."

He pushed her phone map around with his fingertip, trying to get oriented. He didn't think there had been anything where Margot now lived, just seething scrublands that occasionally caught on fire and blackened the skies.

"Did you talk about anything?" he asked.

"Just that we're both excited."

"Mention me?"

"I said you were nervous."

"How did she react?"

"She didn't." Alison took the phone from him. "Daddy, I've told you: if this doesn't amount to anything, it's okay. There's no need to fake it."

"I'm not going to fake it."

"She did say she knew what you were studying when you met her mother—electrochemical activity in amphibian brains."

Mark shrugged. "I ended up wiring big ships. Go figure."

She realized she'd have to push him into the water. He wouldn't dive on his own. "Could we go now?"

"Well, it's what we're here for."

"Good."

They drove the three miles and pulled into an open parking space a few doors down from where Margot lived. A huge man in a basketball jersey, chinos, and flip-flops came down the footpath toward them before they could get out of their car.

"Maybe her husband," Alison said.

The man rapped on the driver's side window with his knuckles. Mark lowered it. The man reached in and grabbed Mark by the shirtfront. It was a violent action, preparatory to getting worse. He said he wanted them gone. "She's gotten this far without you, okay? So beat it." He let go and backed up a step to see if Mark understood.

Mark was no match for this guy in either size or age. He said, "Yeah, I got it," and turned on the car.

Alison said, "Daddy, no!"

Mark backed out of the slot and drove away with Alison yelling at him. Two blocks later he pulled over and rested his forehead against the steering wheel. "What in the hell? That's not worth it." Sweating again, despite the car's air conditioning.

Alison's phone rang. Margot. Alison relayed to Mark what she said. "She's sorry. Things are not good at home."

"I think we saw that," Mark said.

Alison returned to the phone: "Is there anywhere else we could meet?" she asked.

Mark tried to interrupt: "Alison, be careful now."

"Like a mall, or a park, somewhere he wouldn't ... I see, yes, right ... Okay, yes, we can find it. Tomorrow at ten ... Yes, see you then."

On her end, Margot disconnected and came out of the bedroom where she'd gone for privacy. She told herself she hadn't had a father or sister her entire life so she could live without them another day.

Philip started right away. "You think I went overboard."

"This grabbing people, you'll end up in jail."

"He's threatening that?"

"Of course not."

"I don't want you to see him."

Margot said, "I don't care what you want. They flew 1500 miles to get here."

She had been waiting for them with iced tea and sandwiches and thought when Philip saw them at the front door, he'd see two human beings, just two uncertain, brave but a little afraid human beings. What emerged, however, was not two human beings. What emerged before they even reached the door was one threatened beast. Philip started to say that he hadn't wanted them close enough to the house for the kids to see him chase them away. She cut him off. The kids, she knew, were only pretending to be occupied in the TV room, Sissy, the five-year-old, with Eric, the two-year-old, in her lap, and Roger, the four-year-old, ramming a red and yellow truck back and forth while making a growling sound that could be an imitation of a truck or could just as well be an imitation of Philip.

"Don't let's discuss it anymore, okay?" Margot said to Philip. "Because there's nothing to discuss. I wouldn't know what to say." Which wasn't true. She was upside down with things to say, bursting with them. That had been her father and sister out there. Not mirrors. Something real, something physically her.

***

Philip left for work the next morning and Margot left the children with Petra, their Venezuelan helper. She drove first to the university and parked outside the lab. Her mother was letting a grey rat snake slither down into her blouse and come out the sleeve of her left arm. A rat snake always wanted cover and always was surprised when the cover gave out. Paula laughed as she grasped its head and pulled it straight through. The odour of the place was especially pungent that morning.

"Did something die in here last night?" Margot asked.

Paula lowered the rat snake into its terrarium; it curlicued onto a tree branch and slithered quickly down into its subterranean lair. "Charlie Croc didn't finish his dinner."

Margot looked toward the crocodile pen. Half a juvenile wild hog had been stuffed under a piece of driftwood in the croc's bathing pool; its intestines floated on the surface of the water in long, mottled streamers.

"Can you come with me for an hour?" she asked Paula. "I'm going to meet my father and half-sister."

Paula laughed again, the sound drifting out of her like the hog's intestines. "I couldn't. I'd have to shower and change."

"Then shower and change. There's time."

"Where are you going to meet them?"

Margot said the Sunburst Mall because Philip had chased them away from the house yesterday. Paula rubbed her temple. She was thinking about this. That was clear, but no, she didn't think so.

"Really?" Margot asked.

"Baby, the relationship I had with that man was almost thirty years ago. I don't want to renew it."

"It wouldn't be worse than letting a snake crawl into your blouse."

Paula almost said the man had been in her blouse and elsewhere. She almost said they had sex like crazy and some days she smelled worse than this lab. She almost said her past was her business and she'd been good enough for her grandchildren by herself so far and would have to be forever.

But all she really said was, "I don't want to see him. He left. I didn't. Maybe that's why I prefer snakes."

Margot knew she couldn't prevail. "All right. I'll go alone."

The Sunburst Mall's central fountain pool surrounded an island upon which all the vegetation that grew in Gainesville struggled to coexist under the skylight. Lots of pennies, tarnished and bright, shimmered under the flow of water spouting out of the fountain.

Alison had had no better luck persuading Mark to come along than Margot had had with Paula. He said he preferred not to, not after yesterday. Alison said that's why the meeting would be in a public place, so Margot's husband wouldn't dare do anything. And Paula *might* come, to which Mark said that was of no consequence, Margot would be much more important.

"But not important enough to meet? Your own daughter?"

"You meet her. If it works ... I don't know. You could be disappointed, remember. You may not match up."

"We've long since been matched up. Because of you."

The prospect mortified him. He hadn't really unpacked, was more prepared to leave than stay. When Allison went downstairs to the rental car, he called Eve.

"She's meeting Margot at a mall."

"Where are you?"

"In my room. There was some unpleasantness yesterday. Margot's husband is against this."

"And the mother?"

"I probably feel just like Margot's husband. He doesn't want to lose Margot, and I don't want to lose Alison to a mistake I made before she was born."

"Mark, you won't lose her, and human beings aren't mistakes."

"Okay, but I prepared myself to face that yesterday, and I just can't manage it two days in a row."

"Once they meet, there will be a whole new evolution to this. We'll all get drawn in. You know that, don't you?"

"Because of the damn Internet."

"More than that."

They disconnected. He stretched out on the bed and stared at the ceiling. He remembered he had had eight amphibians in his project and mastered inserting sensors into their tiny brains. He remembered watching Paula leap off a boat naked once, and he didn't follow. Someone had to remain aboard to help her scrabble back in. And also to scan the swamp grass for the bulbous brown eyes of an alligator or croc, the ominous parting of the grass as the animal slid in. He'd gone through one year of graduate school but the second year threw him. Paula threw him. She only had her bachelor's degree and yet knew more than he ever would except for his tiny little specialty. He had the feeling that when he moved on, she'd stay and take up with the next guy like him and the one after, or if he didn't move on, he'd sink; in fact, he already was sinking in the bad idea of staying at the same school where he'd been an undergraduate; you couldn't hang around smoking dope and having sex forever without going under. That's what he thought then. He still thought it, but soon, Eve was right, things would evolve right past his thoughts.

The two young women saw one another at about fifty feet. Margot was sitting on the rim of the fountain pool, a human figure naturally complementing the thick vegetation on the little island behind her. When she rose, it turned out that she was several inches taller than Alison, though they looked, obviously, like sisters. Then the distance between them disappeared. They were embracing, ensnared in one another's bodies, salty tears drenching their eyes and cheeks, their hair commingled, their arms wrapped around one another, not trying to get out of an egg but into it, through its membrane, into the vital liquids and harmonies of a future more than a past.

into the dark soil

Katherine didn't know anyone was coming, only that Frank was in jail in Buenos Aires, pending extradition to Italy. She hadn't known he would be in Buenos Aires, either. Someone named Phil from the embassy in Rome called her. "But sit tight. We're working this out."

She fixed fruit, bread and tea for breakfast and didn't look for more information on the Internet, not that difficult to resist in her small stuccoed home with its patio, swimming pool, and big garden outside medieval Viterbo. At Wellesley she was a passionate classics major. The opportunity for Frank to have his final tour in Milan and then settle in Viterbo thrilled her. Everything old in her life was new, everything new was old. Her knowledge of Latin and the Romans was old, but coming into direct contact with all that now made it raw and vital.

She was a silver-haired woman of sixty with a nose that bespoke her Italian heritage (her maiden name was Agnelli, like the industrialists) who had lived in eight Spanish-speaking countries and spoke fluent Spanish but poor Italian and could hardly read Latin or Greek anymore. She had two grown daughters in the States and Frank in Buenos Aires and knew that panic was pointless. If she cut and buttered her bread cleanly, likewise her fruit, and let the tea steep and sat on the patio and looked over the flower beds and performed her mental exercises, she could hold onto some of her naturally calm self.

There were two exercises. First, you could half shut your eyes and let the blurriness draw the colours and shapes of what you were looking at into semi-abstract patterns that generated emotional effects you named: "jarring," "consoling," "intriguing," "sumptuous." This led you away from life's problems, and Katherine did it for a while. They had found the place, which extended beyond the garden to a crooked stream and then a hillside they didn't cultivate but might at some time. They said yes right away; that was how they beat the Roman money that probably would have outbid them. It still was expensive, but they sold their house in Maryland and rummaged an investment account, and now Katherine half focused on the scarf of flowers along the patio wall, the bright slash of lawn interrupted by the turquoise summons of the pool's water and then the garden's rows of Vergilian order. Georgics, that was the word she came up with.

This led her to the second mental exercise, which led to Frank, who was the gardener, and had been when she met him. The exercise was to go back in time and summon the specifics of the past. You could pick an event, buying vegetables from Frank at a roadside stand in South Jersey, for instance. Then you could recall the date by the model year of the car you were driving and you could recall he had the same sly, greedy grin then that he had now, and you were wearing a skirt and a swimsuit under it because you and your friends—two of them, Toni and Mary—would want to go straight to the beach when you got there, just whip off your skirts, grab the towels and trek through the hot grassy dunes that led to the flat plane of the beach and the white froth and green sea water and hazy horizon … and he said, "When you head home, stop again. We sell fresh all summer. You cook?"

"Yes, I cook," she said.

"Not bad for a girl your age."

"My age? I'm eighteen. How old are you?"

The sly greedy grin: "Nineteen. Gotcha there."

That kind of exchange … fragments, but real … the coconut scent of the suntan lotion … noticing every show-off, flirty boy on the beach but wanting to be with your girlfriends and even as teenagers basing your conversations on memories. So much happened before you were seventeen, eighteen. Unimportant but intimate things, tender things, frightening things, all shared in a kind of rattle of words between dips in the suspect waters of the Atlantic full of seaweed and who knew what else. They did stop again to see this cute, cheery guy and buy vegetables from him. He asked for her phone number, and she said, quite practically, "Look, I live in Morristown. It's a long way from here." "What, you don't think I have a car?" Actually, he didn't. He had a 1957 Chevy pick-up truck, or his family did.

From the patio she saw a car turn onto their drive. It came straight at her for twenty seconds, purling plumes of dust and stopping with a crunch. Then there was a spot of silence while the man inside seemed to be consulting something in his lap. Then he got out and introduced himself, Tim Garner, Frank's lawyer. He wore loose slacks, huaraches and a guayabera. He was pleasant, self-confident, and focused on her, not Frank. Are you okay? Do you have access to funds? Has anyone explained the nature of this case to you? How did you manage to make this property so beautiful, so natural? Was Italy always your dream? Friendly, Katherine-centred questions, verging on but not quite patronizing. He was being sensitive, she could see that, trying to soothe her before delivering his news.

"It's better I don't go into the details with you, but I expect that the policia di stato will be here shortly. They haven't come already, right?"

"I've only heard from Phil at the embassy. He said everything would be fine."

"You're okay with that?"

"I'm not okay with any of this, whatever it is."

"Not to worry, totally understandable. Look, they're going to ask you one question, but before that they're going to threaten you with seizing your property and evicting you pending the trial because you're either lying or not cooperating."

"What trial? Aren't you getting him out of Buenos Aires?"

"That's underway. Not going to be a trial. He's a retired agricultural attaché and whatever happened in Milan had highest level approval from the previous Italian government."

Another car turned into Katherine's driveway. Four officers of the policia di stato got out and introduced themselves. Two seemed fluent in English, two didn't.

Tim had given her a look of "Here we go" before those introductions and then settled back down and chatted with the English-speakers as she watched from the kitchen, preparing them all tea. There always had been two Franks. When he majored in plant science at Rutgers, she accepted the fact that he would think differently and impenetrably about almost everything. He'd take the material world as the foundation of all things and even go deeper, into the dark soil beneath, whereas she'd see mankind as life's foundation. So he was obscure to her but she didn't mind, even after he went into the government and became more obscure. That didn't matter because for many years he maintained those greedy, flattering feelings toward her, and these she understood. She had the same feelings toward him: lust, being turned on, wanting more touching, dancing, fucking, drinking, seeing one another at a distance, seeing one another face-to-face, smelling each other, enjoying escaping their families. Her father was in the markets, an executive at a stock brokerage, and he thought farming, which was how he categorized the current and future Frank, was not smart. Frank was strong enough to let him have his fun. And Katherine was strong enough to sit with Frank's parents—Alberto and Letitia Locheri—in their Sears house in South Jersey and insist that nothing had no point, including her obsession with Vergil and Catullus and Hesiod. She had begun studying Latin in tenth grade, Greek freshman year in college. The classes were tiny, the instructors sweet zealots. Some sang poems, some chanted. No one else knew what they did in those classrooms, but they knew they were keeping endangered humanity alive, cherishing the same desires and passions and conflicts that had sprung up, season after season, from the times of the gods themselves.

As the decades passed, Frank and Katherine's bond drifted from the erotic into the familial—not entirely but substantially. Their parents died, one, two, three, four. Their two girls left home, married, and had children. This was where the house outside Viterbo came in and Katherine had found peace there. Initially, while he was establishing the garden (and she was redoing the house and furnishing it) Frank seemed peaceful, too, but then he said there were some lucrative things he could do back in Latin America. The word was "consult." She gave him leave. She'd given him leave the whole time. He did something extra throughout his career as an agricultural attaché; she knew what it was in general but didn't want to know the specifics. Her apparent indifference to Frank often being away puzzled and even irritated other embassy wives. Katherine never opened up. Frank was an agricultural attaché; that's what she said no matter who asked. So of course he had projects in the turbulent regions of country after country, connections with legitimate farmers and agribusiness types, and deep insight into the drug and political culture where embassy officers seldom dared to travel. But Frank did, and she knew, because he was so smart, that whatever he was doing, he was doing it expertly. Which was why, no doubt, he found that having retired and established the garden, he had to go back and do some more. Which led to this.

The lead Italian was Captain Franco Di Blasio. He spoke at length, indictment-style. "Mrs Agnelli, you are married to Mr Frank Locheri. On April 13th last year, Mr Locheri and five other men kidnapped an Egyptian Muslim imam named Alim Sa'id from a street in Milan, where he was a legal resident. They flew him to Cairo. In Cairo he was tortured to reveal information about Islamic extremists with whom he allegedly had associations. I do not know what he revealed, but when he returned to Milan last month he brought suit against your husband. He is blind in one eye; he suffers constant pain in his shoulders; and he is undergoing hip and knee replacements. Your husband participated in this criminal affair because he worked for the United States government as an intelligence agent. The United States government says it had the Italian government's agreement. The newly elected Italian government points out the fundamental incapacity of any government to agree to such actions." Captain Di Blasio paused on this point, letting it settle in. "For all these reasons, we have asked Interpol to detain your husband in Buenos Aires. From there he will return to Italy for trial. I come to ask you only one question. Your truthful answer to that question will weigh in the Italian government's decision as to whether this property should be seized pending resolution of Mr Locheri's trial. If it is seized, you will be expelled from Italy."

The precision with which Captain Di Blasio spoke revealed nothing about his investment in this case, i.e., whether he was simply carrying out orders or disliked American foreign policy or saw a good chance to advance his career. In a sense he was simply a round-faced fellow with a mole on his left nostril and short arms and short legs who was patrolling the perimeter of whatever was going on. He was not a decision maker. Didn't pretend to be. Ignored the tea Katherine made him until he finished speaking and then drank it in one long swallow, so perhaps he was more nervous than he let on, or perhaps not.

For her part, Katherine realized she had attitudes of indifference toward the officials of other countries that might once have been justified—they had diplomatic immunity, they lived in official housing, they could always leave a country in twenty-four hours or less (and had once), but she didn't have immunity anymore.

"We own this house, my husband and I both. Whatever you allege has nothing to do with me."

Captain Di Blasio said, "Under these extraordinary circumstances, you might find that is not true."

She looked to Tim, who had made no effort to intervene, and realized that he was the United States government's lawyer, not Frank's and certainly not hers. But at last he said, "The question?"

Captain Di Blasio asked, "Where was Frank Locheri on April 13 of last year, Mrs Agnelli?"

Katherine said, "What is the law in Italy about the privacy privileges of husbands and wives?"

Captain Di Blasio said, "We are not in a court of law. We are conducting an investigation before entering a court of law. If you do not know where Frank Locheri was on April 13th of last year, or if you do, this is fact, not privacy."

"I certainly can tell you Frank didn't work for the United States government on April 13th of last year."

"Are you certain of that?"

Katherine realized she couldn't be. She only knew this: "His official retirement and pension began in June of the previous year."

"But he could have been reemployed, could he not?"

"I thought you said you had one question."

"You did say that," Tim now said helpfully.

Captain Di Blasio swallowed. Was *that* emotion, drawing excess saliva down one's throat? Katherine looked at the colleague immediately to his left; this man, with a blade of an aquiline nose, was taking notes. The other two men, she now realized, were bodyguards or flunkies of some other kind. She squinted at the foursome and explored their dark effect; they were like the extended wings of a bat or a dead limb that hadn't yet fallen. Nothing good. In any case they obstructed her view of the flowers, lawn, pool, garden and hillside where she thought they ought to let a local farmer graze his sheep. They'd been asked about that once but declined because Frank had grapes in mind for that hillside, part of his rationale for pursuing the consulting money. Indeed, her impression was that they weren't popular in the neighbourhood because Frank did his own gardening and she didn't have a full-time maid. Maybe someone who didn't like them already had said something about April 13th, and they were trying to catch her in a lie. Also, they did their shopping in Viterbo proper, not stores speckling the countryside. She treated Viterbo proper as her little Rome. It was a fort to begin with, Castrum Viterbii. Pope Eugene III lived there in 1145. She loved the blue grey Palace of the Popes and the bell tower of St. Lawrence cathedral and the little Gothic church of Santa Maria della Saluta.

"What day of the month was April 13 last year?"

"A Saturday."

Tim leant forward to whisper: "Do you have any receipts, phone records, photographs, or checks that might link Frank to being here on April 13?"

Katherine didn't answer. She thought, first, that no one knew what had happened on a normal day a year ago unless it was a birthday or holiday or anniversary. Then she began to do her second exercise as a remedy. April … April … what was the difference between one day in April and the next? Was Frank even in the country then, bringing back an airplane stub from somewhere? No, that work in Latin America had begun in the summer. She swam alone all summer, or most of it.

Normally she didn't do her second exercise with audiences watching. There they steeped, like tea, the water of time darkening with currents of intertwining events.

Captain Di Blasio said, "Of course, if you do not know, you do not know."

She asked if she could have a moment alone. Captain Di Blasio said that if she meant to go into the house, he would like to accompany her. She *had* meant to go into the house, but she didn't want him there, so she said, no, she only wanted to step out by the pool.

"It would help."

"How would it help?" Captain Di Blasio asked.

Tim said again, "Isn't Mrs Agnelli's request reasonable? One question, remember?"

Captain Di Blasio wasn't going to be toyed with. "Yes, but the question hasn't been answered." He gestured toward the pool. "What out there will provide an answer? Isn't the answer more likely in the house, to be preserved or destroyed?"

Katherine got up anyway and took the path through the flower beds to the pool. Frank had suggested replacing it; it was an old pool with lots of patching and an antiquated filtration system. Katherine had said in response, just the way she would say something, "Now, really, Frank, why would you do that?" She meant change the patina of the entire property. The old house, old walls, old patios and so forth required a complementary old pool with a yellow-tiled Neptune on one side wall eyeing green and blue-tiled mermaids on the other side wall. "Go do your gardening, leave everything else to me."

She realized the five men had trailed her, so she walked farther, toward the garden: long rows of tomato plants, the green tops of carrots, spindly pepper plants with tiny peppers forming, spreading eggplant and squash and cucumber vines …

She turned to Di Blasio. "He worked on the garden on Saturdays. That's what he was doing here on April 13th last year."

Captain DiBlasio disagreed. "No, he drove to Milan, donned a balaclava, and joined his old comrades in this illegal activity."

"He was an agricultural attaché, don't be ridiculous."

"Madam, excuse me, we know for a fact what he was. We have a message with his name on it, an advisory to the US intelligence station's counterparts."

"You mean sent to the Italian intelligence agencies? What did they say? Okay?"

"They had no authority to say okay."

"Maybe not, maybe they wouldn't dare, so you must mean higher, someone in Rome. Who? The minister of interior? The minister of justice? The prime minister?"

Captain Di Blasio said sharply, "I am not here to debate. I have asked you a question. You have answered. Now, is there any way you can prove what you say? This is a part of my question, perhaps the decisive part. A person can say anything, but what is the proof? If there is no proof, it is unlikely that you will retain possession of this house, these grounds, and that garden."

At the moment Katherine assumed Frank was heading to the US, and she worried that no matter what she said, he might never come back here again, but she didn't want to live in a rented apartment in DC with all their money tied up in Italy. It wasn't the plan. It wasn't what they had fallen in love with. Frank had established the garden and wanted to terrace the hillside and grow grapes there. That was the truth of it. Would they eat the grapes? Some, yes. Preserve the grapes, turn them into jelly? Some, yes. But sell them and eventually figure out how to transform them into wine? If they lived long enough, that would be the "final miracle," as Frank put it, his ultimate transition from truck gardener to vintner. He'd get wine out of the dirt. "Neat trick for a South Jersey boy."

She walked between the tomato plants to get farther away from the men trailing her. It was like a chase, but a very little chase. She was prey, they were predators, each a stand-in for something else: she for brutal US government counterterrorism tactics, they for offended Italian sovereignty. That was it. The new Italian government was trying to undo everything the old government had done because the old government was headed by slime in a suit.

She said *April* to herself and thought of the weather and continued her second mental exercise. He liked to garden on weekends because throughout their peregrinations weekends had been the only time he'd been able to do so. He'd done it in suburban backyards, on apartment balconies and rooftops, and in communal gardens fringing Bogota and Mexico City. And in April in Viterbo the highs and lows would have been receptive to his rake and trowel and hand cultivator and old leather apron festooned with seed pockets. One morning very, very early, she recalled, she awakened and he wasn't in bed.

Where was he? She looked toward the bathroom, no light. She went into the sitting room. No light. She looked out the back window and there in the distance was a bright LED headlamp moving along in the garden. Frank was planting seeds in the pitch dark. Why? Who knew? She went back to bed. When she awoke, he was gone. The note said, "Probably back tonight." That night he returned past her bedtime, but she heard him, got up and looked out the back window. Once again, the LED headlamp shone on the ground where Frank slipped his trowel into the dark soil and slipped in tomato seeds … tomatoes because he was where the tomatoes grew, lots of them, which Katherine turned into sauces and soups and juice and canned for the winter and Frank liked to eat fresh off the vine. He'd go out in the garden in August with a salt shaker, pluck a few, bite, salt and bite again. When he was sated he might kneel and press his face into the tomato plants because he loved their smell in the hot sun so much.

So he may or may not have done what they said, and if he did, how could he be so stupid? He was supposed to be out of that. But the imam, if that's what he was, what could she do for him? What did he deserve? Katherine had no idea. She saw no justice in any of this—these men, this question, the destruction of her life. When Frank began consulting, she had taken over the gardening. At first she resented it. She preferred cooking and reading and writing letters and swimming and playing with Latin and Greek vocabulary cards and doing all the things necessary to making the household go. It was her home and felt like it always had been. But eventually she came to enjoy the smells of the plants and the earth and the feel of the tools in her hands and the scraping crunch of digging and the magic of the tiny seeds and the way the plants perked up when she watered them, their leaves fattening with life.

She turned to Captain Di Blasio and said, "Follow me." She then led the five men to the patio and told them, "Sit down, gentlemen. I'll only be a minute getting you proof."

She returned with Frank's worn green ledger and paged back

through it, certain of what she'd find, none of it involving spying or counter-terrorism. All the entries were dated. Some had to do with too much or too little rain, or pests, or soil conditions, or the growth rates of various vegetables, one kind of squash versus another. He'd measure their length and girth and used his old scale to weigh them. And every time he planted seeds, he made notes. What could be more important than when you planted your seeds?

On April 13 of the previous year the notes read: "Got all the tomato seeds in. Big, big job. Exhausted. Knees ache. 125 plants. Will have to buy more stakes but first want to know how many will have to be thinned so we don't crowd out the Brussels sprouts."

Captain Di Blasio asked if he could take the ledger. Katherine pulled it away. This ledger was the most important document in Frank's life, more important than birth, marriage, or death certificates. Whatever he did elsewhere, he did not record or discuss. But he'd pore over this book, writing the main observations in his neat tiny lettering on the right hand page and additional notes on the left hand page. "Thomas Jefferson used to keep a book like this," he once told her. "It's my travelling garden. Some day I'll have a permanent one. This will tell me what to do with it."

Captain Di Blasio pressed her. "We will give you a receipt and possibly return it to you, although I frankly doubt it. Now we have evidence, and evidence is permanent."

Captain Di Blasio's English-speaking lieutenant volunteered to photograph it.

"The whole thing?" Katherine asked.

"I can do that, too," Tim said, "and I'll definitely get you a copy."

The two men used cell phone cameras to take pictures of the 137 pages that had been used in the 160 page ledger. When they were finished, Captain Di Blasio apologized for taking up so much of her time.

Katherine said, "You *should* apologize. And you should

apologize for threatening to seize my home. You're no better than the last government no matter what you may think."

Captain Di Blasio accepted this verbal slap with no comment. He led his men to their cars. They raised a trail of dust on the way out.

Katherine said to Tim, "Where is he now?"

Tim looked at his watch. "Miami? Probably spend the night. Then DC I can get you a ticket, no problem."

With Captain Di Blasio gone, Katherine let herself go, too. She had a sickening intuition that if she left this little place outside Viterbo, she'd never see it again. She knew Frank would promise her something else. Maybe in Colombia, maybe in Guatemala. She could hear him swear he'd find a way to make that happen, but she didn't want it. She wanted to stay in her new old past. It felt right. It felt like her. This, always this to the end.

"No. Just tell him I'm here, or I'll tell him if he calls me before you see him."

"I think you should leave, Katherine," Tim said. "Today we won but tomorrow …?"

She didn't have a "tomorrow" exercise, but if she had enough time and peace she would invent one.

"No thanks. I'm staying."

She watched another plume of dust rise behind Tim's departing car. Then she went to the tool shed and got her sun hat, long gloves, and hand cultivator. She'd weed and redirect some rambunctious eggplant and squash vines. As she worked, the sun would warm her like a hand spread across her back, pressing her down face-to-face with the rich dark soil, making her perspire, but that was okay. After she finished, she'd swim.

acknowledgements

Many of these stories first appeared in literary magazines. My thanks goes to their editors and readers: "Trouble Sleeping"/ Consequence; "You Must Tell Us" originally appeared as "A Little about Love" in Atticus Review; "The Woman in Yemen"/Atticus Review; "Through the Ice" appeared in Tryst3 as "Only in the Moment of Creation"; "After Apple-Picking"/ The Literary Review; "The Frying Pan"/ The Newer York; "Who Has a Real Castle Where I Can Hide?"/The Missing Slate; "Monkey Girl"/Black and White; "With Her Ear Pressed to the Earth"/34thParallel; "Birth"/Quarterly West; "The Woods"/Ginosko; "A Life"/The Missing Slate; "The Door"/The Feathered Flounder; "On Being a Woman"/S/tick; "Pivot Point"/Steel Toe Review; "The Only Good Thing about Getting Older"/december; "Into the Dark Soil"/Rathalla Review. I also would like to thank everyone at Vine Leaves Press, especially Jessica Bell, publisher, and Lindsay Adkins, editor, for their enthusiasm, skill, and support.

vine leaves press

Enjoyed this book?
Go to *vineleavespress.com* to find more.